Treachery
IN THE
HIGHLANDS

Other Books by Anna Durand

Dangerous in a Kilt (Hot Scots, Book One)
Wicked in a Kilt (Hot Scots, Book Two)
Scandalous in a Kilt (Hot Scots, Book Three)
Gift-Wrapped in a Kilt (Hot Scots, Book Four)
Notorious in a Kilt (Hot Scots, Book Five)
Insatiable in a Kilt (Hot Scots, Book Six)
Lethal in a Kilt (Hot Scots, Book Seven)
Irresistible in a Kilt (Hot Scots, Book Eight)
Devastating in a Kilt (Hot Scots, Book Nine)
Spellbound in a Kilt (Hot Scots, Book Ten)
Relentless in a Kilt (Hot Scots, Book Eleven)
Incendiary in a Kilt (Hot Scots, Book Twelve)
Wild in a Kilt (Hot Scots, Book Thirteen)
Unstoppable in a Kilt (Book Fourteen)
Valentine in a Kilt (Book Fifiteen)
Electrifying in a Kilt (Book Sixteen)
Lachlan in a Kilt (The Ballachulish Trilogy, Book One)
Aidan in a Kilt (The Ballachulish Trilogy, Book Two)
Rory in a Kilt (The Ballachulish Trilogy, Book Three)
The American Wives Club (A Hot Brits/Hot Scots/Au Naturel Crossover)
Brit vs. Scot (A Hot Brits/Hot Scots/Au Naturel Crossover)
A Novel Secret (A Hot Brits/Hot Scots/Au Naturel Crossover)
One Hot Chance (Hot Brits, Book One)
One Hot Roommie (Hot Brits, Book Two)
One Hot Crush (Hot Brits, Book Three)
One Hot Escape (Hot Brits, Book Four)
One Hot Rumor (Hot Brits, Book Five)
One Hot Christmas (Hot Brits, Book Six)
One Hot Scandal (Hot Brits, Book Seven)
One Hot Deal (Hot Brits, Book Eight)
One Hot Favor (Hot Brits, Book Nine)
One Hot Bash (Hot Brits, Book Ten)
One Hot Moment (Hot Brits, Book Eleven)
One Hot Chase (Hot Brits, Book Twelve)
Natural Obsession (Au Naturel Nights, Book One)
Natural Passion (Au Naturel Trilogy, Book One)
Natural Impulse (Au Naturel Trilogy, Book Two)
Natural Satisfaction (Au Naturel Trilogy, Book Three)
Fired Up (standalone romance)

Treachery IN THE HIGHLANDS

A Hot Scots Prequel

ANNA DURAND

JACOBSVILLE BOOKS · CHESTERHILL, OHIO

TREACHERY THE HIGHLANDS

ISBN: 978-1-964417-59-2 (paperback)
ISBN: 978-1-964417-60-8 (ebook)
ISBN: 978-1-964417-61-5 (retail audiobook)
ISBN: 978-1-964417-62-2 (library audiobook)

Manufactured in the United States.

Jacobsville Books
www.JacobsvilleBooks.com

Publisher's Cataloging-in-Publication Data
provided by Five Rainbows Cataloging Services

Names: Durand, Anna, author.
Title: Treachery in the Highlands / Anna Durand.
Description: Chesterhill, OH : Jacobsville Books, 2025. | Series: Hot Scots prequel.
Identifiers: ISBN 978-1-964417-59-2 (paperback) | ISBN 978-1-964417-60-8 (ebook) | ISBN 978-1-964417-61-5 (retail audiobook) | ISBN 978-1-964417-62-2 (library audiobook)
Subjects: LCCN 2025906461 | LCSH: Thieves--Fiction. | Highlands (Scotland)--Fiction. |Time travel--Fiction. | Middle Ages--Fiction. | Man-woman relationships--Fiction. | Historical fiction. | Romance fiction. | BISAC: FICTION / Romance / Time Travel. | FICTION / Romance / Historical / Scottish. | FICTION / Romance / Historical / Medieval. | Paranormal / Witches. | GSAFD: Love stories. | Historical fiction.
Classification: LCC PS3604.U724 W55 2023 (print) | LCC PS3604.U724 (ebook) | DDC 813/.6--dc23.

Chapter One

Joey

The city sprawls out below me, a glittering tapestry of lights and shadows. I crouch on the edge of the rooftop, wearing my trusty leather jacket as I lean forward. My gaze locks onto the pawn shop nestled between a bodega and a laundromat. *Bingo.*

"All right, Finnegan," I mutter to myself. "Let's see what we're working with here."

I pull out a pair of compact binoculars, scanning the building's facade. Two cameras, one above the door and another at the corner. Child's play. The streetlights flicker to life, casting pools of sickly yellow that barely penetrate the gloom. I drum my fingers on the concrete ledge as I weigh my options—take a chance on this shop, or head back to the dump I call home.

You know what you want to do, Finnegan. Why are you hesitating? Just go for it, dumbass. I stand, stretching my arms above my head. The wind whips around me, threatening to throw me off balance, but I've danced this jig too many times to falter now. As I make my way across the rooftop, in my mind, I tick off every step of the plan. *Disable the cameras, pick the lock, slip inside. In and out in ten minutes flat. Easy as it gets.*

But a nagging doubt creeps in. What if something goes wrong? What if this is the job that finally catches up to me?

I shake my head, banishing those thoughts. "Get it together, Finnegan. You've done this a hundred times, at least."

Now that I've given myself a mini motivational speech, I'm ready to go. My movements are fluid and practiced. Every step, every gesture has been honed by years on the streets. I'm a ghost, a shadow, invisible to all but the most observant eyes.

And in this city? No one's watching that closely.

Just as I reach for the fire escape ladder, a memory ambushes me, as sharp and unwelcome as a knife to the gut. Foster home number...what was it? Four? Five? The details blur, but the ache remains even after all these years.

"You're nothing but trouble, Joey," Mrs. Whoever-She-Was had sneered, her bony finger jabbing my chest. "A petty thief who doesn't care about anyone but himself. No wonder your parents left you."

That old crone had been right. I am a thief, and all I steal is trinkets. It had been sweets—candy bars, mostly—that I coveted all those years ago. Now...the candy has become bracelets and lockets. Nothing much has changed. Yeah, I'm pathetic. But tonight, that all changes. One last score, the biggest yet, and I'm outta here.

I swallow hard, pushing down the lump in my throat, and take several slow, deep breaths until the old anxiety fades away. Ancient history, I assure myself, but the words ring hollow.

My hands clamp around the cold metal of the ladder as muscle memory takes over. One rung, two, three...I descend with the grace of a cat burglar which, I suppose, is what I am. Maybe if my parents hadn't kicked the bucket, or if my foster mother had stuck around, I wouldn't be scaling buildings in the dead of night.

But they did scram. And here I am, a product of New York's unforgiving streets, about to rob a pawn shop.

My feet hit the alley pavement with a soft thud. I pause, listening for any sign that I've been detected. Nothing but the distant wail of sirens and the ever-present hum of the city.

"All right, Mr. Finnegan. Time to prove what a petty thief can do. It's showtime."

I slink toward the back of the pawn shop, my movements a fluid dance of shadows and stealth. Every step is calculated, my body instinctively avoiding loose gravel or anything that might give me away.

You're good at this, a traitorous voice in my head whispers. *Wonder what Mom and Dad would think of their little boy now?*

I grit my teeth and hiss, "Shut up and focus on the job."

Maybe I should worry about why I'm talking to myself, but I shove those thoughts aside.

As I reach the back door and hover my hand over the lock, I can't shake the feeling that somewhere out there, two ghosts are watching me with disappointment in their eyes.

I shake off the phantom disapproval and get to work. The lock is a simple tumbler—almost too easy. I work the mechanism deftly as I feel for the sweet spots, and within a minute, two at most, I hear the soft click that means I've accomplished my task. As I slip inside the shop, the darkness embraces me like an old friend. The air is thick with the musty scent of forgotten treasures and broken dreams, things normal people had to pawn to feed their families. Shadows loom large, cast by the faint glow of streetlights filtering through grimy windows.

The item I'm looking for wasn't pawned by a poor person. Nope, this little beauty is way too pricey for that.

I navigate the cluttered aisles with practiced ease, my feet finding clear paths where others might stumble. Glass cases loom on either side, their contents glinting dully in the low light. The antiquated security system might as well have been designed by a monkey. I disable it swiftly.

While I search for the item I want, I can't help but imagine how different things might have been. In another life, maybe these clever fingers would be saving lives in an operating room instead of picking locks and disabling alarms.

But that's not my story, is it? This is who I am, and there's no point in denying the truth. A bad seed never grows into a flower.

Just as I'm about to start my sweep of the shop, a sudden vibration in my pocket nearly makes me jump out of my skin. My heart races as I freeze, listening intently for any sign that the noise has alerted someone. Silence, that's all. I exhale slowly, fishing out my phone with trembling fingers.

The text on screen sends a shiver up my spine: *Did you really think you could get away from us, Finnegan?*

Aw, shit. How did Fulvio Barbieri find me? I covered my tracks like a pro—or so I thought—but now Damiano Zanetti's enforcer has hunted me down. I wish I'd never met anyone in the Zanetti crime family. My heart pounds in my chest as I stare at the glowing screen. This can't be happening. Not now. Not when I'm so close to getting out of the Zanettis' clutches.

I hover my fingers hover over the phone, itching to reply, to tell Fulvio where he can shove his threats. But I know better. Engaging will only make things worse. I shove the device back into my pocket, trying to ignore the way it suddenly feels like it weighs a tone.

Focus, idiot. You've got a job to do.

I force myself to breathe, to push aside the panic threatening to overwhelm me. The familiar weight of my lockpicks in my hand grounds me as I move through the shop, my eyes scanning for the most valuable items. Then a glint of gold catches my attention. *Jackpot.* I carefully lift the delicate gold chain of the diamond necklace, removing it from its velvet nest. The way it catches the faint light is…kind of beautiful. The necklace probably cost a small fortune. Just what I need to fund my escape.

While I'm slipping the necklace into my satchel, another vibration nearly makes me drop the bag. My heart races as I fumble for the phone, dreading what I might see.

Ticktock, Finnegan. Hand over the proceeds or…

Fulvio will murder me. That's what he means. But he'll do that anyway. My pulse accelerates, and my breaths shorten. No one crosses the Zanetti family.

Another message appears on screen: *I'm coming for you now, Joey boy.*

I sling my bag over my shoulder and zigzag through the shop, heading for the back door with adrenaline surging through me with a sharp burn. The weight of the stolen necklace feels like a noose around my neck, but I can't afford to leave it behind. It's my ticket out of this mess. As I burst into the alley, the cool night air hits my face like a slap. I pause for a split second, ears straining for any sign of pursuit.

But I can't hear anything.

I sprint down the alley, my footsteps echoing off the brick walls. My mind races faster than my feet. How did Fulvio find me? I'd been so careful, covered my tracks like a pro. But clearly, I'd slipped up somewhere. A car engine roars to life nearby, and I instinctively duck behind a dumpster. The stench of rotting garbage assaults my nostrils, but I barely notice as I press myself against the slimy metal.

The car engine grows louder, headlights sweeping across the mouth of the alley. I hold my breath, praying to whatever god might be listening that it's just a random passerby. No such luck. The car slows to a crawl, tires crunching over broken glass and debris. I risk a peek around the edge of the dumpster—and my blood runs cold. It's a sleek black Audi.

Fulvio's ride of choice.

"Come out, come out, wherever you are," a familiar voice calls, dripping with false cheer. "You can't hide forever, Joey boy."

I bite back a curse. How the hell did he find me so fast? I scan the alley, desperate for an escape route. The fire escape I used earlier is too far, and there's no way I can make it without being spotted. My gaze lands on a rusty ladder leading up to the roof of the adjacent building. It's a long shot, but it's my only chance. I take a deep breath, steeling myself for what's to come. The moment Fulvio's car passes the dumpster, I spring into action. My feet barely touch the ground as I sprint for the ladder, my heart pounding so hard I wouldn't be surprised if Fulvio can hear it.

"There you are, you fucking rat!" Fulvio's voice booms behind me, followed by the screech of tires.

I don't look back, focusing all my energy on climbing. The rusted metal bites into my palms, but I ignore the pain. I haul myself up the ladder, my muscles on fire, sweat drenching me. The sound of car doors slamming and footsteps pounding the pavement below only spurs me to go faster.

"You can't run forever, Joey boy!" Fulvio's voice echoes off the brick walls. "Damiano wants his money, and I aim to collect—one way or another. You shouldn't have swiped those greenbacks from us."

Yeah, lifting that money had been dumb. But I needed cab fare to get to the pawn shop.

The moment I reach the rooftop, I sprint across it. My breaths come in ragged gasps. The cool night air whips against my face as I leap to the next building, tucking into a roll as I land. The impact jars my bones, but I can't afford to slow down.

Behind me, I hear grunts of exertion as Fulvio and his goons chase after me. They're in better shape than I expected, but I've got desperation on my side. I vault over an air conditioning unit, my feet barely touching the ground as I sprint across the rooftop and leap to the next building, my heart in my throat as I soar through the air. For a moment, I'm suspended between earth and sky, caught in the liminal space between freedom and capture.

I zigzag across the rooftops, vaulting over vents and ducking under clotheslines. I need to get off the roof. Luckily, I glance down to see an open dumpster full of garbage bags. I leap off the ledge, sailing down for a relatively soft landing. Climbing out of the dumpster, I dart down a narrow alley with my pulse pounding in my ears. The shouts of Fulvio and his goons echo behind me, growing fainter as I increase the distance between us by leaps and bounds.

As I weave through the labyrinth of back streets, my feet seem to run on autopilot. Years of navigating these urban canyons have etched the map into my psyche. Left, right, duck under a low-hanging fire escape, vault over a chain-link fence. My lungs burn, but I can't afford to slow down.

Glancing back, I can't see any evidence of my pursuers.

After a quick trip to another pawn shop, one that's actually open this late, I get rid of the necklace. Fortunately, the shop owner isn't picky about provenance. Now that I've got fifteen hundred dollars in my pocket, I huddle in another alley while I book a trip on my phone, choosing the cheapest fare available and the first available flight. That takes me across the Atlantic to…

Scotland.

That'll do just fine.

Twelve hours later, I stumble off the plane at Inverness Airport, bleary-eyed and disoriented. The cheap fare had gotten me an equally cheap, uncomfortable seat, and a bonehead beside me who shared his whole boring life story with me.

I stretch and yawn as I exit the plane. The crisp Scottish air wakes me up as I exit the terminal, a stark contrast to the stifling heat of New York City. I pull my leather jacket tighter around me, suddenly grateful for its battered warmth.

"Welcome to Scotland, jackass," I say to myself, scanning the unfamiliar landscape. Rolling hills of green stretch out before me, dotted with ancient stone buildings that look like they've been plucked straight out of a fairytale. It's beautiful, sure, but it's also completely foreign. I feel exposed and almost…vulnerable.

Nah, that's bullshit.

My phone buzzes in my pocket, and I flinch, half-expecting another threatening message from Fulvio. Instead, it's a notification from a local news app I downloaded during the flight. My eyes widen as I read the headline.

Recent Excavations at Dùndubhan Castle Uncover a Treasure Trove of Priceless Artifacts.

As I climb into my rental car, visions of piles of money dance in my head. I hadn't planned on stealing anything here, but I can't resist the siren call of snatching some loot. Oh-ho, yeah. This country just might lead me to the score of a lifetime—and get Fulvio off my ass for good.

Chapter Two

Rachel

I stand atop the battlements of Dùndubhan Castle, my hair whipping about my face as I gaze out at the vast expanse of wilderness that surrounds the fortress. The wind carries the crisp scent of heather and pine, a familiar fragrance that usually soothes my restless spirit. But today, it only fuels my longing for something more than the cloistered life I've always lived. I might as well have grown up in a nunnery.

Adventure? Excitement? Romance? Nay, I have no such opportunities. I have only my parents and my great-aunts to converse with, and they are all considerably older than I am. No one has come here for such a long time that I feel certain I will never again see another stranger or even a long-lost friend. Well, my grandparents visit us occasionally, though they prefer to remain in the village of Loch Fairbairn. I am not permitted to go there.

Why? Because my family believes I must be cloistered for my own protection.

Not that any miscreants have ever attempted to harm me. My mother and father are overly protective.

My gaze travels toward the waters of Loch Fairbairn in the distance as I imagine what lies beyond the forest—and the hills I can see in the distance. Nothing of much interest lies o'er the mountains far yonder. But I do know what awaits in another time, another millennium that I cannot reach. My mother was born there. Her world bustles with cities filled with towering buildings that scrape the sky. That's why they call them skyscrapers. Those busy streets are filled with people from all corners of the world and adventures waiting to unfold.

Ne're shall I see that strange other world.

I sigh, resting my arms on the stone parapet. As I gaze at the horizon, I speak to myself. "Oh, to spread my wings and fly far from this gilded cage."

I wince at my ungrateful thought. My mother and father have encouraged me to spread my wings however I choose—as long as I don't visit the village of Loch Fairbairn. I understand why they fetter me so. It's because they love me. And I am grateful for this life I share with my family. Though I lament my lack of excitement, I must admit that I have enjoyed second-hand adventures. Guarin Abadie has come to our home twice in my life, and the Frenchman told wonderful stories about faraway places like France and England and even the Far East.

Och, how I wish I could see the world.

The Highlands are beautiful, wild, and magical—and the only home I've ever known. But lately, the hills of Scotland feel confining, as if I wear a corset that's pulled too tight. I yearn to break free, to experience life beyond these ancient walls and mist-shrouded lochs.

"Careful, sweetie," a familiar voice warns. "Lean over any more, and your wish to fly away might become a reality."

At the sound of my mother's voice, I spin round in surprise, feeling my cheeks grow warm, as if she's caught me doing something wicked. She strides toward me, wearing a motherly smile as her beautiful auburn hair glistens in the afternoon light.

"*Màthair*! I didn't even hear you approach." I struggle to hide my embarrassment with a forced laugh.

She joins me at the wall, bumping my shoulder affectionately. "Lost in those daydreams again, huh? I swear, sometimes I think your head's so full of dreams in the clouds that there's barely room for your brain."

I roll my eyes but can't help smiling. "Says the bean who frequently regales us with tales of skyscrapers and subways. Bean means woman, in case you've forgotten."

"Nope, I haven't forgotten," my mother concedes with a wink. "Speaking of which, want to hear about another adventure in the concrete jungle?"

My heart leaps at the prospect of another story from the modern world. "Always. You know I adore every tale you share with me."

"You're my best audience." She winks, then launches into her story. "Picture this: I'm visiting New York on business and decide to power walk down Fifth Avenue. I've got my laptop bag slung over one shoulder and a venti latte in hand—because in New York, caffeine is essentially a food group..."

I listen, enthralled, as my mother weaves her tale. The way she describes the towering buildings, the constant hum of activity, the sheer energy of the city…it's intoxicating. I can almost smell the street vendor's pretzels and hear the cacophony of honking taxis.

"…and then this guy in a hot dog costume—don't ask, it's a long story—comes barreling around the corner. Next thing I know, I'm wearing my venti latte and doing an impromptu tango with Mr. Wiener!"

I burst out laughing, the sound echoing off the stone walls. "Och, *Màthair*! Only you could turn a simple coffee run into such chaos."

"Sweetie, I love it when you call me Mother in Gaelic."

"After so many years in Scotland, ye still haven't learned the entire Gaelic language. But I wouldnae wish to change you. Now, please, please tell me the rest of your New York tale."

Màthair grins, clearly pleased with my reaction, and regales me with more mishaps in the Big Apple. When she's done, she shrugs. "What can I say? I lived life on the edge…of complete disaster, usually."

I know she has embellished her tales, but I've loved her stories ever since I was old enough to understand them.

As our laughter fades, I turn back to the loch. A familiar ache settles in my chest, and my voice grows softer. "It sounds wonderful. All of it. Even the disasters."

My mother rests her hand on my shoulder, and the warm, comforting feeling soothes me. "Hey now, sweetie, don't go getting that faraway look again. Your adventures are waiting for you too, sweetie. They just might not come packaged quite how you expect."

I try to take her words to heart and not let my dreams get the better of me. Yet as I gaze out at the familiar landscape, I can't help but wonder. Will my own story ever be as thrilling as the ones my family tell?

I'm about to respond to what *Màthair* said when heavy footsteps clap behind us, coming closer. I turn, my heart skipping a beat as I see my father, Kieran, striding down the walkway. His imposing figure is silhouetted against the setting sun, but as he draws closer, I notice the hint of a smile softening his usually stern features.

"There ye are, lasses," he rumbles, his deep voice carrying a mixture of affection and authority. "I've news for ye both."

I straighten instinctively, my curiosity piqued. "What is it, *Athairich*?"

Aye, I often use the Gaelic terms for mother and father. I'm quite proud of my Highland heritage.

My father clasps his hands behind his back, his golden eyes gleaming, and smiles. "The clan gathering's been set for the next full moon. We've much to prepare."

My breath catches. The clan gathering? We haven't been invited to that event in all my life. It's been years since the last one, and I know what it's like only because my great-aunts shared their tales with me. The gathering is a whirlwind of tartans, music, and age-old traditions. I feel a surge of excitement, quickly followed by a twinge of...something else. Disappointment? Dread?

A thrill rushes through me at the thought of seeing and speaking to other MacTaggarts, not to mention other clans. But my excitement dies quickly. The last full moon won't arise for nearly a month. We must wait that long for the gathering.

"Why would they invite us?" *Màthair* says.

"Aye, that's the question, isn't it?" *Athairich*'s brow furrows as he strokes his beard. It's only a slight beard since Alyssa Vescovi refuses to kiss her husband unless he trimmed his facial hair. "The Buchanans have extended the invitation, though I cannae say why after all these years."

I exchange a glance with my mother, seeing my own mix of eagerness and wariness reflected in her eyes. The clan gathering is an opportunity, certainly, but one that could bring danger as well as new ventures.

"Will we attend?" I ask, trying to hide the eagerness in my voice.

My father's gaze narrows on mine, but then his expression softens. "Aye, lass, we must. It would be an insult if we skipped the event, and in these times, we can ill afford to make enemies."

My mind is already racing with possibilities. The gathering means a chance to meet people from beyond our castle walls, to hear stories of the wider world. But it also means I'll need to be on my guard, to keep my nascent powers hidden. We MacTaggarts are witches, after all—save for *Màthair*.

"We'll need to prepare," my mother says, her tone thoughtful. "Rachel, you'll need a new dress. And we should review proper etiquette for—"

"Aye, and ye'll need to mind yer tongue, lass," my father interjects, his gaze stern but not unkind. "No talk of yer mother's world or any...unusual abilities. We cannae risk drawing attention."

I feel a pang of disappointment but solemnly nod my agreement. "I understand, *Athairich*. I'll be the very picture of a proper Highland lass."

Father smiles tenderly. "I know ye will, mo nighean. Ye always make us proud."

As he turns to leave, Mother gives my hand a reassuring squeeze. "Don't worry, sweetie-pie. There will still be plenty of excitement, even if we have to keep some things under wraps."

The clan gathering may not be New York City, but it's a step into a wider world. And who knows what adventures—or dangers—might await me there?

Over the next few days, Dùndubhan buzzes with activity. *Màthair* and *Athairich* along with myself and my three elderly aunts, all scurry about in a whirlwind of activity. My father airs out his great kilt, and Mother irons out the kilt and his best shirt for him. *Màthair* fusses over my new gown, making sure every seam is perfect. And I…well, I try my best to stay out of trouble.

But on the third morning, as the sun peeks over the misty hills, I find myself drawn to the shores of Loch Fairbairn. I sneak away before the others have woken so I can enjoy a bit of solitude. The water laps gently at the pebbled beach, its surface a mirror of the pink-tinged sky above. I glance over my shoulder, making sure I'm alone, before closing my eyes and taking a deep breath. Focusing my mind, I extend my hand toward the loch. At first, nothing happens. Then, ever so slightly, a tendril of water rises from the surface, twisting and curling in the air like a translucent serpent.

"Come hither," I whisper, willing the water to obey. The tendril grows thicker, rising higher. I smile as I guide it through the air, making it dance and swirl around me.

But then the magical serpent dissipates and splashes back down into the water. *Bod an Donais*, why have my powers still not reached the level of Efrica, Morna, and Lachina?

When I return to the castle, my father gives me his patented stern look, his arms crossed over his cheat. "How many times I've asked ye not to go beyond Dùndubhan land? It's unwise."

I shrug. "But I need priobairneach."

"No one requires excitement, lass. Vow you will never go beyond Dùndubhan land again. Please, Rachel."

My father watches out for us all, and 'tis a hard job with so many magical women on the premises. So, I give in. "I vow it, Father."

"Thank you, mo nighean." He offers me his arm as we enter the castle where the rest of the family is already waiting. "The clan gathering 'tis a grand occasion. Rachel, you shall have a special role this time. We've all agreed that you should lead our contingent in the welcoming ceremony."

I swallow hard. "Me? But…that's always been your duty, Father."

"And now 'tis time for you to take your place at the head of our procession along with me and your mother. Our people look to us, Rachel. We must uphold the old ways, even as the world changes around us."

"Of course, you're right. I won't let you down."

While my whole family begins to discuss the preparations, my mind wanders as it often does. I love my clan and my family. But I still yearn for more—for adventure, for the unknown, for something wonderful to happen. I close my eyes, picturing myself in my mother's New York, navigating crowded streets and towering buildings. Mayhap I would explore ancient ruins in Egypt or trek through lush jungles. She told me about those things too.

As our evening meal winds down, I make my excuses and head for my chamber, my mind buzzing with fresh ideas for things to try tomorrow. What if I could master my powers in time for the gathering? Mayhap then I could use them to help my family, or even impress the Buchanans. They have always viewed my family as being beneath them.

Och, how I wish I had a modern mattress like the ones my mother has told me about. Medieval beds aren't "cushy," as she would say. I flop onto my bed, staring up at the stone ceiling, thinking about all the stories Mother shared—about her life before she was transported here, about the wonders of the modern world. Would I be as brave as she was, plunging into an unknown future with nothing but her wits?

"What if..." I whisper to myself, grinning at my thoughts. "What if I could use water to travel? To see other times, other places?"

The thought sends a thrill through me. I may not have mastered my powers yet, but I can feel it. Something monumental is coming. And whatever it is, I'll be ready.

I drift off to sleep, dreaming of lochs that stretch across centuries and adventures yet to come.

Chapter Three

Joey

What can I say? Scotland is amazing. I grew up on the streets of New York, where I was more likely to see a drunk vomiting on the sidewalk than to have cheerful people chatting with me. I'm not the most…friendly looking guy. Goatee, worn leather jacket, eyes that have seen too much—yeah, I'm that guy you probably cross the street to avoid. But here? These Highlanders don't seem to care that I resemble a hoodlum. They've probably never heard that word before.

"Halò, laddie! Care for a dram?" A burly man with a beard that could house small animals beckons me into a pub that looks older than most American cities.

"Uh, sure," I holler, uncertain of how to handle this unexpected kindness.

The bartender slides a tumbler of amber liquid across the worn wooden bar. I take a cautious sip, and the whisky burns down my throat in the best way. It's smoky, peaty, and unlike anything I've tasted before. I'm no slouch when it comes to knocking back a glass of hard liquor, but this stuff makes me cough. "That's some strong stuff. I like it."

"What brings ye to our wee corner of the world?" the bartender asks, his thick brogue making me strain to understand him.

I hesitate, unsure of how much I should reveal. So, I go with vagueness. "Just…exploring."

One thing I learned in foster homes was that a kid should never say too much. Though I'm not a child anymore, I can't seem to shake off the remnants of my past.

The bartender seems satisfied with my non-answer. "Aye, plenty to explore 'round these parts. Mind yerself in the hills after dark. Strange things happen when the mist rolls in."

I raise an eyebrow, intrigued despite myself. "Strange things?"

He leans in closer, whispering to me. "Aye, laddie. The old ones say the veil between worlds grows thin in these parts. Some claim they've seen ghostly figures dancing in the mist or heard the wail of bagpipes when no piper was near."

I shake my head. "Come on. Ghosts and magical mist? You don't really believe in that shit, do you?"

The bartender's eyes narrow, and for a moment, I worry I've offended him. But then he breaks into a hearty laugh. "Believe? No, not me. But there are those who do, and who am I to say they're wrong?" He winks. "Besides, it's good for tourism."

"Uh-huh. That sounds more believable than ghosts."

The man sitting on the next stool over leans toward me, crooking a finger. "You would do well not to mock what ye dinnae understand, laddie. These lands are old, more ancient than ye can imagine. The magic here runs deep in the earth, in the stones, in the very air ye breathe."

I'm about to brush off his warning when a chill slithers down my spine. The pub suddenly feels colder, and the shadows in the corners seem to deepen. The other patrons have gone quiet, their eyes fixed on me with a strange intensity. I shift on my barstool, unable to get comfortable though I can't pinpoint why. Have I stepped into a Twilight Zone episode?

The burly man's intense gaze doesn't waver, and I find myself struggling to maintain my usual cocky demeanor.

Swallowing hard, I try to shake off that eerie feeling and give the thumbs-up sign to prove I'm not rattled. "Right, magic. Got it."

I take another swig of whisky, hoping it'll calm my nerves.

The burly man leans in closer, his breath hot on my ear. "Ye think ye're clever, don't ye? But mark my words, lad. The Highlands have a way of humbling even the most skeptical of souls."

A gust of wind howls outside, rattling the discolored windows. The flames in the fireplace flicker and dance, casting eerie shadows across the room that seem like they might spring to life at any second. I can't shake the feeling that something's changed, like the air itself has become charged with energy I can't explain.

The bartender slides another dram my way. "On the house, laddie. Ye might be needin' it."

I contemplate the whisky, wondering if these people plan on giving me a mickey. But then I shrug and knock it back in one gulp. The burn helps to ground me, pushing back the unsettling atmosphere in the pub. I slap a few Scottish notes on the bar, then rush out the door, letting it slam shut behind me.

As I head for my car, I notice a faint shimmer in the air, like heat rising from pavement on a scorching day. But it's chilly this evening, and the shimmer seems to be moving or…swirling around me like an invisible halo. That whisky must have marijuana in it. Do they even have that in Scotland? Doesn't matter. I'm suffering from jet lag and lack of sleep, that's all.

I rub my eyes and yawn as I reach for the car door. The second my fingers touch the handle, a jolt of static electricity zaps me. I yelp and jump back, massaging my hand. "What the hell? I need to get outta here before one of those crazy Scots kills me."

The shimmering in the air intensifies, swirling faster around me like a transparent cyclone. My heart thuds as I try to make sense of what's going on. This can't be real. It's just the whisky, the jet lag, the Scottish weed, my overactive imagination…

But then the ground beneath my feet begins to tremble. The world spins, colors blurring together like a kaleidoscope gone haywire. I stumble, trying to grab onto something, anything, to steady myself. But there's nothing solid left to grab onto anymore.

"Help!" I shout. My voice echoes like I'm inside the Grand Canyon, my cries distorted even to my own ears. "Somebody help me!"

The last thing I see before everything goes black is the fucking pub.

A cold hand smacks my face. "Wakey-wakey, *macan*. Did ye hit yer head?"

That voice. It's the bartender.

I push up into a sitting position, blinking swiftly. "Uh, I'm okay. Must've been jetlag or low blood sugar."

The bartender squints at me, a flicker of something—concern, or maybe suspicion—crossing his weathered features. "Aye, must've been."

His tone suggests he doesn't believe me for a second.

I glance around, still disoriented. I'm lying on the cold, damp ground outside the pub, but something's off. The air feels different, heavier somehow, and there's a strange scent I can't quite place. Woodsmoke, maybe? And something else, earthy and ancient.

As I struggle to stand up, the bartender gives me a hand. "I'm okay now, I swear. Just need a good night's sleep."

He lifts his brows but then turns to head back into the pub.

Since I hadn't booked a motel, I'll need to drive until I spot someplace. The map on my phone is malfunctioning, so it's no help. Just my luck, right? Or this might be divine my punishment for letting myself get sucked into the Zanetti crime family. I can't even find a freaking gas station. Next, Rod Serling will appear in the passenger seat to tell me I've driven into The Twilight Zone.

When I start to veer toward the ditch alongside the road, I realize I must find a motel—now. But I have no idea how to find one in the dark. All I can do is pull over, curl up in the backseat, and try to catch some z's. Amazingly, I do fall asleep. In the morning, I stop at a gas station to clean myself up as best I can in the bathroom.

But as I'm climbing back into the rental car, I notice a piece of paper lying on the floor on the passenger side. When I pick it up, I realize it's an advertisement for that castle—Dùndubhan. As I stare at the flyer, my hands shake slightly. How the hell did that paper get inside my car? Maybe somebody from the bar slipped it in there while I was having a weird conversation with a Scottish bartender.

This is all too weird, and I'm too tired to think about…anything. I should find a motel and get some sleep. But my eyes keep gravitating to the flyer.

Screw it. I need answers, and the castle seems like as good a place as any to start searching. I fire up the rental car and pull out onto the narrow road, following the vague directions on the flyer. As I drive, the landscape grows wilder, more rugged, and yet beautiful too. The paved road gives way to a dirt track, winding its way through misty glens and over craggy hills.

Finally, I round a bend—and there it is. Dùndubhan.

I park in the designated grassy area behind the castle. A cheerful young woman with a Scottish accent tells me to follow the signs that will lead me to the main entrance where I can sign up for a tour or look around on my own. I choose the solo option, unsure of what the hell I'm doing here. After a quick perusal of the ground floor hallway, where I find nothing of interest to a petty thief like me, I head up to the great hall on the first floor. That's boring too, so I climb the stairs up to the third level—which is, apparently, the second floor. Weird. Scots don't know how to name things properly.

At last, I reach the long gallery, where I'm surrounded by artifacts from various periods that line every wall, and the middle of the room too. Every relic rests inside a glass case and has a sign explaining its importance. My thievery has always been centered around jewelry and other trinkets. Here, I discover historical treasures from the medieval world, most of which were found on the castle grounds. Yeah, this stuff is way outside my wheelhouse. But I browse the old junk anyway.

My attention stalls at a glass case that houses a big sword, though I'm not sure why. I study it intently, reading the words engraved on a placard: "*The claymore belonging to Ciaran Amhlaigh mac in tSagairt (Kieran Aulay MacTaggart), the last laird of Dùndubhan.*"

As I lean in to examine the sword more closely, a strange sensation shivers through me. The glass case seems to shimmer and distort, like heat waves rising from hot pavement. It's too much like what happened last night, but all I can do is squeeze my eyes shut until the craziness passes. But my head starts to spin, and I stumble backwards, trying to shake off the dizziness.

"Look out!" a woman shouts. "He's coming for you!"

Before I can understand what's happening, a large body tackles me to the ground. A rough voice snarls, "Gotcha, Joey boy. Did you really think you'd get away from us?"

"Fulvio? What the hell?"

He hoists me off the floor, grinning like the maniac he is.

I struggle against Fulvio's iron grip, my mind reeling. How the fuck did he find me here? In this castle? In the long gallery?

"Let go of me, you stupid gorilla!" I shout, twisting and kicking with every ounce of strength I have. "Somebody call the cops!"

Fulvio just laughs, a cold, mirthless sound. "Not a chance, Joey boy. The boss wants a word with you."

I'm about to tell him exactly where he can shove his threats when suddenly, the air begins to shimmer and warp. Not again. But something's different this time. The walls of the castle seem to ripple and fade, replaced by swirling mist.

Fulvio's grip on me loosens as he gawks at the surroundings as if he's completely dumbfounded. "What the fuck is going on? How are you doing this?"

He shakes me again, but his grip isn't as ironclad now. For a moment, he just stands there, completely flummoxed.

And he loses his grip on me.

I seize my chance, wrenching free and stumbling backward. My hand brushes against the glass case holding the ancient sword. With a blinding flash of light, the glass case shatters. Shards litter the floor and tourists flee, ignoring the glass shards on the floor that crunch beneath their feet. Without thinking, I grab the sword, its weight unfamiliar yet somehow right in my hand.

Fulvio lunges at me, his face contorted with rage. "You little shit!"

I swing the sword wildly, more out of instinct than skill. To my shock, the blade connects with Fulvio's arm, slicing into his flesh and drawing blood. He howls in pain, stumbling backward. The mist around us thickens, swirling faster and faster, on the verge of becoming a miniature hurricane. I can barely see Fulvio now. He's just a dark shape in the fog. The floor beneath our feet seems to shift and tilt wildly.

"What the hell did you do?" Fulvio shouts, his voice sharp with fear.

Before I can answer, a deafening roar fills the long gallery. The mist parts briefly, and I catch a glimpse of something impossible. A vast, swirling vortex of energy, pulsing with an otherworldly light. It's creepier than what happened to me last night, and it's like nothing I've ever seen before. The supernatural whatsit grows larger by the second, and soon, I might not be able to escape. I need to get out of here. Now.

But it's too late. The vortex expands rapidly, engulfing me while Fulvio's form recedes from my view. The sword falls out of my hands, clattering to the floor, as I feel myself being lifted off my feet, spinning wildly through the air. Then I feel the sword's hilt clutched tightly in my hand again and glance down at it. The metal is glowing with an eerie blue light. Fulvio's screams fade into the distance as we're pulled apart by the force of the vortex.

The world around me becomes a blur of color and sound. I can't tell which way is up or down. My stomach lurches as I'm thrown through the air, spinning wildly, my limbs flailing like I'm a ragdoll. The sword vibrates in my hand, pulsing with that eerie blue light. Just when I think I'm going to be sick from the dizzying motion, everything stops.

I crash into deep, dark waters and plummet down, down, down with no way to escape my fate. Yet somehow, my fall was cushioned by something…inexplicable. But I have a worse problem than how I got here and why I'm not dead.

Because I can't swim.

Chapter Four

Rachel
A Few Moments Ago

I stroll along the banks of Dùndubhan's moat, crossing over the drawbridge on my way back to the castle. Pausing halfway there, I turn to gaze down at the murky depths. My father would be shocked to find out what sorts of tales I dream up in my mind to pass the time. A lass like me should never venture out on her own, that's what most folk believe. Even my mother, a woman from the future, believes I must be coddled like a bairn. I love them for them for caring so much about me, but I do sometimes feel a wee bit…stifled.

I've often dreamed of a mysterious stranger who would sweep me away to thrilling places and whisk me away on breathtaking adventures. A lad who would make my pulse quicken and give me a warm slickness between my thighs. A lad with a wicked streak.

Ah, but 'twill never happen. Mayhap if I squeeze my eyes shut and wish with all my might…

I stride onto the far bank and lean against a large, ancient stone that lies beside the drawbridge. The water below ripples, and for a moment, I swear I see a face gazing back at me. Not my own, mind you, but that of a man with dark hair, whisky-brown eyes, and a strange-looking beard that covers only a small area around his mouth. But when I blink, the image is gone.

"An Diabhal fhéin!" I whisper, staring into the murky depths. My heart races as I try to make sense of the vision. Who was that man, and why did he appear to me? Mayhap I shouldn't have invoked the devil when cursing my rotten fortune, but I cannae help it.

Wind whips my hair around my face, and I pull my cloak tighter. The air feels charged, as if the very fabric of time is stretching thin. I've heard tales of such occurrences from my great-aunts, though I've never experienced anything like that myself. Glancing back at the castle, I debate whether to share my vision with anyone. Would anyone believe me? Even among witches, this manner of sightings is rare and often dismissed as fanciful imaginings.

Och, of course my family would believe me.

I take a deep breath, preparing myself for what I'm about to do. With a quick glance 'round to ensure I'm alone, I kneel at the water's edge. My fingers tremble as I trace ancient symbols in the damp earth, whispering incantations passed down through generations of MacTaggart witches.

"Show me," I say, my voice barely audible above the gentle lapping of the moat. "Show me the truth behind the vision."

The water begins to swirl, slowly at first, then faster. Colors dance across its surface—flashes of silver, streaks of gold, and bursts of vibrant blue. My heart pounds as I lean closer, straining to make sense of the chaotic images. Suddenly, the swirling water stills, and the man's face reappears, clearer this time. His gaze, filled with a mix of confusion and annoyance, seems to lock onto mine. I gasp, nearly losing my balance as I tilt even closer.

"Who are you?" I wonder aloud.

As if in response, the vision expands. I see the man stumbling through a dark alley, desperate to escape from…something. He glances over his shoulder, fear etched across his face as an angry brute gives chase.

My breath catches in my throat. This isn't merely a vision of the past or present. Somehow, I'm seeing a glimpse of the future.

The scene shifts again. Now the man stands before Dùndubhan, ambling into the castle where other men and women wander about. The vision wavers, and I struggle to maintain my focus.

"Rachel!" My father's booming voice shatters my concentration. The water of the moat instantly stills, the mysterious man's face vanishing like mist in the morning sun. I scramble to my feet, hastily brushing dirt from my skirts. I have ne'er been blessed with dà-shealladh like Great-Aunt Lachina, so I cannae understand what came over me.

"Coming, *Athairich*!" I shout, my voice a touch too high-pitched to be natural.

As I turn toward the castle, I see my father's imposing figure striding through the open gates and onto the drawbridge. His brow is furrowed, golden eyes narrowed with concern and a hint of suspicion.

"What mischief are ye up to now, lass?" he asks while sweeping his gaze over the moat and the disturbed earth at my feet.

I force a smile, hoping it doesn't appear as nervous as I feel. "No mischief, Father. I wished for a wee bit of fresh air, that's all."

He raises an eyebrow, clearly unconvinced. "Aye, and your mother is a selkie. By God's bones, Rachel. I know that look in your eye. What have ye seen?"

I hesitate, torn between my desire to confide in him and the fear that I might have imagined the incident. I think I'll wait a wee while to find out if the vision returns. It might be nothing at all. But I cannae deny that man's face intrigued me and stirred something within me that felt warm, liquid, and delicious.

Father sighs, running a hand through his graying hair. "Ah, lass, why cannae ye be satisfied with the life you have? Ye constantly seek adventure, and I worry your desire for that will lead you astray."

My father turns toward the gates and begins walking, only to halt after a few paces. He glances back at me, his brows furrowed. "Are ye coming, lass?"

"Not yet. I'd like to sit on the riverbank for a spell, if that's acceptable."

"As you wish, mo nighean."

He smiles and heads back inside the castle walls.

As I settle in on the riverbank with my feet dangling, I close my eyes to hear all the sounds of nature. Birds twittering. The moat splashing faintly. The warmth of the sun on my face feels lovely, and I begin to hum an old song as I picture the face of that strangely alluring man from my vision.

Every hair on my body stiffens in anticipation, and I glance 'round, watching for…something.

I swear I hear a faint echo of my own humming, as if it's bouncing back from some unseen barrier. My eyes fly open, as I inspect the area. The moat's surface has gone eerily still, like glass, reflecting the cloudy sky above.

A ripple appears in the center of the water, spreading outward in concentric circles. My breath catches in my throat as I lean forward, half-expecting to see the mysterious man's face again. Instead, the ripples grow more intense, churning the water into a frothy whirlpool. A blast of wind whips around me, tugging at my skirts and hair. The air crackles with an energy I've never felt before—raw and wild, like lightning barely contained. My heart races as I scramble to my feet, torn between fleeing and staying to witness whatever is about to happen.

The whirlpool grows larger, its churning waters now spanning the width of the moat, while a violent tempest emerges in the sky, writhing like a wild serpent, dipping down toward the earth. But it doesn't touch down, merely hovering several feet above my head. A low, rumbling sound emanates from its depths, vibrating through the ground beneath my feet. I take an involuntary step back, my eyes wide with a mixture of fear and fascination.

Abruptly, the tempest aloft evaporates.

I return my focus to the whirlpool. But as I watch, it dissipates within a moment or two at most, and silence reigns once more.

How very strange.

I'm about to turn away, until a throaty caterwauling erupts overhead, drawing my attention to the blue sky—and the beast that's plummeting downward. "*Iasg is feòil!*"

My curse, "fish and flesh," hardly seems appropriate, though. That is clearly a man plunging toward the earth, not a giant fish. And he will surely die. Swiftly, I issue a magical incantation—praying the man will survive.

I freeze, paralyzed by the sight of the falling man. His arms flail wildly as he dives toward the moat, his dark hair whipping about his face. In the split second before he hits the water, our eyes meet. His are whisky brown. Just like in my vision.

He crashes into the moat with a tremendous splash, sending water arcing high into the air, and vanishes beneath the waves. Without thinking, I hitch up my skirts and wade in after him in the shallows. The icy water shocks me, but I charge forward, searching desperately for any sign of the stranger.

"Halò?" I call out, my voice trembling. "Can ye hear me? Are ye injured?"

For a heart-stopping moment, there's nothing but silence. Then, a few yards away, the surface of the water breaks. The man has sprung up out of the water, gasping and sputtering. He thrashes about, clearly disoriented, seeming on the verge of going under again.

"Hold on!" I shout, plunging deeper into the frigid water. "I'm coming to fetch you!"

The man's wild eyes lock onto mine as I swim toward him. His lips move, but I can't make out the words over the splashing. As I draw closer, I see panic etched across his face.

"Take my hand!" I shout, stretching my arm out.

He hesitates for only a moment before grasping my hand tightly. His grip is strong, his desperation obvious. I pull him toward me, wrapping my arm about his chest to keep his head above water.

"I've got you," I assure him. "Relax and allow me to guide us back to shore."

The stranger nods weakly, his body shivering violently against mine as I slowly swim us back to shore. By the time we reach the bank, my arms and legs are burning from exertion, but I manage to haul us both onto solid ground. We collapse onto the muddy shore, gasping for air.

"Are ye unharmed?" I ask between breaths, glancing at the mysterious man.

He's lying on his back, chest heaving, eyes squeezed shut. His strange clothes—unlike any I've ever seen—are soaked through and clinging to his body.

As I watch, he slowly opens his eyes and turns his head to meet my gaze. "How am I not dead? I fell from way up high, got thrown around like a ragdoll, and sank deep into the water. I should be a red smear on the grass."

"But ye aren't, and I'm grateful for that." My magics must have saved him, but I cannae tell him that yet. He might panic, or worse, try to murder me. Witchcraft is performed in secret. Witchfinders have been known to haunt the Highlands in search of witches to burn.

"Where am I?" he croaks, his accent unfamiliar to my ears, though it reminds me somewhat of my mother's manner of speech.

"You're at Dùndubhan Castle," I reply, pushing myself up to a sitting position. "In the Highlands of Scotland."

He pushes up on his elbows to study his new surroundings. "Where did all the tourists go?"

Tourists? I know what the word means, but I dinnae think it's wise to let this man see that I know. I learned it from my mother, who was a tourist in the twenty-first century, until she was pulled into the past.

The man's brow furrows in confusion as he takes in my words and appearance. He sits up fully, wincing slightly, and runs a hand through his dripping hair.

The man blinks repeatedly, seeming even more bewildered than before. "Tourists are…um, people visiting from far away?"

He waves his hand vaguely in the air.

"Oh!" I behave as if I have no idea what a tourist is, even though I do understand. "Well, Dùndubhan is not that sort of place. 'Tis our family seat."

"Family…" His voice trails off as he attempts to process my words. Wincing, he raises a shaking hand to his head. "Damn, what happened to me?"

I shrug. "Something very strange. 'Tis all I know."

He wipes a hand over his face and sighs. "What's your name?"

I stare at him with my brows wrinkled. Should I tell him who I am? Nay, I should not. Or mayhap I should. His presence has made me terribly confused which might explain what I say next. "I am Rachel MacTaggart. And you are…"

"Joey Finnegan."

An Irish lad? No, he doesn't seem at all like an Irishman aside from his surname. His accent is quite unusual—to me, at least.

"I don't understand," Joey says, his voice hoarse. "I was just...Fulvio grabbed me and then...crazy shit happened." He trails off, shaking his head as if to clear his mind. "This can't be real. Am I dreaming?"

I reach out hesitantly, placing a hand on his arm.

He flinches at the contact but doesn't pull away.

"I assure ye, this is quite real, Joey," I tell him. "Though I cannae explain how ye came to be here. A tempest pulled you down from the sky, then you fell into a whirlpool."

Guilt settles in my heart as I wonder if I should explain who and what I am. But my parents would lock me away in the tower bedroom if I confessed everything to a stranger.

Joey aims his golden eyes at me once more, and I'm struck by the intensity of his gaze. I sense fear there, yes, but also a sharp intelligence that makes me wonder who this man is.

Joey stares at me for a long moment before he speaks again. "A tempest? A whirlpool? That's impossible." He shakes his head, sending droplets of water flying. "Look, I appreciate you fishing me out of that moat, but this has to be some kind of elaborate prank. Where are the cameras?"

I tilt my head, not understanding his strange words. "Cameras? I know not what ye speak of. There's only you and I here on this bank, Joey Finnegan."

He scrambles to his feet, swaying slightly as he takes in his surroundings. I rise too and watch as his eyes widen and he notices the looming stone walls of Dùndubhan Castle, the ancient drawbridge, the wooden gates, and the dense forest beyond.

"No," he mutters, shaking his head. "No, no, no. This isn't right. Where's the parking lot? The gift shop? The moat is where the driveway was, but..." He scratches his head. "I must be dreaming."

"I know not of these things you speak of. There is only the castle, the forest, and the village beyond."

Joey knifes his hands through his hair, his eyes wild. The poor laddie seems incapable of comprehending the situation.

"What year is it?" he demands suddenly, grabbing my shoulders.

I recoil slightly at his touch, surprised by the intimate contact, but hold my ground. "The year of Our Lord 1621."

His jaw drops.

Chapter Five

Joey

I stumble backward, feeling as if I've been smacked down by a large, angry lumberjack. I'm kind of dizzy too, but that's ridiculous. Men don't get light-headed. "Look, Rachel whoever-you-are, what you're saying is impossible. This is the year 2025."

"Are ye certain of that, Joey Finnegan?"

"Yeah, absolutely."

Rachel seems oddly delighted by this turn of events. Maybe she doesn't get out much. Insane asylums are full of nutjobs who think they're Cleopatra or Joan of Arc, so this girl might think she's Mary Queen of Scots.

"This is bullshit," I declare as if I have a frigging clue what's happening to me. "You must be pulling my leg. The year is 2025."

"Afraid not, Joey." The certainty in her voice and on her face is damn convincing. "I once met a laddie who had calculated years greater than three thousand. But that's a tale for another day. Right now, we need to get you inside and dried off before anyone else sees you."

A shout rings out from the direction of the castle. "Rachel! Where are ye, lass?"

"Och, it's my father," she hisses, grabbing my arm. "Quickly now, we must hide you. Kieran MacTaggart willnae be pleased to see what his daughter has brought home."

My head is spinning now for sure. I've never felt this bewildered before, and so I let Rachel pull along with her a cluster of bushes near the moat's edge. We crouch down just as more heavy footsteps approach.

"Rachel MacTaggart! I told ye to come inside, not go for a swim! Ye look like ye jumped into the moat."

No, it wasn't Rachel who did that.

She peeks through the branches, where we can both see her father's imposing figure as he scans the area.

"I'm here, *Athairich*!" she hollers, sounding remarkably steady. "I'll be along in a moment. I, um…dropped something in the water and had to fetch it out."

I shift my position minutely, and Rachel throws me a warning glance over her shoulder. I mouth, "Sorry."

"Ye'll catch your death in those wet clothes," Big Daddy grumbles. "Come inside now, lass. Whatever ye've lost can wait until tomorrow."

"Aye, I'll be there shortly," she replies, and I'd swear she's rifling her brain for a way to smuggle her new toy into the castle undetected.

As Big Daddy's footsteps retreat, Rachel turns to me. "We need to get ye inside without anyone seeing. There's a secret corridor I found a few years ago, and no one else knows about it."

"It's not a dungeon, is it?"

"No, ye dafty." She sighs and grabs my hand. "Dinnae fash. I won't hurt you."

My life in the twenty-first century wasn't exactly awesome, so I guess letting this crazy girl lock me up couldn't be as bad as what Fulvio would've done to me. Yeah, I've lost my mind.

I wave toward…wherever we're going. "Lead the way."

We creep along the edge of the moat, staying low and using the bushes for cover. As we near the corner of the castle walls, Rachel seems to spot something, though all I see is ivy climbing up the bricks. But she pulls open a small wooden door that had been masked by the vines.

"There," she says, smiling and pointing at the door. "We'll slip inside here and find ye some dry clothes."

Rachel walks behind me as we head for who knows where.

What else can I do? I follow close behind the hot medieval girl as she eases the door open, wincing when the hinges creak. The narrow passageway beyond is dark and musty. Doesn't this place have an HVAC system? No, I guess it wouldn't. If I believe this is the past. I must be dreaming, right? A beautiful, sexy girl didn't pull me out of a moat, and she definitely didn't check out my ass a minute ago.

Finally, she halts and fishes a key out of her skirts. There must be a pocket inside there, though I couldn't see enough of it to be sure. As she eases the door inward, I wonder again if she plans to lock me in her private dungeon. But instead, Rachel plucks a lantern off the wall, where I can see a hook has been installed. She lights the wick, and the golden glow spreads throughout the room.

"Mind the step," she warns, taking my hand to guide me.

"In ye go," Rachel whispers, her lilting accent making my dick twitch—not enough for her to notice, thankfully. "And mind yer head, Joey."

I duck through the low doorway, my eyes adjusting to the dim light. It's not a dungeon, thank God, but a small chamber with rough stone walls. A fire crackles in a hearth and casts dancing shadows across the room. The smell of herbs and something earthy fills my nostrils.

"Sit," she commands, pointing to a wooden stool.

I obey, watching as she bustles around the room, grabbing jars and vials from shelves I hadn't noticed before.

"So, uh, what is this place?" I ask, trying to sound casual and not like a guy who just fell through time or…something. "And what are you doing with those vials and stuff? Are you trying to brainwash me?"

"Nay," Rachel says with a faint chuckle. She pauses in her work, holding a bundle of dried plants in her hand. Her blue eyes lock onto mine, and I swear I see a spark of humor dancing within them. "This, my dear time traveler, is where we figure out just how ye managed to tumble into our century."

I chuckle nervously. "Right, because that's totally a normal thing that happens."

"Och, ye'd be surprised," Rachel quips, tossing the herbs into a mortar and beginning to grind them with a pestle. "Though I must admit, it's usually old relics or magical artifacts that find their way through time, not handsome gentlemen."

I'm no gentleman. But she doesn't need to know that. "So, you, uh, deal with this kind of thing often?"

Rachel's laugh is like music, echoing off the stone walls. "Not exactly. But my great-aunts, now they've seen their fair share of oddities. I'm simply the apprentice, trying to muddle through." She pauses her grinding and looks at me thoughtfully. "Though I must say, you're by far the most interesting thing that's stumbled into Dùndubhan in quite some time."

I shift on the stool, unsure whether to be flattered or concerned, and I mumble, "Lucky me."

Rachel resumes her work, adding liquids from various vials to her concoction, humming tunelessly all the while. The aroma intensifies, filling my nostrils with a mix of earth and spice like nothing I've experienced before. While I watch her fiddling with potions and herbs, I can't stop myself from babbling.

"No offense, Rachel, but the gunk you're whipping up smells like a pig's ass."

Her delicate laughter reminds me of tiny bells. "Dinnae fash, Joey. 'Twill smell much better once I'm finished."

"How long will that take?"

The hottest girl I've ever met casually shrugs one shoulder. "It takes as long as it takes."

Yeah, that's an incredibly helpful statement.

"Have you always been a witch?" I ask, just for something to do.

"Not quite always." She grinds the herbs with a mortar and pestle, sighing wistfully. "My work would go much faster with fewer accidents if I had the MacTaggart witches' book. Unfortunately, 'twas lost many moons ago, before anyone can remember."

I want to ask her more about that, but I don't get the chance.

"All right, Joey Finnegan," Rachel says, her accent wrapping around my name like a lover's caress, "care to tell me what brought ye to our humble castle in the first place?"

I hesitate, weighing my options. How much should I reveal? This girl—this woman—seems genuine, but I've learned the hard way not to trust the way things appear to be. Damiano Zanetti had seemed like a nice, fatherly guy. I learned too late he was a godfather, the kind who sinks his claws into you and never lets go.

While Rachel keeps doing whatever the fuck she's doing, I might as well try to get a little information out of her. "You've got a bed and chairs and other furniture, so this must be your private hideout."

"Aye, 'tis my wee sanctuary," Rachel says, slipping in behind me and securing the door. "We can speak freely here."

"Do you drug all the guys you find in the moat and hide them in your secret room?"

"Ahmno drugging you. But why aren't ye more afeard of what's happened to ye?"

I shrug one shoulder. "After all the shit I've been through, starting from the time I was a boy, I guess time travel doesn't seem so scary—or so bad."

Especially with a woman like Rachel tending to me.

"What travails have beset ye, Joey? If ye dinnae mind me asking."

"That's okay." I scratch that back of my neck, thinking back on my not-so-excellent adventures. "I ran away from my old life and flew to Scotland, hoping to escape from some evil bastards. But one of them caught up to me. In this castle, actually. The modern version of it, anyway."

"How intriguing. What happened next?"

Rachel is a very strange girl, and she might slightly insane. But I kinda like that about her.

"Well, I was standing in front of a glass case that held a medieval sword that was labeled as 'The sword of *Ciaran mac in tSagairt.*' That means Kieran Aulay MacTaggart. Hey, that's your last name too—MacTaggart."

Her eyes go wide. She doesn't blink, but her lips fall open.

"What's wrong, Rachel?"

She flaps her head several times. "That sword belongs to my father. Ye must have seen a similar sword in your time."

"Huh." That's all I can manage to say. Was I destined to find that sword? Nah, I don't believe in fate. Says the guy who traveled through time.

Rachel clears her throat and goes back to work.

I spin around, taking in the cluttered shelves lining the walls. Jars of mysterious substances, bundles of dried plants, and what look suspiciously like animal bones are crammed into every available space. A worn wooden table dominates the center of the room, its surface covered in open books and scattered parchments.

"Look, I appreciate the hospitality and all, but what the hell is going on?" I demand as my New York instincts kick in. "One minute I'm running from the mob, the next I'm in some medieval cosplay nightmare."

Rachel's blue eyes sparkle with amusement. "Ye think this a game, do ye? I assure ye, Joey Finnegan, 'tis all too real. I'm only an apprentice, trying to muddle through. I cannae deny that you are the most fascinating specimen I've ever encountered."

Now I'm a specimen. That's just perfect.

Rachel goes back to her work, mixing up who knows what. Probably something designed to turn me into her sex slave. Not that I'd mind being at her mercy. But I forget about that as the smell of her potion intensifies, a mix of earth and spice that makes my head swim.

Damn, she's hot. Or maybe her witch's brew is getting to me.

She eyes me sideways, her lips curling in the slightest smile. "Tell me, Joey, how do you think you came to be in the past? Magic must have brought you here, but the how and why are unknown to me."

I swallow hard, weighing my options. This girl seems genuine, but I've been burned before. Still, if I'm really stuck in the past, I need allies. So, I give her a sanitized version of the truth.

"I was...in some trouble back home. Unsavory people were after me, and I needed to lay low for a while. Scotland seemed as good a place as any to disappear." I push a hand through my hair, which is still slightly damp from my unexpected swim. "I found the castle by accident. Couldn't believe how many tourists were there checking out the artifacts."

Rachel raises an eyebrow, her hands never pausing in their work. "Danger-ous people, I take it?"

"Bingo." I realize she might not understand that word, so I explain. "That means yes."

"You came from New York City," she says as if she's not sure she knows how to pronounce the name. "Now, tell me about the trouble you got your-self into."

"Let's just say I got mixed up with the wrong crowd back in New York. Thought I could handle it, but..." I trail off, not wanting to relive those memories.

"Och, ye poor laddie."

Rachel moves closer. Too close. The scent of her turns me on, but the way her bodice pushes the mounds of her tits up might just turn me into a rampaging animal. She's hot, yes. But there's something else about her, something I can't quite describe, that makes me want to pull her into my arms and rip that bodice open.

Rachel stretches her hand out to me, nearly touching my shoulder be-fore she seems to think better of it. Her blue eyes search mine. "Ye've been through the ringer, haven't ye?"

I shrug, trying to play it cool even while eying the concoction she's been working on. "It's nothing I couldn't have handled before I fell through some kind of weird whirlpool. Things are different now, way different." I peer down at her vials. "What exactly are you brewing there, anyway? Some kind of truth serum?"

Rachel laughs, and the musical sound enchanting. "Nothing so sinister, I assure ye. 'Tis a potion to help anchor ye to our time. Without it, ye might just slip right back to yer own century."

"Wait, you're serious? This isn't some elaborate prank?"

"I'm afraid not, Joey," Rachel says. "You have truly traveled through time, and now you're here in seventeenth century Scotland. Though I can-nae say how or why just yet. Someone must have thrown you into this world for a reason, whether it was nefarious or not."

"What if I'm stuck here?"

She shrugs one shoulder. "I'm fair certain ye will adapt. Ye dinnae seem like the sort who would simply lie down and die."

Rachel continues to stir her concoction. "And as for being stuck, well, that remains to be seen. First, we need to stabilize your presence here."

Finally, she lifts the mortar, which is now filled with a swirling, irides-cent liquid. Then she commands me to "drink this" while holding it out to me.

I squirm at the sight of the orangish liquid. "Uh, no offense, but I'm not in the habit of drinking mystery brews offered to me by strangers. Not even beautiful ones."

She gives me an exasperated look, shaking her head.

I gaze down at the mystery brew that still faintly bubbles. This must be an alternate universe, but I guess I'd better get used to it.

Chapter Six

I roll my eyes at Joey. "Och, ye daft man. If I wanted to harm ye, I'd have left ye to drown in the moat. Now drink up before ye fade away entirely."

"And if I don't swallow your witch's brew?"

"Then ye might find yourself slipping back through time, perhaps to somewhere in the middle of a Viking raid—or worse. Is that what ye prefer?"

I cannae hold back my exasperation. Joey is behaving in a quite uncooperative and ungrateful manner.

He scrunches up his face. "Uh…no, I guess?"

I release my frustration with a blustering sigh. Joey Finnegan is the most obstinate man I have ever met. Well, after Alisdair MacLeod, that is. But I dinnae want to think about that cacan right now. Aye, Alisdair is a wee shit, despite being quite large.

Joey folds his arms over his chest. "About that MacTaggart book of magic…has anyone tried to find it?"

I roll my eyes and huff. "Do ye think MacTaggarts are stupid? Aye, every generation has hunted for the book, but it's gone. Or mayhap hidden by a cloaking spell at the bottom of a well. An evil witch stole it, according to the legend. But who knows what the truth might be?"

"Sorry. I didn't mean to offend you. Just thought I might be able to help."

He gives up on conversation and instead picks at the blanket on the bed.

I've just bent over to sniff my potion, inhaling deeply and smiling as the steam washes over me, when I notice Joey staring at my bodice.

"What's the bother now, Mr. Finnegan?"

He winces and scratches his cheek. "Your bodice is…awfully tight. And, uh…" He makes a cupping gesture with his hands. "Your mounds might be on the verge of spilling out."

Mounds? What in the world is he talking about?

But then he swerves his gaze away from me, seeming to force himself to focus on the task at hand. He groans miserably and grabs the mortar. "Bottom's up, I guess."

"Drink every bit of it, please."

He glowers at me but at last finishes off the potion.

"There's a good laddie," I say, patting his shoulder. "Now, let's see if that does the trick."

"Will I sprout wings or turn into a frog?"

I can't help laughing. "No, ye daft man."

"So, uh, did it work?" he asks, handing the empty mortar back to me.

"Aye, I believe it has. You're looking more…solid now."

He wipes a hand across his brow in a sarcastic gesture. "Okay. At least I won't need to keep rocks in my pockets to anchor me." He sticks his tongue out repeatedly while his lip curls. "Are you sure that shit wasn't excrement from a cow? I might start mooing."

"Dinnae be ridiculous. You'll need different clothes, though."

"Please don't dress me up in a kilt. Skirts aren't my thing."

I burst out laughing. "Skirts?"

"What the hell is so damn funny?" Joey demands in a growly tone, his expression rather petulant and not all what I expected from a pirate who emerged from the depths of the moat. Aye, when I first saw Joey, I wondered if he were a pirate and hoped he might whisk me away on a swashbuckling adventure. "Don't you have any clothes that won't make me look like a douche?"

"A doosh?" I ask. "Mayhap you can explain that word to me."

He scrunches up his face and averts his gaze. "Never mind."

"As you wish. But you need proper clothing." I scrutinize his body, feeling his arms and thighs—strictly to gauge his clothing sizes, of course. "We need to get ye proper attire. Can't have ye wandering about the castle in those strange clothes. Then, we could perhaps introduce you to the family."

He looks down at his strange blue trews and leather jacket. "What's wrong with my clothes?"

Cannae help laughing again. "Nothing, if ye want to be mistaken for a witch or worse. Come now, I have some old clothes that might fit ye."

"No way will I wear a dress."

"But gowns are quite comfortable."

He twists his mouth into a wry smile. "You're teasing me, aren't you? I don't mind that."

I lead Joey to a trunk in the corner and begin rummaging through it. He watches me with a mixture of curiosity and trepidation.

"Here we are," I pronounce triumphantly, pulling out a bundle of clothes. "These belonged to my grandfather, Uilleam, who died before I was born. They should fit ye well enough."

"Hand-me-downs?" he says, his lips pursed. "I had my fill of those when I was a kid. My parents, and later my foster moms, never cared if I was wearing threadbare junk. But I'm in a different century now, so I'll need to adjust."

He accepts the clothes, feeling the texture of the homespun wool. "Uh, thanks. Where can I change?"

I point to a folding screen in the corner. "Behind there. And be quick about it. We dinnae want anyone stumbling upon ye in those strange garments."

Joey returns a moment later, now properly dressed. But he fusses with his clothing while making odd faces, then sighs heavily. "Guess I'm doomed to look like a court jester."

"Nay, you look nothing like that. You're quite handsome, actually."

He smirks. "Thanks. I appreciate the compliment. You are absolutely beautiful, by the way."

The way his voice deepened inspires my loins to grow...warm and slick in an unseemly manner. I find myself squirming, though not from discomfort, not precisely. Once, I saw my parents kissing in the garden, and I did not understand the strange fervor that I witnessed on that day. But I began to get an inkling when I happened upon an indecent book that someone had left in the cellar—centuries ago, based on the amount of yellowing. The pages of the dusty tome had faded somewhat, but I could figure out what the deliciously craven images depicted. And ever since, I've been, um...pleasuring myself inside my secret chamber.

And sometimes, I employ magics to do that.

Joey's annoyance evaporates. He tips his head to the side, studying me with renewed interest. "Have you ever been kissed, Rachel?"

There's something about the way his whisky-brown eyes explore every detail of my face, shivering a thrill down my spine that leaves me feeling as if I'm standing on the edge of a precipice. "Ye've got a smoldering fire in your eyes, Joey Finnegan."

The words had spilled out before I could catch them. How foolish did I sound? Very, I'm fair certain.

He quirks an eyebrow, one corner of his mouth lifting in a maddening half-smile. "And you, Rachel MacTaggart, have an innocent way of behaving, but there's a glint in your eye that says otherwise."

A blush warms my cheeks—partly from his words, partly from the fact that my body is humming with a wicked desire that, until now, I've known only in my dreams or in the privacy of my secret chamber. I've never been kissed before. The very thought sets my heart to racing like a deer escaping from a bear, rushing through the heather, only to be devoured in the most delicious manner. And Joey, with his dark hair tousled just so and that rogue's jacket that tells tales of city life I can only imagine, is every bit the man I'd dreamt would steal that first kiss.

"Have you ever been kissed before, Joey?" The words had slipped out bold as brass, and for a moment, I worry I've gone too far. But then his gaze darkens with something that resembles hunger. And suddenly, the slickness in my loins is dribbling down my inner thighs. An unusual scent wafts from down there too.

"Of course I've been kissed. I'm an expert on that topic—and on popping cherries."

My brows wrinkle. "What do cherries have to do with anything?"

Before I can take another breath, Joey closes the distance between us, his hands framing my face with a tenderness that belies the fierce need in his gaze. He crushes his lips to mine, igniting a fire that coils a slow, slithering fire low in my belly. My toes curl into the worn rug beneath us as I clung to him, lost in the sensation of his mouth moving against mine, the stubble of his jaw grazing my skin.

Pressed against him, I feel a hard, insistent lump bulging against my belly. Somehow that lump arouses me even more. A gasp escapes me, the sound smothered by the heat of our kiss. What would making love be like? The question flashes through my mind, leaving a trail of warmth and a tingling between my thighs that I've never experienced before.

"Tha mi ag iarraidh barrachd," I whisper as he moves his lips a touch, just enough that I could say those words. It was the Gaelic phrase for 'I want more' slipping out instinctively.

Something wild and fierce that rises within me, spurred on by the taste of him, the smell of leather and man, and the rush of emotions that made my head spin. Our breaths mingle, fast and ragged, as we navigate this unfamiliar territory together. Every brush of his lips fans the flames of my curiosity, kindling something deeper within us both. Breathing hard, with our kiss still simmering on my lips, I take a step back from Joey. His chest heaves in the dim light of my secret room, his gaze as piercing as a hawk's.

"What am I to do with ye, Joseph Finnegan?" I muse aloud, tucking a stray lock of hair behind my ear.

"Hmm, what would you like to do, Rachel MacTaggart?" he asks, a half-grin lifting the corner of his mouth. His gaze flicks down to my chest where my nipples are visible beneath the fabric.

"What if I fancy keeping ye all to myself?" The words slipped out before I could stop them, revealing more than I intended. I like having this man from another world hidden away in a secret place where no one will ever see or hear what we might do in this room. 'Tis a secret thrill that sets my heart to racing.

"Your family will start wondering where you've gone," Joey says, leaning against the bedpost, his arms folded so that the muscles and sinews beneath his shirt flex with every movement. "Are you going to keep me here forever?"

Bod an Donais, I do want that. And when I glance up at Joey, I can think only one word: mèinn. Aye, I want this craven man for my own, if only for tonight. I bite my lip, releasing it slowly. "Forever is a long while, Joey."

He takes a step toward me.

But I back away, clucking my tongue. "Nay, I shall be the one in control of you tonight."

"What exactly do you have in mind?"

A thrill runs through me at his words, at the way his gaze rakes over every inch of me. I've never felt so bold, so wanton. It's as if his presence has awakened something primal within me.

"First," I say, my tone calmer than I feel, "You will remove your clothing. Slowly."

He quirks an eyebrow but complies, shrugging off the clothing I'd found for him with a fluid grace that makes my mouth water. The thin fabric of his undershirt clings to his muscled chest, and I find myself transfixed by the roughhewn beauty of him. A few small scars on his chest only serve to make him even more fascinating. How did he acquire the scars? I'll ask him later. Once I'm done with him. But it's the bulge in his trews that leaves me speechless and tingly in my nether regions.

Oh, aye, he is a large man in every way.

"Like what you see?" he teases, his cocky grin causing wetness to slicken my thighs even more and to create a sucking sound whenever I move.

I swallow hard, willing my voice not to waver. "*Bod an Donais*, I dinnae like it. I love it. Now get rid of the rest, please, immediately."

"Mind explaining that phrase you just spoke first?"

"Oh, aye. It literally means 'the devil's penis.' However, it's used as curse word."

Joey's hands move to the waistband of his trews, his eyes never leaving mine as he slowly unlaces them. The tension in the room is palpable, crackling like lightning before a storm. As the fabric slides down his legs, revealing more of his tanned skin, I feel a rush of heat flood my cheeks. I've never seen a man fully unclothed before, and the sight of Joey standing before me, bare as the day he was born, sends a shiver of excitement through me. He's all lean muscle and sharp angles, a stark contrast to the softness of my own form.

The thickness of his cock makes my mouth water, and I drag my tongue over my lips—three times. The tip of his arousal is rosy red, with a drop of clear liquid poised on the tip.

"Your turn," he declares, his voice low and gravelly, his chest rising and falling heavily.

I hesitate for a moment, then I begin fumbling with the laces of my bodice.

Joey steps forward, his breaths warm against my ear. "Let me do that."

With deft fingers, Joey delicately unlaces my bodice, his knuckles grazing my skin with every movement. As the fabric falls away, exposing my breasts to the cool air, I fight the urge to cover myself. My nipples have pearled, and the tightness of them gives me a shivery sensation. My own juices dribble down my thighs.

Joey groans deeply as he roams his gaze over my body. "You are so fucking beautiful. And the scent of your lust is making my dick stiffen even more."

His words embolden me. I let my skirts pool at my feet, standing before him as naked as he is. The vulnerability of the moment is both thrilling and terrifying, and I can't believe I'm doing this with a stranger. Yet oddly, he doesn't feel like a stranger to me.

"Now what?" Joey asks.

"Lie down on the bed."

His lips stretch into a sensual smile as he follows my command, stretching out on the narrow bed. The candlelight flickers across his sculpted body, casting enticing shadows. I hesitate for a moment, overcome by the sight of him. With trembling fingers, I reach out to trace the hard planes of his chest. His skin is warm beneath my touch, and I marvel at the way his muscles tense and relax. Joey's breath hitches as I explore lower, following the trail of dark hair that leads to his impressive manhood.

"Rachel," he groans, his hips lifting slightly off the bed.

"Oh, Joey," I breathe, my fingers tracing the hard planes of his chest. "I…I'm not sure what to do next."

His eyes soften as he gently grasps my hand. "We don't have to do anything you're not ready for. Just lie down beside me."

I slide onto the narrow bed, keenly aware of every point where our skin touches. Joey wraps an arm around me, drawing me close against his warm body. The feeling of his bare skin against mine sends tingles racing across my flesh. Joey's hand traces lazy circles on my back as we lie here, our breathing slowly syncing. The initial urgency fades into a comfortable intimacy.

"Tell me more about where ye come from," I say, nestling closer to Joey's warmth. His scent envelops me, a heady mix of leather, spice, and something uniquely him.

His hand stills on my back for a moment before resuming its gentle caress. "It's…different from here. Louder. Faster. There are machines that can take you anywhere in the world in a matter of hours. Buildings that reach so high they seem to touch the sky."

I try to imagine such wonders, but my mind struggles to comprehend them. "It sounds magical."

He chuckles, the rumble vibrating through his chest. "Some might say that. But it has its downsides too. People are always in a rush, always connected to their devices—little machines that can show you destinations beyond the reach of the human eye. Sometimes I think technology has made us lose touch with what's really important."

"And what do ye think is important?"

Joey remains quiet for a moment. "Connection. Real, human connection. The kind where you can look into someone's eyes and see their soul. The kind we're sharing right now."

His words send a shiver through me, and I tilt my head up to meet his gaze. The intensity I find there takes my breath away. Without thinking, I lean in and press my lips to his. Our kiss is different from the first one—slower, deeper, filled with a tenderness that makes my heart ache. But for now, I'm content to bask in his warmth and the quiet intimacy that surrounds us.

Abruptly, he peels his mouth away from mine. "You should be in charge, Rachel. Do whatever wicked things you want to me, and I guarantee I'll love every minute of it. When you're ready, I'll fuck you until the sun comes up."

Oh my, I cannae wait for that.

Chapter Seven

Joey

The look on Rachel's face makes me want to pounce on her like a wild jaguar that hasn't mated with a female in years. To see the sweet virgin gazing at me with intense hunger, her focus locked on my groin, is the hottest thing I've ever seen. Should I be doing this with her? A good man would say no. We just met today. But I've never been a particularly good man, and doing bad things is my forte.

I need to fuck Rachel.

But as I raise my head, she places a hand on my forehead to push me back down. "I will control the situation, Joey, if you please."

"Sure. Whatever you want."

Rachel hops off the bed, making her tits bounced wildly. I can't help groaning. Damn, I need to suck those little buds until she cries out. But I can't do anything. She tied me up, and I don't care. Rachel MacTaggart is so fucking beautiful, and her small yet plump lips make me want to claim that mouth and then that body. Damn, it's been too long since I had sex. Now I'm the secret boy toy of a medieval girl who treats me like I'm a curiosity. When she brushes her hands over her bodice, my dick twitches, and suddenly, I'm breathing harder.

She hunts around in a dresser drawer and brings out several ropes. Her naughty expression makes my breath hitch. But when she catches one corner of her mouth between her teeth, releasing it slowly, my dick twitches like it can't wait to be inside her. Climbing onto the bed again, she straddles my body with her hips and sets the ropes down beside her.

Then she takes hold of one rope with both hands, stretching it taut. "Would you mind if I tie you up, Joey?"

"Don't ask, Rach. Command me."

"You want that?"

"Hell yeah, baby."

She bites her lip again, considering me while running her hands up and down the rope. "After I've given you pleasure, mayhap you will do the same for me."

"You can bet on it. I'll fuck you like a maniac."

She leans forward, her breath hot against my ear. "Then let the games begin, Joey Finnegan."

"You're awfully casual about having sex with a stranger."

Rachel bites her lip, letting it slide free gradually. "I reckon I should be worried, but I…trust you not to hurt me."

I lift my head as much as I can while tied up. "Rachel, that's not—"

She seals my lips with one finger. "Shh, gràidh. Let me enjoy you."

How can I say no to that? She's the cutest sexpot I've ever met. I should turn down her offer to fuck me, but my brain shut down the second she said she wants to enjoy me. I've never had the best judgment when it comes to screwing women I barely know. But Rachel is the first girl who ever made me want to do that.

But I have to ask a question. "What does *gràidh* mean?"

"Darling."

She called me that? It's probably a term Scots use casually.

With deft movements, Rachel snatches up two ropes and loops them around my wrists, binding me to the headboard. The soft hemp fibers ensure I won't get chafed. Rachel's fingers trail down my arms, leaving goosebumps in their wake, and I grip the ropes harder.

"Is this too tight?" she whispers in her enchanting Scottish accent that makes me so hot for her.

"It's perfect," I growl, reflexively straining against the bonds. My cock feels like it might explode, that's how much I want her.

Rachel smirks, clearly pleased with herself. She reaches for two more ropes, this time securing my ankles to the bedposts. I'm spread-eagled before her, completely at her mercy. The vulnerability should terrify me, but instead, it only heightens my lust. Her fingers dance over my chest, teasing and exploring, dipping into my navel occasionally and generally driving me crazy. I lift my hips, desperate for her to remove my bonds and touch her, but she tuts softly.

"Patience, my gallant time traveler. Good things come to those who wait."

Rachel's nimble fingers work at the button and zipper, her movements torturously slow. When she finally peels the denim down my thighs, I blow out a relieved breath.

Her eyes widen as she takes in the sight of my fully aroused cock waving before her. She stares at it, her eyes wide and her chest heaving. A sexy blush stains her cheeks. "My, my, what a magnificent beast you are."

I can't help the cocky grin that spreads across my face. Not that I wanted to stop it. "Like what you see, my dirty-sexy Highland beauty?"

She drags her tongue across her lips, back and forth, back and forth.

I grit my teeth, fighting against the primal urge to break free of my bonds and take Rachel right here and now. But I force myself to remain still, to let her explore my body at her own pace. Her delicate fingers trail along my inner thighs, making me hiss in a breath because this feels so damn good.

Rachel wraps her hand around my erection, sliding it up and down, up and down, driving me crazy. I let out a strangled groan. Her grip is tentative at first, experimental, but grows bolder with every stroke as she glides her tongue over her lips repeatedly. I think she wants to devour me, and I wouldn't mind that at all. But I can't stop myself from straining against the ropes, desperate to touch her, to kiss her, to flip her over and bury myself inside her until we're both spent and glistening with sweat.

"Rachel," I pant. "Please, you're killing me."

She pauses, her hand stilling on my throbbing length. "Please what, Joey?"

Her simple question belies the glint in her eye that's anything but innocent.

I swallow hard, struggling to form coherent thoughts as my lust for her grows hotter and harder, shortening my breaths and speeding up my pulse. "Fuck, Rachel...I need more. I need to be inside you."

She licks her lips again—and winks at me.

Then, with agonizing slowness, Rachel lowers her head, her silky golden-brown hair tickling my thighs. Her warm breath ghosts over my sensitive skin, making me shudder. When her tongue darts out to taste me, I nearly come undone right then and there.

"Rachel," I groan, my voice hoarse with need.

She looks up at me through her lashes. "Hush now. Let me savor you, Joey."

The naughty lass lowers her mouth again, this time taking me fully between her lips. The wet heat engulfs me, and I arch off the bed, straining against my bonds. Rachel hums her approval. Shockwaves of pleasure course through my body, and when she starts to suck gently, I splutter and thrash.

"Not like that, Rach," I hiss. "Do it hard, or I'll go off before either of us wants."

Her inexperience is evident, but what she lacks in technique she makes up for in enthusiasm. Her tongue swirls around my dick as she bobs her head, sucking greedily, finding a rhythm that has my heart thudding and my ears ringing. I want to thread my fingers through her hair, to guide her movements, but the ropes hold me fast.

"God, baby," I pant. "That feels incredible."

She releases me gradually, a wicked grin on her face. "I'm pleased you're enjoying yourself. But I believe it's time we moved on to the main course, don't you agree?"

Unable to speak thanks that blowjob, all I can do is flap my head like a moron while Rachel straddles my hips. I can feel her heat hovering just above me, and I smell her cream wafting around me. The scent is tantalizing and maddening.

"Are you ready for me, Joey?"

"Shit, yes," I groan, straining against the ropes. "Fuck me hard before I have a heart attack."

Rachel smirks, clearly enjoying having me at her mercy. With agonizing slowness, she lowers herself onto me, enveloping my cock in her tight, wet heat. We both gasp at the sensation.

"Oh, Joey," she breathes, her eyes fluttering shut. "I love the way you feel inside me. Never knew it would be so….exhilarating."

She begins to move, rolling her hips in a sensual rhythm. I buck up to meet her thrusts, desperate for more friction. The bed creaks beneath us as we find our rhythm together. Rachel braces her hands on my chest, her nails digging into my skin as she rides me with increasing urgency. The liquid sucking sound of my cock sliding in and out of her, over and over, has me grunting and thrashing. The vision of her rose-dappled chest and her tits bounding in my face drives me insane.

"Ah, fuck, Rachel," I groan, straining against the ropes. "You feel so good."

She throws her head back, suddenly going rigid.

I dig my nails into the bed, clenching my jaw, transfixed by her stunned expression. The second her inner muscles clamp onto me, I use all my strength to buck up into her repeatedly until she blows her top. Rachel slaps her palms on my chest and fucks me so wildly that I can't help but thrust my hips into her movements. Not even the ropes could stop me now.

Rachel screams, her cries echoing off the stone walls and her nails raking my chest.

My cock explodes. I shout and thrash while my come jets into her womb. She increases her pace, her breasts bouncing hypnotically with each thrust. I ache to touch them, to take a rosy nipple between my teeth, but the bonds hold me fast. All I can do is watch in awe while this Highland beauty takes her pleasure from me.

As our frenzied movements slow, Rachel collapses onto my chest, her breath coming in ragged gasps. I long to wrap my arms around her, but the ropes still bind me. She nuzzles my neck, placing soft kisses along my jaw, her delicate breaths tickling my shadow beard. For a moment, we simply lie here, basking in the afterglow.

She lies on top of me, her expression dazed. "That was…wonderful. Your member is magical indeed."

I chuckle. "I'm good, but not that good. Thanks for the compliment, though, Rach. You were absolutely incredible, and that's not hyperbole."

She lifts her head, a shy smile playing on her lips. "Truly? You're not simply saying that to make me feel better?"

"Trust me, I've never experienced anything like that before. And I've had my fair share of sexual encounters."

A flicker of something, maybe jealousy, passes across her face before she irons out her expression. "Well then, I suppose I should feel quite proud of myself."

"You should, for sure."

Rachel traces lazy patterns on my chest with one finger, then flicks her fingernail over my nipple, making me gasp. "Perhaps we should untie you now, hmm?"

I grin, tugging at the ropes. "As much as I enjoyed being at your mercy, I'd love to get my hands on you."

She giggles and reaches up to loosen the knots. As soon as my hands are free, I wrap my arms around her, dragging her in for a deep, hot kiss. Rachel melts against me.

When we finally break apart, I cup her face gently. "You are the sexiest woman I've ever been with, Rach."

She smiles shyly. "I like that you've begun to call me Rach. I've never had a nickname before."

"Well, it's about damn time you got one."

"Now that you're free, what do you plan to do with me, Mr. Finnegan?"

I growl playfully, flipping us over so she's pinned beneath me. "Oh, I've got lots of ideas. And every single one is filthy."

She grins.

I'm just about to lean in and claim those lips when a loud pounding on the door makes us both freeze. Whoever that is, they seem like they want to kick the door down.

"Rachel! Are ye in there?" A man's gruff voice booms from the other side.

"Shite," Rachel hisses, her eyes wide. "It's my father!"

We scramble to disentangle ourselves, frantically searching for our discarded clothes. I've barely managed to pull on my funky looking trousers—the ones Rachel called "trews"—when the door handle starts to rattle. With her help, I just barely manage to pull on everything including my medieval boots.

But we forgot about my modern clothes. Shit. It's too late to worry about that, though.

"Rachel! Open this door right now!"

She throws me a desperate look, then her gaze darts around the room frantically. She shoves me toward a large wooden wardrobe and whispers, "Quick, hide!"

I stumble toward the wardrobe, still dizzy from our passionate encounter. As I try to cram myself inside the tight space, the aroma of musty furs and old leather engulfs me. Rachel tosses my modern clothes and boots in after me and slams the wardrobe doors shut. I hug my clothes to my chest.

"One moment, *Athairich*! I am in a state of undress."

At last, the pounding ceases. Big Daddy's voice is softer now, almost apologetic. "Oh, I see. I will wait here until you have covered yourself."

Through a tiny crack, I watch her hastily pull on a chemise and smooth down her hair. Rachel then digs through a wooden chest until she finds the dress she wants and hastily pulls it on over her head. As she smooths out the dress, she takes a deep breath to compose herself before she opens the heavy chamber door.

"Father, what a surprise," she says, her voice unnaturally high. "I was… asleep."

Kieran MacTaggart stomps into the room, his imposing figure casting a long shadow across the room. Even from my hiding spot, I can feel the intensity of his anger radiating off him.

Big Daddy squints at his daughter. "Resting? That's what ye were doing, eh?"

Rachel stands her ground, chin lifted defiantly. "Aye, 'twas what I was doing. Is that a crime now, Father?"

Kieran's gaze narrows as he surveys the room. "I heard voices. Yours and a man's voice."

"You must be mistaken," Rachel says, but I can see her hands trembling slightly. "Perhaps 'twas the wind playing tricks on your ears."

Kieran grunts, clearly unconvinced. He stalks around the room, his gaze roving over every surface. My heart pounds so loudly I'm certain he'll hear it. Hiding in a wardrobe reminds me of all the times I got stealing trinkets when I was a boy, and I'd have to hide in a closet until my foster mom number whatever gave up on trying to find and punish me.

"And what of these?" Kieran snatches up my discarded T-shirt, jeans, and leather jacket from the floor. "Ne'er have I seen such garments, and I'm fair certain they dinnae belong to you."

Oh, damn. In our haste, we'd forgotten about my modern threads.

Rachel pales visibly. "Well, you see, I...found them. In the forest. I brought them back to examine them more closely."

Kieran MacTaggart isn't buying that story. I can't leave Rachel out there alone to deal with her dad.

So, I hastily pull on my medieval clothes—somehow without either Rachel or Kieran noticing it—and burst out of the closet. I drop my medieval garb on the floor. Then I dust myself off casually, as if men pop out of closets in women's bedrooms all the time. "Hey there, you must be Rachel's father. I'm Joey Finnegan."

Kieran glowers at me with a seething hatred in his eyes—and a huge sword in his hand.

I adjust my medieval coat and clear my throat. "So, Mr. MacTaggart, is it true that you're the last laird of Dùndubhan?"

"Where did ye get such an asinine idea?"

"I heard it in this castle—back in the twenty-first century, before I was chucked into the Middle Ages."

"Are ye claiming to have traveled through time?" Big Daddy growls. "Rachel might have brought ye to our home, but ahm the one who's about to make certain ye leave."

Oh, crap. Kieran's tone is not friendly. He glares at me with all the seething anger of a man who just found a stranger hiding in the bedroom of his only daughter.

Bye-bye, Joey Finnegan. You are going to die.

Chapter Eight

Rachel

A*thairich*, no!" I place myself between Joey and my father, using my own body as a barricade. The man who gave me blissful pleasure mere moments ago gazes at the laird of Dùndubhan with a smirk playing on his lips and a canny gleam in his eyes. "I said, no, Father. You will not harm this man."

I must stand up to my father. I shan't let him harm Joey.

"Father, how did you find this chamber?" I demand. "No one had entered this room until I stumbled onto it a few years ago."

"Did ye think no one else knew?" He huffs. "Ahm aware of everything that goes on in this castle."

Guidheachan. My private sanctuary is not a secret after all.

Cursing in my mind willnae alter the situation. But I couldn't stop myself from thinking that phrase. It means "son of a bitch."

My father squints at me, then snarls a litany of Gaelic profanities. When he finally gives up, setting the tip of his sword on the floor, all the fight seems to have drained out of him.

I feel a wee bit faint as I stand my ground in a manner I have never done before, not with my father. His eyes dart between Joey and me as if he's figuring out how to handle the situation.

Father swings his claymore in a circular motion as if he's trying to instill fear. He knows that won't work with me. "Rachel, step aside. This interloper has no place here. And what is he doing in your chambers? Has he molested you?"

"Of course not. Do ye think I'd let a stranger into this room without being certain I could trust him? Ahmno a fool." I lift my chin, channeling every ounce of stubbornness I've inherited from him. "Joey stays, Father. He is under my protection now."

Kieran MacTaggart's eyes narrow to slits, and I swear I can see the wheels turning in his mind. "Protection, ye say? And what makes ye think ye have the authority to offer such a thing?"

I take a deep breath, knowing my next words will change everything. "Because I am a MacTaggart witch—just like you."

My father eyes Joey with deep suspicion. "Who is this man? Why did you bring him into our home? And by God's bones, whyever did you invite him into a room I have ne're seen before? 'Tis dangerous, mo nighean. He might be a brigand."

Should I confess to the actual way in which I met Joey Finnegan? I feel Joey's hand brush against my back in a silent show of support. But my father's gaze bores into me, demanding an answer I dare not give. Not yet. I swallow hard against a lump in my throat, knowing I can't reveal the whole truth without risking even more chaos.

"He is…well, he's not from here, Father," I say, carefully choosing my words. "Joey comes from a place far away, and he needs our help."

"Far away?" Father scoffs. "Ye mean he's a Sassenach? An Englishman?"

I shake my head. "No, not English. He's from…somewhere else entirely."

Joey steps forward, his whisky-brown eyes aimed straight at my father. "Mr. MacTaggart, I mean no disrespect to you or your clan. I found myself here by accident, and your daughter has shown me great kindness."

Father's grip on his sword tightens. "Accident? What sort of misadventure brings a man to Dùndubhan, laddie? Even members of my own clan rarely visit us."

"Magic, Father, that's what brought Joey here. The sort of magic our family has guarded for generations."

"You told him of our magics?" He sighs heavily, shaking his head. "Your actions have been very foolish and quite unlike you. Have you no sense of the peril you might have unleashed in our home?"

I bite my lip, frantically scrambling for a plausible explanation.

My father glowers at Joey once again. "What is your vocation, Joey Finnegan?"

"Well, I—" Joey makes a pained face. "In the twenty-first century, I was an orphan who became a petty thief. Not proud of my lifestyle. It's just what I had to do to survive."

My father's face is turning an odd shade of crimson, and I must say something to stop him from ejecting Joey from the castle. But before I can speak, a commotion erupts from the hallway. The door bursts open, and my Great-Aunt Lachina stumbles in, her eyes wild and unfocused.

"The veil!" she cries, her voice raspy and urgent. "The veil between worlds has been torn!"

Father's attention snaps to Lachina. His brows furrow, and his voice abruptly becomes gentler. "What do ye mean, gràidh? Explain so we might all understand your upset."

Lachina's gaze fixes on Joey, and she points an accusing finger at him. "This one…he has crossed through time itself. Dark forces pursue him, Kieran. Forces that threaten us all!"

The room falls silent, save for the crackling of the hearth fire. Never have I known Lachina to be so afeard. Her face is pale, and she wrings her hands.

My mother, who had remained in the background thus far, now clasps Father's hand. "Relax, Kieran. Let's hear what this guy has to say before we toss him down the garderobe shaft."

"Mayhap you are correct, mo chridhe. Your wisdom always exceeds mine."

Joey surreptitiously clasps my hand, squeezing it gently. I can feel the tension radiating from him, but he stands tall, meeting my father's glowering gaze.

"It's true, Mr. MacTaggart," Joey concedes, his voice steady despite the gravity of the situation. "I don't know how I got here, only that I was at the modern version of this castle when—wham!—I got sucked into a tornado and then dropped into a whirlpool in the moat. And I think…well, I'm beginning to realize it must have something to do with your family's magic. Jeez, I can't believe I'm talking about witchcraft."

Father's eyes dart between Joey, Lachina, and me. "Rachel, ye will explain this. Now."

I lay my hands over my belly, lifting my chin. "Joey appeared at Dùndubhan through a portal. One that I suspect our ancestors created long ago, though it had been dormant for many moons. He's from the future, and he escaped to Dùndubhan because bad men were after him."

Before the laird can chastise me, *Màthair* interjects. "Rachel, if Joey is wanted by bad men, maybe there's a good reason for that. How much do you know about him?"

How can I respond to her question? I know so little about the man I allowed to ravish me, yet I know in my bones that he would never harm me. My family remains too skeptical to understand my feelings.

"The threads of fate are becoming entangled," Lachina whispers. "The universe is weaving a new tapestry here at Dùndubhan. I've seen visions of dark figures, men with strange weapons, searching for something...or someone."

Joey steps forward. "Mr. MacTaggart, I—"

"You will call me Laird, ye cacan."

"Sure, whatever." Joey's jaw is clenched, but otherwise he seems almost relaxed. "I know this sounds crazy. Hell, I can barely believe it myself. But I swear to you, I mean no harm to your family or your secrets. I'm just trying to figure out what's going on and how to get back home."

"And where exactly is this 'home' of yours, laddie?"

Joey hesitates, his gaze darting to me before he answers. "New York City. In the year 2025."

A collective gasp echoes through the room. Even Father, usually so stoic, can't hide his shock. "Impossible. Alyssa was brought to this time by my aunts' magics. They did not send you here. Aye, Lachina?"

"Yes, but..." She shakes her head. "Kieran, please believe me. Darkness is coming. The men who sent this laddie here are fearsome enemies."

I seize the moment, pressing our advantage. "Father, Joey needs our help. And if Great-Aunt Lachina's visions are true, we might need his help as well. Whatever forces are pursuing him could be a threat to all of us."

Father studies Joey with the intensity of a hawk eyeing its prey. "And what skills do ye possess that could possibly aid us against such a threat?"

Joey straightens his shoulders, meeting Father's gaze with a determination that makes my heart swell with pride. "I may not have magic, but I know the future these men come from. Their weapons, their tactics. I can help you prepare for what's coming."

A tense silence falls over the room as my father considers Joey's words. I hold my breath, acutely aware of the weight of this moment. Finally, Father's shoulders slump ever so slightly, and he nods.

"Very well," he says, his voice gruff. "Ye may stay, for now. But know this—if I catch even a whiff of treachery from ye, I'll not hesitate to run ye through myself."

Joey lifts one brow, and his lips curl into a cocky slant. "Understood, Mr. Laird Man. You have my word."

Should I or my family trust a thief? Joey has been good to me, but we met only this morn.

Father turns to me, his expression stern. "Rachel, you will no longer enter this hidden room. Henceforth, you shall remain within sight of at least two members of the family at all times." He turns to Joey. "I will accept responsibility for ensuring our guest does not attempt to escape. If anyone approaches the castle, we will keep Joey out of sight and make sure he doesn't cause any trouble." Father grasps my shoulders, pulling me closer to glare into my eyes. "But you, Rachel, are not to consort with him under any circumstances. Do you understand?"

"Yes, Father."

Just as the tension in the room begins to ease, Lachina suddenly gasps, her hand flying to her mouth as if to stifle a scream. Her eyes roll back in her head, and she sways precariously on her feet like a reed caught in a sudden gale. I rush to her side, catching her just as she begins to collapse.

"Great-Aunt Lachina!" I cry, my heart racing. The room, which had been uncomfortably warm from the hearth's blaze, now feels as cold as the North Sea. Every eye is on us, the silence thick with dread.

Lachina's body is rigid, her breathing shallow and rapid. I lower her gently to the floor, cradling her head in my lap. Her normally serene face is contorted with fear and pain, and a thin sheen of sweat glistens on her forehead. My mind races through the possibilities—has the strain of her earlier vision been too much for her? Or is this something even more dire?

"Someone fetch water!" I shout, but no one moves. They're all too stunned, too paralyzed by the sight of the clan's most revered seer in such a state. Even my father, who usually springs into action in a crisis, stands rooted to the spot, his face a mask of concern and helplessness.

Lachina's lips begin to move, forming soundless words. I lean in closer, straining to hear her. Is she trying to tell us something? To warn us? Every second stretches into an eternity as we wait for her to speak, to give us some clue about what she's seen.

"What have you seen, Lachina?" I exclaim. "Please tell us!"

Her voice comes out in a raspy whisper, barely audible. "They're coming. The men from the future. They are perilously close to discovering the portal through which Joey came."

A bone-chilling wind whips through the chamber, extinguishing the fire and plunging us into darkness. The stone walls seem to groan and shift around us. I clutch Lachina tighter, my heart pounding so hard I fear it might burst from my chest.

"Father!" I cry out, reaching blindly in the darkness.

"Stay where ye are!" his voice booms.

I feel Joey slipping his fingers between mine, and I'm grateful for the contact. I hear shuffling and muffled curses as everyone tries to orient themselves in the pitch black. Then, a blinding flash of light erupts from the center of the room. As my eyes adjust, I see a swirling vortex of blue and silver energy, crackling with electricity.

"Holy shit," Joey breathes beside me. "It's happening again."

The vortex grows larger, its howling wind drowning out all other sounds. I cling to Joey, and he clings to me. But just when it seems we might all be spirited away to another realm, the portal is snuffed out like the wee flame of a candle. Golden light spreads throughout the room, and I see that my father has lit my lantern.

As the glow flickers across the room, it reveals the shocked and fearful faces of my loved ones. Whatever transpired a moment ago, the situation has returned to normal now. Yet a chill lingers inside this chamber. And the anxiety generated by the tumult remains on the faces of us all.

What if the magics I invoked to save Joey from drowning have caused this frightful occurrence?

"Come," Father commands. "We shall all retire to the solar to discuss the situation as well as to alert Efrica and Morna of the danger. They are waiting for us there."

I help Lachina to her feet, supporting her as we make our way to the solar. Joey hovers close by, his eyes darting around warily as if he expects more otherworldly intrusions. Father leads the way, his broad shoulders tense, one hand resting on the hilt of his sword.

The solar is warm and inviting, a stark contrast to the chill that still clings to my bones. Great-Aunts Efrica and Morna are here, their weathered faces creased with concern. As soon as we enter, they rush to Lachina's side, fussing over her like mother hens. She is the youngest of the aunts, after all.

"What happened?" Efrica demands, her voice sharp with worry. "We felt a disturbance in the very air itself."

Father raises a hand, silencing the room. "Dark powers may have attempted to invade Dùndubhan, and we must protect ourselves."

Guidheachan. As my Gaelic curse suggests, I wish ill fortune on whomever is determined to harm our family. What further intrusions must we endure? And what will the evil ones from the future attempt to do next?

We have many questions, but no answers.

Father seizes Joey by the throat. "You must have caused a portal to appear and sent Lachina into a fevered trance. You are no friend of the Mac-Taggarts."

Chapter Nine

Joey

Kieran MacTaggart hoists me off my feet and leaves me dangling in midair. He also scowls at me while snarling words between his teeth. "I should ne'er have allowed you to remain with us, much less remain alive. Whatever foul spells you have invoked caused pain for Lachina. And ye no doubt bespelled my daughter too. Why shouldnae I kill you this instant?"

"Uh, because I didn't do anything to Rachel or Lachina. You'd be murdering an innocent man." My voice is hoarse thanks to Kieran's iron grip on my throat.

His eyes narrow to slits. "Innocent? Ye appeared through the mists on our sacred ground. Naught but dark magic could have brought ye there."

"I didn't 'appear through the mist,' sir. I was ejected from a twister and plunged into the moat. I would've drowned if Rachel hadn't saved me."

I try to twist free, but it's like wrestling with a granite statue. My lungs burn for air, and black spots dance at the edges of my vision. Great. I can see the headlines now. Joey Finnegan, dead in medieval Scotland, strangled by an angry Highlander with trust issues.

"Father, stop!" Rachel's voice cuts through the tension like a blade.

Kieran's grip loosens just enough for me to gulp down precious oxygen. I catch sight of Rachel rushing toward us, her hair flying behind her like streamers of gold and bronze.

"He's telling the truth," she insists. "Joey didnae hurt Lachina. I was with him when it happened. We all were."

"Then who conjured the portal?" Kieran's voice rumbles like thunder. His gaze bores into mine with such intensity I swear he's trying to drill into my soul. "If not you, then whom?"

"I don't know," I wheeze. "I know nothing about portals or magic or whatever's happening here. One minute I was running from—" I catch myself before mentioning the mafia goons who'd chased me to Dùndubhan. Something tells me explaining modern organized crime to a medieval Scottish warrior might not help my case. "—from trouble. Next thing I knew, I was drowning in your moat. Until your daughter saved me."

Kieran's massive hand tightens again, almost choking me. "Ye expect me to believe ye simply materialized? A stranger with peculiar clothes and even more peculiar speech who appeared on the very day when Lachina fell ill?"

"Great-Aunt Lachina is not ill, Father," Rachel explains. "Not in the manner you suggest. Please dinnae blame Joey for an inexplicable event none of us understand. Instead of harassing him, try listening to him."

Kieran's grip wavers, but he doesn't release me. I swear I can see his internal struggle in those golden eyes.

"Father," Rachel says, her voice softer now, but no less determined. "Do ye remember what Great-Aunt Lachina herself said about strangers? 'Not all who come unbidden bring disaster.'"

Something flickers in Kieran's golden eyes—recognition, perhaps, or memory. His jaw works beneath his beard as he considers his daughter's words.

"Aye," he finally mutters. "She did say that."

He drops me unceremoniously, and I collapse to my knees, gasping like a fish tossed onto the land. My throat feels raw, as if I've swallowed broken glass.

Alyssa steps up beside her husband and lays a steading hand on his arm. "You didn't trust me either when we first met. Why not give Joey a chance?"

"Cannae do that, not with our precious daughter." Kieran straightens his clothing and lifts his chin. "Mayhap what Lachina said was true. But this man who looks like a fiend from Hell will get nowhere near you, Rachel. Not until I'm satisfied 'tis safe."

Rachel's eyes flash with a defiance that matches her father's intensity. "Father, I am not a wee bairn to be sheltered. I have dà-shealladh, same as Great-Aunt Lachina. If Joey meant harm, don't ye think I would ken it?"

Kieran grumbles. "Your second sight is not as strong as Lachina's."

"Not yet."

I push myself to my feet, still massaging my throat. "Look, I understand your suspicion. I'd be suspicious too if some strange guy fell into my..." I gesture vaguely at the castle surroundings, "...medieval fortress. But I swear on whatever you hold sacred, I mean no harm to your family."

Kieran's massive frame looms over me like a mountain ready to avalanche. "Ye speak of our ways as if they're foreign to ye. Another reason to distrust ye."

"Because they are foreign to me," I blurt out before I can stop myself. "Where I come from, we don't have castles and moats and people wearing..." I gesture at his kilt. "Whatever that's called."

Kieran's nostrils flare. "Ye mock our dress now?"

"No, no, I'm not mocking anything. I'm just trying to explain that I'm...not from around here. The kilts I saw back in the twenty-first century were shorter and, well, just different."

Rachel steps between us. "Father, Joey isnae only from another land. I believe he's from another time."

Wasn't I just explaining that? Nobody listens to me.

And now I'm whining in my head. Terrific.

The silence that follows is so complete I can hear the wind whistling through the stone battlements above us. Kieran's face darkens like storm clouds gathering over the mountains.

"Witchcraft," he spits. "Time magic is forbidden. Ye know that, Rachel. And yet ye engaged in such witchery."

"I didnae intend to, Father. But I wished for—well, it doesnae matter."

"Tell me what ye wished for, mo nighean."

She bows her head and bites her lip.

Kieran's nostrils flare. "I see. My daughter yearned for a strange man from the future to whisk her away to...who knows where. Fairyland, mayhap." A sigh blusters out of him. "I thought ye were more intelligent than that. Now I must do what is necessary to separate you from this fiend until I have proof that he's no threat to us."

Uh-oh. I'm getting a bad feeling about Big Daddy's intentions. He wants to "seperate" me from Rachel. That doesn't sound like an invitation to dinner tonight.

The laird swivels his head toward me, his eyes mere slits. Then he marches over to a chest and brings out a small sword, returning to stand in front of me. "This dirk could slice ye in half, laddie. Best be careful with your words and actions."

"Uh, okay."

He seizes my arm. "Yer going to spend the night in the tower bedroom. Alone. In the morn, we'll discuss the situation again."

"Tower bedroom?" I choke out. "That sounds...homey."

Actually, it sounds like a torture chamber.

Kieran's grip tightens like a vise. "Tis more than ye deserve."

As he drags me out of the solar, Rachel follows tries to follow. But Big Daddy gives her a hard look, and she backs away. "Father, there's no need for this. Joey has done nothing wrong!"

"Silence!" Kieran's voice booms throughout the castle. "Ye've been bewitched by this man, and I'll not hear another word on it." He frowns. "Until I've made my decision, that is."

We climb a narrow spiral staircase, going up, up, and up while my legs begin to burn with every step. Kieran shoves me forward, seemingly unbothered by the endless climb. Medieval Scots must have thighs of steel.

"Here," he finally announces, pushing open a heavy wooden door that groans in protest. "Yer quarters for the night."

The "tower bedroom" turns out to be a chamber that's about as welcoming as a prison cell. A narrow cot sits beneath an arrow-slit window, and a rickety table holds a single stub of candle. A threadbare rug covers part of the stone floor, and the whole place smells of mildew and despair.

"Cozy," I mumble.

Kieran grunts. "Be grateful ye have a roof. I considered dropping you down the garderobe shaft."

Do I want to know what a garderobe is? Doubtful.

I lean forward, glancing around the room. "This isn't the dungeon?"

The laird's massive hand shoves me further into the room. "Dinnae test my patience, laddie. The door will be barred from the outside. If ye attempt to escape..."

He pats the dirk at his side meaningfully.

"Got it. Stay put or get skewered."

"Ye mock our ways again."

I wait a moment, allowing myself time to get over the initial shock and disappointment. So what if Big Daddy hates me? He couldn't hurt me any worse than my foster moms had. A nine-year-old on the streets, alone, hungry, treated like a mongrel dog...yeah, the tower room will do just fine.

"Not mocking anything," I say, my voice stronger now. "Go ahead and lock me in. I'll see you in the morning."

Kieran studies me for a moment, tipping his head to the side. Then he walks out the door, hesitating on the threshold, and finally shuts the door.

I hear the heavy wooden bar slide into place, and Kieran's footsteps fade away as tromps down the staircase. The silence that follows feels like a physical presence in the room.

"Well, Finnegan," I say to myself, "you've really done it this time."

I slump onto the cot, wincing as something that feels suspiciously like a rock digs into my back through the thin mattress. The last rays of sunset filter through the arrow-slit, casting long shadows across the stone floor. My throat still burns from Kieran's grip, and I gingerly touch the tender skin, wondering if I'll have a necklace of bruises by morning.

If I live to see morning.

Shortly after Kieran's footfalls fade away, I hear someone removing the wooden bar that keeps me in. I glance around for anything I might use as a weapon, but of course, I find nothing.

The door swings open—and Alyssa hurries inside. She makes a shushing motion with her finger.

If she's trying to seduce me...yeah, sure, Finnegan, that's what she wants. What a moron.

The lady of the house approaches me. She speaks in a half whisper. "I'm going out that door to grab a few things for you."

"No offense, ma'am, but your husband will slice and dice me if you do that."

She shakes her head. "Not that door. The one behind you."

Turning in that direction, I suddenly understand. "A secret door?"

"Yes. Now wait here."

Alyssa disappears through the hidden doorway.

I stand and pace the small room, five steps one way, five steps back. Medieval prison cells aren't known for their spaciousness, I guess. The stone walls seem to close in, but I take slow, deep breaths to calm myself.

The secret door swings open. Alyssa gently pushes it shut with one foot while clinging to the large bundle in her arms.

I move to help with her burden.

She shakes her head again.

All I can do is lean against the wall while she does...whatever. As she unfolds her bundle, things become clearer. I whisper, "Is that a different mattress?"

She nods.

"And decent sheets?"

She nods again.

Alyssa swiftly replaces the mattress, then changes the linens. Once she's done, she points toward the far corner. Still speaking softly, she tells me, "That chamber pot in the corner is for relieving yourself. The jug on the table is full of water."

"How did you sneak that in here?"

"I didn't. Lachina sometimes comes up here to be alone and think. She left the water and chamber pot here." Alyssa tiptoes to the door but pauses with her hand on the knob. "Sleep tight, Joey."

"Why on earth would you help me?"

"Because Kieran is freaking out for no reason, and he'll figure that out in the morning." She gives me a tight smile. "Rachel was very upset about the situation, but she'll be fine, don't worry. MacTaggart women are tough."

Alyssa walks out, shutting the door and sliding the wooden bar into place.

Shuffling over to the cot, I settle onto it and grab the water jug, sipping the contents. It tastes like water. No obvious poison. So, I'll probably live to see another day in medieval Scotland.

Woo-hoo.

Chapter Ten

Rachel

Last night, after my mother sneaked into the tower bedroom to make Joey more comfortable, I considered sneaking in there myself. Mother undoubtedly assumed no one had seen her entering and exiting the tower. She also must have believed I didnae catch on to her plan.

My motives were…less altruistic than hers.

I love Mother all the more for worrying about Joey. Whatever my father believes, I'm convinced that Joey is a good man deep down. So what if he was a thief back in New York City? Everyone deserves a second chance.

After dressing and fixing my hair, I rush downstairs to the great hall for breakfast.

Father and Joey haven't come down yet. Neither have the aunts. My grandparents left for Loch Fairbairn early this morn, which I know because I was already awake and waiting to say goodbye. Mother sits alone at the table, calmly sipping her morning tea. She looks up at me with those knowing eyes that always seem to read my thoughts before I've even formed them properly.

"Good morning, sweetie," she says, her voice lilting with that musical quality that makes even the simplest greeting sound delightful. "You're up early."

I slide onto the bench across from her, trying to appear casual. "Just hungry is all."

"Mmm." The sound she makes is noncommittal, but her eyes twinkle. "Nothing to do with our guest, then?"

Heat rises in my cheeks. "I dinnae know what you mean."

"Of course not." She pushes a plate of bannocks toward me. "Though I suspect our Mr. Finnegan will be down shortly. He was restless when Kieran checked on him this morning."

I spring off the bench, suddenly feeling a wee bit faint. "Did Father…"

"Beat the shit out of Joey?" She grins, shaking her head. "You don't really believe your father would do that."

I slump back onto the bench. "Nay, I dinnae believe it. I'm anxious to see Joey, that's all."

"Naturally."

Mother's smile widens, and I know I've revealed too much. All I can do to avoid her knowing gaze is busy myself with buttering a bannock.

"Your father may be as stubborn as a Highland mule, but he's not un-reasonable." She clasps my hand. "He's just protective. Give him time, and I'm sure Kieran will come around to our point of view."

"Our view?"

She gives me a quick hug. "I'm on your side, Rachel. Always."

The great hall door swings open. Joey enters, dark hair tousled in that careless way that somehow looks deliberate. He scans the room before his attention lands on me, and something in my chest flutters wildly. Aye, Joey has done that to me.

"Morning," he says. "I slept like a baby last night, if anybody's interested."

Father has just entered the great hall and sat down in his chair at the head of the table. Joey's words were clearly meant for the laird of Dùndubhan. But Father only lifts one brow briefly.

Mother gestures to the empty space beside me. "Join us, Mr. Finnegan. I trust you slept well?"

Joey's gaze flicks to me before he answers, and I wonder if he's remembering my mother's midnight visit. "Better than expected, considering."

"Considering my husband has you sleeping in what amounts to a drafty prison cell?" Mother's tone is light, but I can hear the apology beneath it.

"It has a certain rustic-meets-prison kind of charm." Joey slides onto the bench next to me, close enough that I can feel his warmth radiating into me. "Reminds me of my first apartment in Brooklyn. Except with a better view and fewer cockroaches."

Father grunts, reaching for his tankard. I catch the slight twitch at the corner of his mouth—not quite a smile, but not displeasure either. "The tower room has housed many a visitor. Some more welcome than others."

Joey doesn't flinch under my father's scrutiny. Instead, he meets his gaze steadily, and I feel a flare of admiration for his courage. Most men cower before my father, the great Laird Kieran MacTaggart.

"I appreciate the hospitality," Joey replies breezily, reaching for a bannock. "Even if it comes with a side of suspicion."

I tense, waiting for Father's reaction. To my surprise, he lets out a short bark of laughter.

"At least yer honest about it," Father says. "More than I can say for most strangers who've wandered onto our lands."

"Father," I begin, but Mother shoots me a warning glance.

Joey's leg presses against mine under the table, and ahmno certain if it's accidental or deliberate. Either way, an electrifying warmth courses through me and makes focusing on breakfast nearly impossible. I shift slightly, pretending to reach for the honey, but don't move away from his touch.

"So," Joey says casually, slathering butter on his bannock, "what's on the agenda today? More suspicious glaring? Maybe some light interrogation? Or do I get the full Dùndubhan dungeon treatment?"

"Nothing like that," Mother says with a laugh, cutting through the tension so easily that I'm a wee bit jealous. "We don't have a dungeon, anyway. But Rachel could show you around the grounds. Couldn't you, sweetie?"

Before I can answer, Father claps his tankard down with a thud that resonates through the great hall. "The *macan* can help me sharpen the weapons. If he's to stay here, he'll earn his keep."

Joey's eyebrows shoot up, but I catch the hint of relief in his expression. This is progress—Father offering work instead of outright rejection.

Or threats of murder.

Joey's brows wrinkle. "Sharpen weapons? I've never done that before."

"That's obvious," Father says with a snort. "But ye'll learn."

I watch as Joey straightens his shoulders, meeting Father's challenge with that confident half-smile, the one that makes my stomach flutter and my loins grow slick.

"I'm a quick study," Joey says, taking a bite of his bannock. "Though I should warn you, the last sharp object I handled was a letter opener at the office job I had for about five seconds. Didn't end well for the potted plant next to my desk."

Mother chokes on her tea, covering her laugh with a cough. Even Father's eyes crinkle slightly at the corners.

Joey sighs melodramatically. "Serves me right for thinking a thief could become a data entry operator. But I'm raring to go when it comes to sharpening dangerous weapons, and I'm sure the laird is too. Just hope I don't accidentally chop off parts of my body that I really need."

"Dinnae worry," Father says, his voice gruff but lacking the earlier edge. "I'll make sure ye dinnae take anyone's eye out. Especially yer own."

Joey glances at me, and for a heartbeat, something lovely passes between us—a shared understanding, perhaps, or mayhap a deeper connection that neither of us wants to name yet. His gaze holds mine for fraction longer than necessary, and I feel that flutter in my chest again.

"I'd rather go with Rachel," Joey says boldly, still looking at me. "See the grounds, get my bearings. If I'm going to be stuck here for a while, I should know the lay of the land."

"Ye'll have plenty of time for that after ye've proven yerself useful."

"Father," I interject. "Joey has already proven himself—to me."

The hall falls silent. Even Mother seems to be holding her breath. Father's jaw works back and forth as he considers my words.

"Aye," he finally concedes, though grudgingly. "That he did."

Joey shifts beside me, our thighs still pressed together. The contact sends a fresh wave of heat through my body, and I wonder if he can feel it too—the ardent desire simmering between us.

"I'll tell ye what," Father says, surprising us all. "The lad can help me with the weapons till midday. After that, Rachel may show him the grounds." He fixes Joey with a pointed stare. "That is, if ye haven't managed to dismember yerself by then."

"Challenge accepted," Joey says, his tone deceptively light. "I promise to return with all fingers intact."

"I'll hold ye to that." Father pushes back from the table. "Meet me at the smithy in a quarter hour."

As Father strides from the hall, Mother rises gracefully. "I'll be in the solar with the aunts. Care to come with me, Rachel?"

"Oh, aye. Is it embroidery day again?"

"Absolutely."

I rise as well and kiss Joey's cheek as he exits the great hall. Mother and I trail after him until we "peel off," as Mother likes to say, and head for the solar. By the time evening comes, we are all too tired to do anything but eat a quick meal and go to bed. Father insists Joey must not share my bed, but he lets our guest sleep in a much nicer bed chamber this time.

Joey defers to my father.

The next afternoon, we receive surprise visitors. My grandparents, Dale and Norma, have returned earlier than expected, and we greet them in the courtyard. They admit to worrying about the situation between me and Joey, as well as what Father might do to him. But I never doubted that Kieran Mac-Taggart would warm up to the time traveler and do the right thing.

My grandparents hug me fiercely and kiss my cheeks. They also fuss over me as if I'm a bairn, cooing and blubbering. This is nothing new, however. I love them to pieces. They can blubber all they like and I willnae complain.

"Are you sure you're okay, honey?" Grandmother asks. "Your father is right. That man does look like a demon, with that goatee and wild hair."

I can't help but laugh. "Grandmother, Joey does not look like a demon! He just has a different style than what you're used to." I lower my voice. "Besides, I think he's quite fetching."

"Oh, I didn't say he wasn't handsome. The most dangerous ones usually are."

"Norma," Grandfather chides gently, "don't go putting ideas in the girl's head."

"I'm fairly certain those ideas are already there," Grandmother says with a knowing smile that makes my cheeks burn.

"Where is this mysterious time traveler now?" Grandfather asks, glancing around as if Joey might materialize from behind a tapestry.

"Father has him repairing the cellar door," I say, unable to keep the pride from my voice. "Joey's surprisingly good with his hands."

Grandmother raises an eyebrow at that, and I feel my cheeks flush again.

"For building things," I clarify quickly. "He's been here three days now. Father insists one harassing him endlessly."

"That's to be expected, honey. You are the only daughter of Kieran Mac-Taggart and Alyssa Vescovi."

"And how does your New York thief feel about manual labor?" Grandfather asks, his tone casual but his eyes shrewd.

"He hasnae complained once," I pronounce, and it's true. Joey has thrown himself into every task Father has assigned, from weapon sharpening to cellar repairs, with determination. "I think he's trying to prove himself."

"To your father?" Grandmother asks, though her knowing smile suggests she already knows the answer.

"To all of us. But aye, mostly to Father."

The large, wooden outer door of the castle flies open, and Kieran Mac-Taggart stomps into the courtyard. He rakes his gaze over all of us. But his harshest glare is reserved for Joey. "Sassenach, 'tis time we finished the discussion we had the other day with the entire family. Ahm glad Norma and Dale are here as well. Gather the aunts and meet me in the solar."

My heart lodges itself somewhere in my throat. The "discussion" Father refers to can only be about Joey's presence at Dùndubhan, and judging by the thunderous expression on his face, I'm not certain it will end well.

"Kieran," Grandmother says, stepping forward with that particular blend of deference and authority that only she can manage with my father. "We've only just arrived. Perhaps we could—"

"Now," Father interrupts, his voice brooking no argument. "The matter cannae wait."

Joey appears behind Father, his hands dirty from the cellar repairs, a smudge of dust across one cheek that somehow makes him even more appealing. Our eyes meet, and I try to convey reassurance I don't entirely feel.

"Should I make myself scarce?" Joey asks, wiping his hands on his borrowed trews. "I'm getting pretty good at this home-repair stuff."

"You are coming with us, Joey Finnegan. Right now."

Chapter Eleven

Joey

The MacTaggarts have taken all the available normal chairs, leaving me with nothing to sit on except some kind of weird box that has spiky things shooting up from both sides. Oh, there's also a super uncomfortable engraved back. To top it off, I barely fit on this contraption, and my ass is already starting to hurt. Not sure what the medieval term is for this hard, wooden thing I'm sitting on. But hey, I'm used to bad furniture and the hard stares of angry men. Nothing Kieran MacTaggart says or does will tick me off.

Probably.

Two more people have entered the room. Kieran nods to the newcomers and introduces them. "Joey, ye might as well know the names of these folk. Meet Dale and Norma Vescovi, Rachel's grandparents. Normally, the first daughter would be named after her mother's mother. But we altered that tradition for our lass. Alyssa chose the name—Rachel Morainn MacTaggart."

Alyssa smiles at her husband lovingly, then glances at me. "Morainn was the first name of Kieran's mother who died a long time ago. She was from the Ross clan."

"Nice to meet you guys," I say to the gray-haired couple. "Were you sucked into the past by magic too?"

"Sort of," Dale confirms. "Kieran's aunts brought us here so we could be with Alyssa."

"Why didn't Alyssa take the MacTaggart name?"

Alyssa herself responds. "Kieran insisted on using the traditional Scottish way in which the wife keeps her family name."

I shift my weight, trying to find a position on this wooden torture device that won't give me sciatica. Rachel catches my eye from across the room and gives me a sympathetic smile. I return it with a half-hearted smile of my own, hoping my discomfort isn't too obvious.

Back in New York, I had cash in my pocket. Guess that's gone now. Even if I could wish for my money to magically appear, what would I do with it?

Kieran MacTaggart's deep, snarly voice snaps my attention back to the gathering. "You have brought peril to my kin, Joseph Finnegan, and I will know what your role is in the dark magics that brought you here."

"Dark magics? You've gotta be shitting me." I gesture at my modern clothes that are slightly battered. They've always been like that, since I could only afford junk I bought at thrift shops. Mobsters aren't known for their magnanimous nature. "I don't know jack about supernatural crap."

Kieran's eyes narrow, and I swear I can see the veins in his forehead pulsing. "You mock our ways, outlander?"

"No, not intentionally," I backpedal, realizing I've stepped in an invisible pile of manure. "I'm just...confused. Where I come from, magic isn't exactly a daily occurrence."

Rachel turns to her father. "*Athairich*, Joey speaks the truth," Rachel says. "He's as bewildered by all of this as we are."

I throw her a grateful smile, but Kieran isn't mollified.

He leans forward, his massive frame casting a shadow over me. "Bewildered or not, your arrival has set in motion circumstances we do not yet understand. The winds whisper of change, and not all change bodes well."

A chill runs down my spine. I've faced down mob enforcers who were less menacing than Kieran MacTaggart when he glares at me. Still, his attitude doesn't scare me the way he must've hoped it would.

"Look, I understand what you're saying, Mr. MacTaggart," I tell him. "You're worried about your family, I get that. But I swear, I'm not here to cause trouble. I just want answers—about how to get home, whether I can ever blend in here, stuff like that."

"You will call me laird, ye cacan."

If I plan to go home somehow, I probably shouldn't have let his daughter fuck me. Well, my judgment has never been the best.

Kieran's eyes narrow further, if that's even possible. "And how do we know you speak true? How do we know you're not in league with our enemies? The ones we cannot yet identify?"

I can't stop the bitter laugh that spills out of me. "Trust me, big guy, I've got enough enemies of my own without adding yours to the mix."

Rachel steps forward, lifting her chin. "Father, I believe him. I've spent time with Joey, and I sense no deception in him. I believe his arrival is not a threat. We should worry not about Joey, but about the beings Lachina spoke of."

Kieran's gaze softens slightly as he looks at his daughter, but the suspicion doesn't leave his eyes. "Your heart is kind, gràidh, yet sometimes you are too trusting. We cannot afford to be naive when unknown forces might be plotting against us."

I bite my tongue, resisting the urge to point out that trusting me hadn't exactly been Rachel's only motivation for our…interactions. Instead, I tell Kieran, "Look, I get why you don't trust me. I'm a stranger who appeared out of nowhere. But I'm just as lost as you are. If there are dark forces at work here, I have a vested interest in helping to stop them."

Kieran's golden eyes bore into mine. "And why would you wish to aid us? What stake do you have in our affairs?"

I meet his gaze steadily. "Because whatever brought me here might be my only way back home. And if that's the case, then I need to understand what's going on just as much as you do."

The laird's expression remains stern, but I notice a flicker of something in his eyes that might be curiosity. "You speak boldly for one in such a precarious position."

I shrug, trying to appear more nonchalant than I feel. "Bold speech is about all I've got going for me right now."

A snort of laughter escapes Rachel before she can stifle it. Her father shoots her a disapproving look, but I catch the hint of a smile tugging at the corner of his mouth.

"Very well," Kieran says after a moment of contemplation. "You may stay, for now. But know this, Joseph Finnegan—I'll be watching you closely. One false move, and you'll wish you'd never set foot in the Highlands."

Even I know better than to push my luck in this situation. "Understood, sir. Thank you."

"Only knights are called 'sir' in this time."

Does Kieran have chain mail armor? It wouldn't surprise me since he does have a big sword.

The laird of the castle rises to his full height, towering over me—because I'm sitting down. Even when I stand, I'm a few inches shorter than Kieran. When he strides up to me, where I sit on this horrid chair contraption, he leans over to make sure I get the picture. He's Big Daddy, I'm the flea he can squash under his boot anytime he likes.

He jabs a finger at me. "You will wait here in the solar. Lasses, come with me."

Kieran swings the door open, gesturing for the women to obey his command. Alyssa rolls her eyes as she walks past her husband, and the great-aunts follow her. Rachel hesitates beside my torture chair, biting one side of her lip as her gaze flicks between me and Big Daddy.

Kieran squints at his daughter. "Come, Rachel. Now."

A wistful sigh rushes out of her. Then she walks out of the room, and Kieran shuts the door behind them both.

I'm alone in this room.

The solar is decorated with all sorts of knickknacks that would probably net a small fortune at some high-end antiques auction in the twenty-first century. I'm talking about stuff like tapestries depicting faded scenes of battles. Those hang from stone walls, and a wooden chest in the corner looks like it might contain either priceless heirlooms or severed heads. With my luck, it's probably the latter. But I also see smaller items that I could nab no problem.

Just thinking about fleecing these people, especially Rachel, gives me a strange queasy feeling in my belly.

Since I have nothing else to do, I jump up from the torture chair—which I now realize must been meant to impress important people. That's ironic given my current status as "suspicious time-traveling intruder." I stretch my cramped legs and stiff neck. The room is surprisingly warm thanks to a hearth burning in the corner. It casts flickering shadows throughout the room.

I begin to hear muffled voices from beyond the thick wooden door. The MacTaggarts are arguing about me, no doubt. I've been the subject of many heated discussions in my life, though usually they involved whether I should be beaten or sold to a human trafficker because of what I'd stolen that week.

As I edge closer to the door, I press my ear against the rough wood. Old habits are tough to break, and stolen information has saved my skin more times than I can count.

"—cannot simply trust him because you find the laddie comely, Rachel!" Kieran's voice booms, even through the thick door.

"I trust him because I've seen into his heart, Athair," Rachel fires back. "My second sight may not be as strong as Great-Aunt Lachina's, but even I can sense he means us no harm."

I flatten my ear against the door but then nearly lose my balance in the process. If Kieran has second sight, I'm cooked. He would surely get a vision of me getting freaky with Big Daddy's little girl. Rachel's an adult, but I doubt Kieran would accept that as an excuse.

"Aye, and what else have ye seen of his heart?" Kieran's tone drips with suspicion. "Or perhaps 'tis not his heart you've been examining so closely."

I freeze, unable to even breathe. Jesus, has Kieran figured out I did the bump and grind with daughter? Should've kept it in your pants, moron.

"Kieran," Alyssa's voice cuts in, sharp and commanding. "That's enough. I know you're upset, but snide comments are not helpful. Take a breather, honey, before we go back in there."

He grumbles. "I dinnae trust strangers, especially those from another century."

"Oh? You mean like me, hmm? I guess that's why you locked me up in your little dungeon room when we first met." She sighs with mock wistfulness. "Sometimes I miss my pee bucket."

That's what I call too much information.

"Well, I didnae mean—This situation is different, Alyssa."

"Joey is not the enemy—for now. And I trust Rachel's judgment. Our daughter is a smart, capable woman."

I can't help but smile a little. At least someone's on my side.

A long, uneasy silence beyond the door is punctuated only by what sounds like Kieran's heavy breathing. I imagine him pacing like a caged bear, running his hands through his hair while his wife gives him that look that wives across time seem to have perfected.

"The stranger carries strange energies," comes a new voice—older, throatier, with a lilting cadence that makes the hairs on my arms stand up. Must be one of the great-aunts. I haven't memorized their speech patterns yet. "I sense the ripples around him, like stones cast into still waters. But whether he cast them himself or was merely caught in their wake, I cannot yet determine."

"See, Athair?" That voice is Rachel, and her tone is filled with eagerness. "Even Aunt Lachina doesn't believe Joey is the source of the disturbance."

"She didnae say that that," Kieran grumbles. "Not precisely."

"What I am saying," Lachina's continues, "is that we must look beyond the obvious. The boy may be a symptom, not the disease."

I lean closer, straining to hear more, when suddenly the door swings open. I stumble forward, barely catching myself before faceplanting into Kieran's broad chest.

His eyes blaze with suspicion. "Eavesdropping, are we?"

"No, I was just—" I straighten up, trying to look dignified. "Stretching my legs. That chair is a medieval torture device."

"It's a carver chair," Rachel supplies from behind her father, leaning around his massive arm to see me. Her lips twitch with amusement. "Reserved for honored guests."

"Oh." I clear my throat. "I feel...very honored." And oddly turned on, but I hope Kieran doesn't notice that.

The laird snorts. "Come. We have decided your fate."

"Great," I mutter under my breath as I follow the MacTaggart clan back into the solar. "Nothing ominous about that at all."

The women file in behind me, and I can't help but notice how Rachel's great-aunts watch me with those eerily knowing eyes. Lachina, the one with silver-streaked hair, aims her inquisitive gaze at me like I'm a fascinating insect pinned to a board. Not hostile, just...intensely curious. It makes my skin crawl more than Kieran's outright suspicion.

"Sit," Kieran commands, gesturing to the same medieval torture device—carver chair, whatever—that I'd just escaped.

I eye the spiky monstrosity with disdain. "I'd rather stand, if it's all the same to you."

"It is not all the same to me," Kieran growls, his eyes narrowing. "Sit. Now."

I clench my jaw but lower myself back onto the damn chair. The wooden edges dig into my thighs as I perch on it like a bird on a thorn bush. Rachel catches my eye and gives me an encouraging nod, which doesn't help with the discomfort but does strange things to my chest.

"We have discussed your situation," Kieran announces, standing before me with his arms crossed over his chest. The animal pelt draped across his shoulders makes him look even more massive. I bet he threw that over his shoulder just to intimidate me. "And while I still harbor deep suspicions about your arrival, we have agreed that you are not to be...disposed of. Yet."

"Thanks. I feel all warm and fuzzy inside now. Maybe we should hug it out."

"Do not embrace me unless you wish to die a gruesome death."

Yeah, I don't think Kieran's going to be my buddy anytime soon. I expect frequent cold glares, the occasional threats of death and or dismemberment, and multiple dunks into the moat.

Oh, yeah, my life totally sucks.

Chapter Twelve

Rachel

I enjoy a good night's rest with dreams that leave me wishing I were sharing a bed with Joey instead of my Great-Aunt Morna. We do not have enough beds for all of us. When I wake in the morning, I hope to slink away before Morna awakens, but I have no such luck. She is already awake and insists upon leading me downstairs. She remains by my side as we enter the great hall.

Shortly after our discussion in the solar last night, the laird of Dùndubhan had pronounced that Joey would be confined in the tower bedroom until further notice. He also decreed that only he or Mother will enter the tower bedroom to deliver food and beverages to Joey. Aye, Father is extremely overprotective. The door to that room remains locked all night. I know this because I might have sneaked up to the door in the dead of night.

It wouldn't budge.

Fortunately, the situation has changed this morn. The laird of Dùndubhan has commanded everyone to gather in the great hall for a grand breakfast feast. Naturally, my father sits at the head of the table. Yet I am pleasantly surprised to find Joey seated across from me. I would prefer to have by my side, but I understand that my father still doesn't trust Joey. He will change his mind, I believe that.

I assumed the meal would be delicious but simple, as usual.

But I was wrong. The long table holds various dishes, more than I've seen at breakfast since the last time the laird of Clan Grant arrived one morn for a surprise visit. As we pass the bowls around, taking whatever we like, Joey seems rather confused.

"What fashes ye?" I ask him. "Ye haven't put anything on your plate."

"Not sure what these things are."

I point to an item on my plate. "Surely you recognize barley bread."

"Okay, yeah. That I do know." He reaches for a slice, his movements cautious as if he fears my father might reach across the table to stab him with a dirk.

"And this?" I indicate the dark pudding at the center of my plate.

"Looks like…chocolate cake?" His hopeful tone makes me laugh softly.

"No, 'tis black pudding, ye daft man. Made of oats and blood."

The color drains from his face. "Blood? As in, actual blood?"

"Aye. Sheep's blood," I say, taking a hearty bite. "Most nutritious part of the meal."

Great-Aunt Morna snorts beside me. "The lad eats like a bairn, does he? Mayhap he'd prefer some pottage?"

Joey glances at the steaming bowl of the porridge-like substance being passed round the table, then gives me a sidelong glance, clearly dubious of the meal.

"Aye, pottage might be more to his liking," I tell Morna. "Though Joey will need more than that to keep his strength up in these Highlands."

Joey takes the bowl cautiously, his beautiful whisky-brown eyes narrowing as he inspects the contents. "What exactly is in this…pottage? Not dirt and worms, I hope."

"Nay, of course not." I lean over the table, as close as I can get to Joey, and speak in a hushed voice. "Just oats, milk, and herbs. No blood, I promise."

The relief that washes over his face is almost comical.

"Oh, thank God," he mutters, spooning some into his mouth with surprising eagerness. After swallowing, he nods appreciatively. "This I can handle."

My father watches from the head of the table, his gaze sharp as a hawk's. I can feel his assessment of Joey with every passing moment.

"Finnegan." My father's voice booms across the table, causing Joey to nearly choke on his pottage. "Where did ye say ye hail from again?"

Joey's eyes meet mine in a flash of panic. We hadn't properly rehearsed this part of his story. "New York City. That's in America—the New World. That's what we call it."

I slap my fork down on the table. "Honestly, Father, how many times will you insist upon interrogating Joey?"

"Until I'm certain I can trust him."

I feel heat rising to my cheeks as Joey fumbles with his spoon. Beneath the table, I nudge his boot with my shoe, hoping to convey some measure of reassurance. The gesture does seem to relax him.

"I understand your concern, sir," Joey says, straightening his shoulders in a way that makes him look almost regal. "If a strange man appeared near my home, I'd have questions too."

My father grunts, seemingly caught off guard by Joey's directness. A small victory. I'll take it.

"And what skills do ye possess, laddie? Besides eavesdropping at doors?"

"I apologize for that. But in my defense, I've been very confused ever since I fell into the moat and almost drowned."

Father purses his lips briefly, then exhales a heavy breath. "Mayhap I should give you time to adjust."

Joey seems mildly surprised.

"Oh, Father, that's wonderful," I declare. Grinning, I rush to his chair and throw my arms around him. "Thank you, thank you, thank you so much."

He rolls his eyes.

My family will continue to harbor reservations about Joey. Of that much, I am certain. Mother seems far less skeptical than Father. I pray that no one realizes Joey Finnegan and I enjoyed coitus in my secret room. Oddly, my father has not questioned me any further about how and why Joey was in my room. Whatever he suspects, he's keeping it to himself. I wondered if my mother had figured out what Joey and I did in my secret room. It was quite, um, naughty, and she had conspicuously glanced at the bedsheets.

She might have seen the small spot of blood that revealed what we did. I am no longer a virgin. If my mother noticed the blood, she has not let on.

Do I regret losing my virginity to Joey Finnegan? No, not in the least. My intuition urges me to trust him. No one has ever accused me of having a suspicious nature. Nay, I am the exact opposite—too credulous, as my father often tells me. He is correct. But I cannot change my nature.

Father most definitely did not realize what Joey and I did. If he had, he would have murdered Joey instantly.

After breakfast, Father insists upon locking Joey in the tower bedroom again.

"No, you cannot do that," I tell him emphatically. "Joey has done nothing wrong."

"But he admits to being a thief. That alone makes him a threat."

I roll my yes. "What could he steal here at Dùndubhan? Joey is from the future. If he stole something, he wouldnae know how to sell it."

Father grunts.

My mother steps in to mediate our disagreement. "Kieran, honestly, I agree with Rachel. Joey doesn't have any weapons, and he's been nothing but deferential to you. Don't lock him in. Please, honey."

Father's expression softens at Mother's plea. I've always marveled at how she wields such influence over him with just a few gentle words.

"As you wish," he grumbles, running a hand through his hair. "But he's not to wander about unattended. Someone must keep an eye on him at all times."

"I volunteer," I say quickly—too quickly, judging by the narrowing of Father's eyes.

"Absolutely not," he says, his voice dropping to that dangerously low tone that makes even the bravest clansmen flinch. "Your Great-Aunt Morna will watch him."

Joey's gaze darts to Morna, who smiles at him with all the steely resolve of a warrior. I see him swallow hard.

"I'd be honored," Morna says. "Provided he doesnae try to seduce me."

The twinkle in her eye, and the slight smile on her lips, assures me she's teasing Joey.

I set my hands on my hips. "Och, this is ridiculous. Please let me guard Joey so I can show him around the castle. We will remain within the walls of Dùndubhan."

Father's expression darkens like a Highland storm cloud. "Ye think me a fool, lass? I've seen the way ye look at the man."

"I promise we'll stay where everyone can see us," I plead, trying to sound reasonable rather than desperate.

"Aye, just like ye promised to stay away from the western tower last summer?" Father counters, his eyebrow arched knowingly. "We both remember how that ended."

I had learned my lesson about experimenting with fire magic indoors on that day.

Joey clears his throat. "Sir, if I may—"

"Ye may not," Father cuts him off. "Morna will accompany ye, and that's final."

My great-aunt shifts beside me, her hands folded primly at her waist. "Come along then, young man. I promise I don't bite—unless provoked."

Joey gives me a helpless glance before nodding respectfully to my father. "Thank you for your hospitality, sir. I appreciate not being locked in the tower."

Father merely grunts in response, though he gives a tiny wink too. Joey's polite deference might be working in his favor, if only slightly.

Everyone follows as we exit the great hall and go outside.

As Morna leads Joey away, I linger behind, watching the way his shoulders move beneath his clothing. He looks quite fetching in the clothes I gave him. Even in this impossible situation, he carries himself with a certain grace that makes my heart flutter. When he turns back to steal one last look at me, I feel the familiar warmth rising in my cheeks.

"Stop!"

My mother's harsh cry reverberates from behind us.

Father approaches her, his brows furrowed. "What is it, Alyssa?"

"You're acting like a dictator, Kieran." She grasps a handful of his shirt, rising onto her tiptoes to meet him eye to eye. "Rachel is a grown woman—and a Vescovi, like me, which means we don't obey shouty commands without an explanation. Stop treating our daughter like a child. If she wants to spend time with Joey, you will let her do that. Won't you?"

Father seems…chastised. I've rarely seen that happen.

His nostrils flare, his golden eyes locked with Mother's fierce blue ones. The air between them practically crackles with tension. I hold my breath, watching this battle of wills that I've witnessed countless times throughout my life.

"Alyssa," Father says, his voice dangerously low. "The man is a stranger—"

"The man," Mother interrupts, still clutching his shirt, "has been nothing but respectful. And our daughter clearly cares for him."

Joey shifts uncomfortably under Great-Aunt Morna's watchful eye, clearly trying to pretend he can't hear this very public dispute about him. Poor man. His cheeks have turned a rather fetching shade of pink.

Father exhales heavily. Then he finally concedes. "Aye, all right. But they are not to be alone. Not for a single moment."

Mother releases his shirt with a triumphant smile. "Morna can chaperone from a respectable distance."

"Three paces," Father specifies, his eyes drilling into Joey's. "No more."

Great-Aunt Morna chuckles, the sound rough as highland granite. "I may be old, but my eyes are sharp as an eagle's and my legs swift as a deer's. Don't think ye can outrun me, lad."

Joey nods solemnly. "Wouldn't dream of it, ma'am."

I rush to Joey's side before anyone can change their mind, my heart pounding with excitement. "I'll show you the garden first. It's particularly lovely this time of year."

Joey's lips quirk into that half-smile that makes my stomach flutter. "Lead the way."

As promised, Great-Aunt Morna follows us at precisely three paces, her keen eyes missing nothing. I can feel Father watching us from the doorway of the great hall, his gaze burning into my back until we round the corner of the castle wall.

"So," Joey whispers, leaning closer than is strictly proper, "that was intense. Your mom is... fierce."

I laugh softly. "Aye, she's always been my champion. Father may be laird, but Mother is the true power at Dùndubhan."

"Remind me never to cross her," Joey says, his voice low enough that Morna can't hear.

"Morna is protective, that's all. I am the only child Dùndubhan has seen since my father became laird."

The morning air is crisp against my skin as we walk along the stone path toward the garden. Joey matches his stride to mine, his fingers occasionally brushing against my hand—accidental touches that send sparks racing up my arm. Each time it happens, I hear Great-Aunt Morna clear her throat pointedly.

"So, what's the story with the garden?" Joey asks. "Magical herbs and potions? Secret portals to other dimensions?"

I laugh despite myself. "Not everything in the Highlands is enchanted. Sometimes a garden is merely...a garden."

Chapter Thirteen

Joey

"Are you sure about that?" I ask. Rachel has witchy powers of her own. I know that for a fact since she used those abilities to craft a potion that stopped me from disappearing or whatever she thought might happen to me. "Seems like a garden could be a portal to who knows where."

Rachel laughs in a sweet way that makes me want to kiss her—and do a lot more than that too. "You're not entirely wrong. But it's not just any garden. The ancient stones must be arranged in a specific pattern, and the incantation…" She trails off, watching my face with sudden suspicion. "Why are you so interested in portals all of a sudden?"

I shrug, trying for a casual attitude but probably failing miserably. "Just trying to understand this world I've stumbled into. Knowledge is power and all that."

Her fingers brush against mine, sending that familiar electric current up my arm. "Joey Finnegan, you're a terrible liar."

Before I can defend my honor—or lack thereof—she glances over her shoulder. "We best go back inside, mo *leannan*."

I'm about to ask why, but then I glance back too and finally understand. Efrica just appeared from inside the house, her figure blocking what little light filters through the narrow castle windows. The old woman's gaze remains steadily on me, though her attention doesn't feel mistrustful.

Efrica speaks directly to her niece. "Your father is coming, dearie."

Rachel tenses up, and her eyes widen a touch. "Now? Why didn't you say something sooner?"

"I have told you now, have I not?" Efrica waves toward the doorway behind her. "And here he is, mo *leannan*. I must say your father seems less than pleased with the situation."

The imposing figure of the laird of Dùndubhan emerges from the castle. His boots clomp loudly on the gravel, the sound echoing throughout the courtyard.

Oh, shit.

Kieran MacTaggart looks like he wants to murder me. With his squinty gaze and flexing muscles, he's doing a fantastic impression of an evil bastard who wants to rip my throat out and eat my entrails for dinner. But I'm not buying his act. Not much, that is. No, Big Daddy can't intimidate me. He does have a big old sword in his hand, but that doesn't mean he would actually murder me. Does it?

"Are you going to throw me into the garderobe shaft?"

Kieran chuckles in the evilest way. "No, laddie, I have other plans for you today."

Nope, that doesn't sound ominous at all.

Big Daddy halts right in front of me, keeping his hand on the hilt of his claymore. "Before I let ye spend more time with my daughter, I need to find out what yer made of, *macan*. That means a test, and it willnae be easy. Rachel is my only child, after all. I think ye ken what I mean."

"Yes, sir, I do. May I ask what sort of test it will be?"

Kieran grins with feral glee. "The physical sort, naturally. Can ye handle that, Mr. Finnegan?"

I remember the bartender back in modern times called me *macan* too. "I hate to keep asking these questions, but what does *macan* mean?"

"The term describes a young laddie."

"Okay, thanks."

I get that he needs to test me in the worst ways to make sure I can protect Rachel, and that I won't hurt her for fun. Still, it feels like he's going overboard with these physical tests. But I will endure every torture he puts me through. Why? Because Rachel is amazing.

"Prepare yourself, laddie," Kieran growls, his burly frame looming over me. "Let's see how ye handle yerself in a real fight."

Suddenly, I feel like a trout that's been caught on a fishing line. But he won't scare me away. "Listen, big guy, I appreciate the whole protective father routine, but don't you think we could settle this over a nice cup of tea instead? Or maybe a bottle of whisky?"

Kieran's eyes narrow dangerously. "Ye think this is a game, do ye?"

"No, sir, I don't."

"Good. Remain here."

Before I can ask why, Kieran jogs over to the bakehouse and disappears behind the building. A minute or two later, he emerges. But now, he's carrying a big log over one shoulder.

He drops it on the ground at my feet. "Pick up the caber and toss it clear across the courtyard."

"What? Are you serious?"

"Aye. Deadly serious."

I stare at the massive log lying on the ground, wondering if Kieran's lost his mind. The thing must weigh at least a hundred and seventy-five pounds. I've seen strongman competitions on TV, but I never imagined I'd be expected to hurl a telephone pole myself.

"You're joking, right?" I ask, hoping against hope that this is all some elaborate Scottish prank. I know he wants to test me, but still…

Kieran's face remains impassive. "Does it look like I'm joking, *macan*? Mayhap you're afraid to try. No harm in admitting defeat."

I sigh, resigning myself to my fate. Then I roll my shoulders back and lift my chin. "Okay, laird. I'll give it a shot. But if I throw out my back, you're paying for my chiropractor."

"Your what?"

"Never mind. It's a twenty-first century thing."

Approaching the caber, I wrap my arms around it, trying to find the best grip. With a grunt that would make a wild boar proud, I heave the log onto my shoulder, teetering precariously as I struggle to balance its immense weight. My legs quiver, threatening to buckle under the strain. Sweat beads on my forehead, and I'm pretty sure I've pulled at least three muscles I didn't even know I had.

"Any day now, laddie," Kieran taunts, his arms crossed over his broad chest.

I take a deep breath, summoning every ounce of strength I possess. With a primal yell that probably sounds more like a strangled cat, I charge forward, my steps unsteady under the caber's bulk. At the last moment, I heave upward with all my might, flipping the log end over end.

Time seems to slow as the caber arcs through the air. I hold my breath, silently praying to any Scottish deity who might be listening. By some miracle—or sheer dumb luck—the caber lands with a resounding thud, perfectly upright, before toppling forward. I stand here, panting and wide-eyed, hardly believing what just happened.

Kieran's eyebrows shoot up, a flicker of surprise crossing his stoic features. "Well, I'll be damned," he mutters, stroking his beard thoughtfully. "Ye might have some potential after all, lad."

I try to suppress my grin, not wanting to appear too smug. "Thanks, I think. So, does this mean we're done with the medieval weight-lifting routine?"

Kieran's eyes narrow again, and I immediately regret my sarcastic jibe. "Not even close, boy. That was only the warm-up. Do it again, five more times."

Though I'm still breathing hard from the exertion, I suck in a deep breath and blow it out. Then I hoist the caber again, roaring as I throw it halfway across the courtyard. I fist pump and shout, jumping up and down like lunatic. Rachel claps and cheers. Well, at least she appreciates my effort.

"Not done yet, laddie. I have another test for ye." Kieran gives me that evil grin again. "Something much more dangerous."

Oh, great. I think he's trying to give me a heart attack just to get rid of me.

Kieran leads me back into the house, into the long gallery as it turns out. I haven't seen this room before. It has large windows and three separate sections, unlike the great hall on the lower floor. This room doesn't have any kind of furniture, not even a table. My heart sinks as Kieran gestures to a rack of weapons nearby.

"Now, let's see how ye handle a claymore."

I scrutinize the array of lethal-looking weapons. "A claymore? That's your weapon of choice, huh? You seem like the kind of guy who'd want the biggest, baddest sword around."

"There are larger swords out there—such as the Wallace, the Celtic war sword, and the silver basket hilt. But I prefer my claymore."

"Can't deny it's awesome."

Kieran's lips twitch in what might be the ghost of a smile. "Dinnae fash, *macan.* We'll start ye off with a wooden practice sword."

"Oh, how merciful of you," I mutter under my breath.

I grab the practice sword, nearly dropping it as I underestimate its weight. How can wood be so...hefty. Kieran hoists his own wooden claymore with ease, twirling it like it's made of paper.

Kieran's grin is almost feral as he settles into a fighting stance. "Show me what ye've got, Finnegan."

He proceeds to put me through my paces, challenging me to beat him in this round of swordplay. He nicks me a few times—strictly to show off, I think—then I start to gain the upper hand. I wonder briefly if Kieran is holding back so he won't accidentally hurt me. But I finally decide he's not the type to do that. By the time our practice session ends, we're both sweaty and exhausted—in a good way. I haven't felt this energized...ever.

Kieran studies me with a less bloodthirsty gleam in his eyes this time. "Ye've got potential, laddie. But don't get cocky. There's more to protecting my daughter than swinging a sword."

"Whatever you want me to do, I'm game." I lean on my practice claymore for support. "What's next? Wrestling a bear? Climbing a mountain on hands and knees?"

The corner of Kieran's mouth twitches. "Don't tempt me, Finnegan. I could insist you climb Beann Dealgach exactly that way—on all fours. But for now, we'll work on your tracking skills. The Highlands can be treacherous, and ye need to learn how to navigate them."

"Uh, what was that phrase you spouted? I assume it was Gaelic."

"Aye, 'twas my mother tongue. Beann Dealgach is the mountain on which Dùndubhan resides." Kieran waves toward the gates. "Come with me, Joseph."

Rachel races up to us. "I must go with you, please, Father."

Kieran rolls his eyes and sighs. "No, mo nighean. This is a trial Joseph must undertake without your assistance."

Just as I open my mouth to ask the obvious question, Rachel glances my way and explains. "Mo nighean is the Gaelic version of 'my daughter'. Enjoy your manly time with the laird of the castle."

I follow him, my legs wobbling slightly from the exertion of our sparring match. We make our way to the edge of the castle grounds, where the manicured lawns give way to wild, rugged terrain. The misty Scottish landscape stretches out before us, a patchwork of emerald hills and shadowy glens.

"All right, laddie," Kieran says, crossing his arms over his broad chest. "I'm going to give ye a head start. Ye have five minutes to disappear into the wilderness. Then, I'll come after ye. If ye can evade me for an hour, ye pass this test."

I blink at him, wondering if I've misheard. "You want me to play hide-and-seek in the Scottish wilderness? With you as the seeker?"

"Aye, that's the idea. And I suggest ye start running, laddie. Your time starts now."

Determined to meet Kieran's challenge, I sprint through the woods, tripping over rocks and depressions but never falling despite the uneven terrain. As I push deeper into the forest, I try to think strategically, knowing Kieran will easily track my obvious trail if I just keep running in a straight line. Veering left, I head toward a babbling stream I can hear in the distance. The sound of rushing water grows louder as I approach, and I step carefully into the shallow creek, wincing at the icy cold that seeps through my boots.

Wading upstream for several yards, I hope the water will mask my scent and muddy my trail. When I spot a low-hanging branch from a nearby oak,

I seize my chance. With a grunt of effort, I haul myself up into the tree, scraping my palms on the rough bark. Perched on a sturdy limb about fifteen feet off the ground, I try to catch my breath and calm my racing heart. The mist swirls around me, providing some cover, but I know it won't be enough to fool Kieran for long. I'd guess that man must have the tracking skills of a bloodhound.

Just as I'm starting to think I might have given Kieran the slip, I hear it—the faint crunch of leaves underfoot, too heavy to be an animal.

Kieran's massive form materializes through the mist, his golden eyes scanning the forest floor. I hold my breath, not daring to move a muscle as he pauses directly beneath my perch. He kneels, examining something on the ground that I can't see.

"Clever laddie," he murmurs, a note of approval in his gruff voice. "Using the stream to mask your trail. But not clever enough."

My heart sinks as Kieran's gaze slowly travels upward, his eyes locking onto mine with predatory intensity. A wolfish grin spreads across his face. "Found ye, Finnegan. Ye might want to work on your climbing skills. Ye left quite a few marks on this tree."

I jump down, brushing off my trews, and I grin too.

Kieran folds his brawny arms over his chest. "Ready for the next challenge?"

"I'm up for anything you throw at me."

"Good. Let's go back to the castle."

Once we reach the outer wall, Kieran halts and gestures toward the stone structure. Then he grasps my shoulder and squeezes hard. "Ye haven't climbed the curtain walls yet."

"The whats?"

Kieran holds up one finger, pointing toward the giant stone walls that surround the castle.

Oh, shit.

Chapter Fourteen

Rachel

The moment I hear voices coming from the river path, before I've even glimpsed my father or Joey, I hoist my skirts and race up the trail to meet them. Oh, what if Joey couldn't pass the tests? No, he's quite braw and very determined. But Father…he doesn't trust Joey yet. I do, though I cannae explain why.

Two figures emerge from the wood.

"Joey!" I shout, rushing toward him even faster. I can barely breathe by the time I reach him. "Are you injured?"

"Nope. Did you think I couldn't hack all those tests?"

"No, of course not. I…I was worried, that's all," I admit, my cheeks flushing. Joey's eyes soften, and for a moment I forget my father is standing right there.

"Och, Rachel." Father's gruff voice breaks the spell. "Ye shouldnae be scurrying about like a wee lass. We have important matters to discuss."

I straighten up, trying to look more dignified. "Of course, Father. What happened?"

Joey clears his throat. "Well, your old man here put me through the wringer. Climbing, swimming, even had to wrestle a goat."

I can't help but giggle at the image. "A goat?"

"Nay," Father says, a hint of amusement in his eyes. "The laddie did no such thing. I let him go after the forest run. But that doesnae mean he's earned our trust yet."

Joey raises an eyebrow at my father, a hint of mock challenge in his voice. "What's it gonna take then, huh? Should I slay a dragon or two?"

I aim a warning glance at my father, but he simply grunts, unimpressed by Joey's bravado.

"Ye'll have yer chance to prove yerself soon enough, *macan*," Father says cryptically. "The MacLeods are coming, and trouble will surely follow in their wake."

My heart sinks. The MacLeods. That means Alisdair will be here, with his square jaw and big fists, not to mention his relentless pursuit of my hand. I steal a glance at Joey, wondering how he'll react to this news.

"MacLeods?" Joey asks, his brow furrowing. "Who are they?"

"Our neighbors to the north," I explain quickly. "They are...well, it's complicated." I finished lamely because I dinnae want to dive into the centuries-old feud between our clans again.

Joey's eyes narrow slightly, picking up on my hesitation. "Complicated how?"

Before I can answer, Father interjects, his voice gruff but tinged with weariness. "The MacLeods and the MacTaggarts have a long history, laddie. Not always a peaceful one. But old rivalries must be abandoned, and we need to change with the times."

Joey's eyes flick to and fro minutely as his quick mind pieces together the implications. "So, this visit, it's some kind of peace offering?"

"Aye," Father nods, "or so they claim. My cousin Goraidh called on us the day before you, Joseph Finnegan, crashed into our world. Goraidh came to forewarn us. The MacLeods can be...boisterous. And I trust Eanraig MacLeod precisely as far as I can throw him."

Joey's lips quirk into a wry smile. "And I'm guessing you can't throw him very far."

Father barks out a laugh, surprising me. "Aye, Joey. Ye've got the right of it."

I glance between the men, a flutter of hope in my chest. Mayhap they're warming to each other after all.

"So, what's the plan?" Joey asks, his eyes sharp with interest. "I'm guessing you want me to lay low during this visit."

Father's expression turns serious. "Nay, we cannae hide ye. The MacLeods will be suspicious enough as it is. Ye'll have to play the part of a distant cousin, come to visit."

I nibble on my lip nervously as worry gnaws at me. "But Father, they will wonder about his unusual clothing and his strange accent."

"We'll have him wear the clothing you gave him, and we'll say he's from the Lowlands, where styles are different," Father says, his tone brooking no argument. "It's the best we can do on such short notice. Besides, Alyssa speaks differently too."

Joey nods, his face set with determination. "I can do that. I've played plenty of roles before. Just give me the backstory, and I'll sell it."

Joey was a thief before he came here, and that likely explain why he's so comfortable with deception. But there's no time to dwell on it now.

"Rachel," Father turns to me, his eyes stern. "Ye must be on your guard. Alisdair MacLeod will no doubt try to woo ye again."

My cheeks burn at the mention of Alisdair. I can feel Joey's gaze on me, curious and perhaps a wee bit…jealous? No, that can't be right.

Father claps a hand down on Joey's shoulder. "I give you leave to spend the afternoon with Rachel, so long as you ne'er go past the first bend in the river."

"Aye, Father," I agree, trying to hide my excitement at the prospect of spending time alone with Joey. As Father trudges back toward the castle, I turn to Joey with a mischievous grin. "Well then, shall we make the most of our afternoon?"

Joey's lips quirk upward faintly, and he bows deeply. "Lead the way, my lady. But first, mind telling me more about this Alisdair guy?"

Sighing, I lead Joey down the path toward the river. "Alisdair MacLeod is…persistent. He's been trying to win my hand for years now. He's handsome enough, I suppose, and a skilled warrior, but…"

"But?" Joey prompts, his voice carefully neutral.

I halt at the riverbank, watching the sunlight dance on the water. "But I've never felt anything for him. He sees me as a prize to…" I trail off, unable to fully articulate my feelings about Alisdair.

Joey remains quiet for a moment, skipping a stone across the river's surface. "And your father? What does he think of this Alisdair character?"

I sink down onto a mossy rock. "Father sees the potential alliance. The MacLeods are powerful, and a marriage would ease tensions between our clans. But he's never pushed me toward Alisdair, thank the heavens."

Joey nods, his brow furrowed in thought. "So, this visit… it's not just about diplomacy, is it? They're hoping to seal the deal with you and lover boy."

I stifle my amusement at his description. I let out a frustrated sigh, plucking at blades of grass. "Aye, I suspect that's part of it. Though Father would never force me into a marriage I didnae want. But Alisdair is hardly my 'lover boy.'"

Joey's eyes meet mine. "And what do you want, Rachel?"

My heart quickens at his question. What do I want? The answer feels both terrifying and exhilarating.

"I…I wish to choose my own path," I say softly. "I crave adventure and passion. Not just duty and clan alliances."

Joey moves closer, his hand brushing mine. "I already know you've got a rebellious streak. I mean, you seduced me in your secret room before you knew anything about me."

I laugh, feeling a bit giddy at his nearness. "That is true. Though I fear my rebelliousness may cause trouble with the MacLeods' visit."

"Hey," Joey says, his voice low and reassuring. "We'll figure it out together. I've got your back, Rachel."

His words send a thrill through me, and I find myself leaning closer to him. "Thank you, Joey. I'm glad you're here with me."

For a moment, we gaze deeply into each other's eyes, the air between us charged with unspoken desires. The world seems to slow around us. The rustle of leaves in the breeze, and the gentle babble of the water, create a cocoon of quiet, intimate sounds. I can feel the warmth of Joey's body so close to mine, the electric tingle of his hand when it accidentally brushes against my skin. We don't pull away. Instead, our fingers begin to intertwine, slowly, as if testing the waters of a new and dangerous territory. My mind races ahead to what could happen next. A kiss, perhaps, one that is tender and exploratory, leading to something more passionate. Or mayhap the simple comfort of his arms around me, holding me tight against the uncertainties that loom on the horizon. Potential futures flash before my eyes, each more tantalizing than the last.

Joey leans in ever so slightly, and I close my eyes, bracing for the moment our lips might meet. The air is thick with anticipation, every second stretching into an eternity.

Then Joey clears his throat and steps back a few paces.

"So, tell me more about these MacLeods," he says, his tone lighter. "What should I expect when they arrive?"

I sigh, grateful for the distraction from my conflicting emotions. "Well, they're a proud clan, known for their fierce warriors and... boisterous celebrations. Eanraig MacLeod, the clan chieftain, is a bear of a man with a temper to match."

Joey raises an eyebrow, waiting for me to continue.

I choose my words carefully. "Alisdair can be charming when he wants to be, and he is a skilled warrior. But there's an arrogance to him that I find off-putting." I finally understand how that man affects me so awfully and why. "He sees me as a prize to be won, not a person with her own desires. I doubt he would ever allow me to tie him up while I take pleasure from his body, the way you did."

"Sounds like he's no prince charming," he says dryly. "A sexist jerk seems more like it."

"Aye, that he is. But enough about Alisdair. Tell me, Joey, what sort of adventures did you have before you came here?"

A shadow passes over Joey's face, and for a moment I worry I've touched on a sensitive subject. He turns away slightly, his gaze drifting over the rippling water of the river. "Adventures, huh? I've had my share, I guess. Most of them were not good."

I reach out, gently touching his arm. "You don't have to tell me if you don't want to."

Joey looks back at me, a wry smile tugging at his lips. "Nah, it's okay. Let's just say I've been in some tight spots. I had to learn how to think on my feet, adapt quickly. In my world, I didn't always have the luxury of playing by the rules. Sometimes you gotta do whatever's it takes to survive."

I lean in, intrigued. "What sort of tight spots? Were you an outlaw?"

Joey chuckles, but there's a hint of darkness in his eyes. "Not exactly. Let's just say I've had to do some things I'm not proud of to survive. But that's all in the past now."

He doesn't want to elaborate further, that much I can tell. "I'm glad you're here now. And I have a feeling your quick thinking will come in handy when the MacLeods arrive."

"Speaking of which," Joey says, his tone turning serious, "we should probably head back and prepare. I need to work on my 'distant cousin from the Lowlands' act."

As we walk back toward the castle, I can't help but steal glances at Joey. There's so much mystery surrounding him, and so many questions I long to ask. But for now, I'm content to simply be in his presence, our shoulders occasionally brushing as we navigate the winding path.

The sun is sinking lower in the sky, casting long shadows across the Highland landscape. The air is thick with the scent of heather and pine, and a cool breeze rustles through the trees. It's a perfect moment that I wish I could freeze in time.

"Rachel," Joey says suddenly, breaking the comfortable silence between us. "I want you to know that no matter what happens with the MacLeods, I won't let anybody harass you. I might not understand all the politics and clan rivalries, but I know when someone's trying to force a situation."

His words warm my heart, and I find myself smiling up at him. Oh, aye, falling for Joey Finnegan would be so easy to do. But I cannae help worrying about what the MacLeods might be plotting.

Chapter Fifteen

Joey

Rachel smiles with so much sweetness that I feel a strange ache in my chest just from looking at her. What does that mean? I don't know, and I'm not sure I want to find out. Rachel has been so sweet to me since the moment we met, and I do feel…grateful. It can't be more than that. Can it? Someone like me—an orphan turned loner turned petty thief—shouldn't be so lucky.

A hammer will drop on my head anytime, I'm sure.

Rachel leans back against a large tree, eyeing me with an expression I can't quite describe. Her gaze is lustful, her posture relaxed. She splays her fingers over the tree trunk and pets the bark like she's stroking her lover—me. When she licks her lips, I develop an odd lump in my throat. But more importantly, I'm getting turned on. Big time.

Yeah, any minute my dick will wake up. I shouldn't even think about screwing Rachel now, not with her testy father and a horde of MacLeods poised to descend on the castle.

"So, uh, what's the plan?" I ask, desperate to focus on something—anything—other than the way Rachel's fingers are caressing that tree.

She tilts her head, a mischievous glint in her eye. "Well, Joseph Finnegan, I thought we might take a wee stroll through the forest. There's a place I want to show ye."

Her lilting accent does nothing to calm the storm brewing inside me. I try not to notice the way her bodice pushes her breasts up in tantalizing mounds. I need to devour her nipples until she cries out in ecstasy.

Fuck. I'm getting hard.

Rachel's gaze flicks down to my groin, and she drags her tongue across her lips with a hunger that's palpable.

God, I need to kiss her again. Right now.

My dick takes control, and I find myself moving closer, closer, until my palms land on the tree and I'm framing her body with mine. Both our lips are parted, ready for the kiss I can no longer deny we both need. Her plump, succulent lips lure me in even closer.

And I crush my mouth to hers.

I slant toward her more, until her tits brush against my chest. "Rachel, sweet Rachel. I don't think a walk is what either of us wants right now."

Her eyes have darkened from the lust growing within us both, and I press her against the tree. I set my hands on her lips, then slide them up to her waist. Rachel's skin grows warm through the thin fabric of her dress, and the rapid rise and fall of her chest draws my focus to the lush mounds of her tits.

"Joey," she breathes, her fingers tangling in my hair. "I ken we shouldn't, but I cannae help myself. Ye drive me mad with wanting."

I love the way her accent thickens when she wants me inside her.

Our lips crash together in a searing kiss, all pretense of restraint abandoned. Rachel tastes like wild berries and summer rain, her lips soft yet demanding against mine. My hands roam her curves, memorizing every dip and swell as if I might never get the chance again. And who knows? Maybe I won't.

"Oh, Joey," she moans against my mouth. "We shouldnae do this here. Anyone might stumble upon us."

But her actions betray her words as she hitches her leg around my waist, pulling me closer. I grind against her, relishing the friction and the little gasp it elicits from her. The scent of her desire surrounds and intoxicates me. I feel high, like I've smoked some weed, but I haven't. Rachel's lust might be the most intoxicating drug on earth. I can't stop myself from lifting her skirts just so I can slide my hand under her chemise and push my fingers between her folds.

She's already wet for me, and the realization nearly brings me to my knees. I've never wanted any woman this much. But Rachel is different. I slide one finger inside her, then two, watching her face as her eyes flutter closed and her mouth forms a perfect "O" of pleasure. My breathing grows heavier, and I can't resist petting her inner walls with both fingers until she gasps and moans, her lids fluttering shut.

"Joey!" she cries out, and I know she's getting closer to climax. "We need to be careful. If my father finds out—"

"I know, I know, he'll murder me." I brush my mouth against her neck, tasting the salt of her skin. "Tell me to stop and I will."

But she doesn't tell me to stop. Instead, she reaches between us, her fingers fumbling with the fastenings of my trews. The sensation of her hand wrapping around me nearly makes me lose control then and there.

"Rachel," I groan. "You're killing me."

Her throaty laugh gets me even more turned on. "I want you alive and buried inside my wombgate."

"Your what gate?"

"My vulva."

"Uh-huh." I don't have the brainpower to figure out what she's saying anymore. So instead, I growl, too lust-addled to think straight. "Need to fuck you so hard we'll both see stars."

"Och, Joey, please."

Just as I'm about to suggest we sneak off to some secluded glade, a twig snaps nearby. We freeze, our hearts pounding in unison. I reluctantly pull away from Rachel, zipping up my trews, my body on fire with the need to blow my top inside her sweet body. Can't do that now.

We both strain our ears, listening for any further signs of an intruder.

"Did ye hear that?" Rachel whispers, her eyes wide.

I listen to the delicate sounds of the forest—leaves rustling, birds chirping in the distance. But the dense foliage makes it difficult to see very far, and the lengthening shadows of late afternoon only add to the eerie atmosphere. My hand instinctively goes to my waist, where I'd always kept a pocketknife, but it isn't there. I left it back in New York. Old habits die hard, I suppose.

"We should head back," I say, trying to keep my voice calm. "It's probably nothing, but—"

Another snap, closer this time.

Rachel grabs my hand, twining her fingers with mine.

I have no defensive weapons, not even a dirk, that I could use to protect this woman.

She grips my biceps, whispering urgently. "Joey, I think we should run."

My instincts scream at me to flee, but I hold my ground, positioning myself slightly in front of Rachel. "Wait. Let's see what we're dealing with first."

The forest seems to hold its breath as we listen. Then, I hear leaves rustling, followed by a low growl that sends a chill slithering down my spine. That's no human being stumbling onto our tryst.

"Wolves?" Rachel breathes, her grip on my hand tightening.

I shake my head. "Doesn't sound like it. Whatever that is, it's bigger than a canine."

A massive shape lopes out of the underbrush. My jaw drops as I gape the creature before us—a bear, but unlike any I've ever seen. Its fur is a deep, unnatural purple, and its eyes glow with an eerie green light.

"*Dhia*," Rachel whispers, her voice trembling. "It's a *beithir*."

"A what now?" I hiss, not daring to take my eyes off the beast.

"A *beithir* is a creature composed of magic," she explains hurriedly. "They are rare and dangerous. I didnae know they really existed. We need to—"

Before she can finish her statement, the *beithir* lets out a deafening roar and charges toward us. My body moves on instinct as years of street fights and narrow escapes kick in to guide me. I seize Rachel's hand and bolt, zigzagging through the trees.

"This way!" she shouts, tugging me to the left. "We aren't far from the castle! We must keep running!"

I follow her lead, my heart pounding in my ears. The *beithir*'s thunderous footfalls shake the ground behind us. Branches whip at my face as we tear through the underbrush, but I barely feel the sting. All I can focus on is Rachel's hand in mine and the need to keep her safe.

"Almost there!" Rachel pants, her golden-brown hair streaming behind her like a banner.

Just when I think my lungs might burst, we barrel out of the woods and into the clearing behind the castle, rushing headlong for the wooden door that leads into the garden. I glance back to see the *beithir* still running after us.

I kick the garden door open.

An eerie silence descends on us, the air seeming charged with some sort of energy I can't describe. When I look back...

The *beithir* is gone.

What the hell just happened? A shared hallucination? No, that thing was real—and seriously weird.

Rachel and I stand here panting, our chests heaving as we try to catch our breath. The garden is weirdly silent, the only sounds our ragged breathing and the distant chirping of birds.

I'm still gripping Rachel's hand. Between panting breaths, I ask, "Where did it go?"

Rachel shakes her head. "I dinnae ken, Joey. The *beithir*...it shouldnae have disappeared like that. They're powerful creatures, not known for giving up the chase that easily."

I study the tree line, half-expecting the purple beast to come crashing through at any moment. But the forest has returned to its normal tranquility—unnaturally normal, in fact.

"Could it have been an illusion?" I ask, my mind struggling to make sense of what we just experienced.

Rachel's brow furrows. "Nay, 'twas was real enough as far as magical creatures go. But something strange is afoot here." She turns to me, her blue eyes filled with questions. "Joey, I think we need to speak with my great-aunts. If anyone can make sense of this, it's them."

Shit, I'm so far out of my depth here that I expect to hit the bottom of the ocean.

Right now, though, I'm still trying to catch my breath. "Okay, yeah, let's consult the witches."

Those are words I never imagined I'd speak.

We wend our way through the castle gardens, our hands still clasped tightly together. I can't help but notice how natural it feels, like our fingers were made to intertwine. But I push the thought aside. We have bigger problems right now than my growing feelings for Rachel.

As we march across the courtyard, I spot Rachel's great-aunts huddled near the gates. They turn as we approach, their eyes widening at our disheveled appearance.

"Och, Rachel, *leannan*! What's happened?" the eldest aunt, Efrica, exclaims as we approach.

Rachel squeezes my hand before letting go, much to my disappointment. "Antaidhean, we've just had a frightful encounter in the woods. A *beithir* chased us!"

I murmur into Rachel's ear, "Antaidhean?"

"The term refers to my great-aunts."

"Oh. I get it."

The three older women exchange worried glances. Morna, the middle aunt, steps forward. "A *beithir*, ye say? Are ye certain?"

"Hell yeah, I'm sure," I confirm. "The thing was as big as a bear and had purple fur. Glowing green eyes too. Damn thing nearly had us for lunch."

"Watch your language, young man," Lachina, the youngest great-aunt, chides gently. But her expression is serious as she turns to her sisters. "This is ill news indeed. A *beithir* shouldn't be anywhere near here."

"Aye," Efrica nods gravely. "And more troubling still is how it vanished. A *beithir* doesnae simply disappear."

Rachel steps closer to her great-aunts. "There's more. Joey and I, we felt something strange just before we saw the creature. A sort of...tingling in the air."

I hadn't noticed that at the time, too caught up in our heated moment in the woods. But thinking back, Rachel's right. There had been an odd electricity crackling around us, and not just from our mutual attraction.

Lachina's gaze turns stark, and her voice grows hushed. "Ye felt the magic stirring, then. 'Tis as I feared."

"What do you mean?" I ask, feeling increasingly out of my depth. "I don't understand any of this."

The three great-aunts exchange another meaningful look before Morna speaks. "The veil between worlds is thinning. And with it, creatures and magics long dormant might awaken as well."

I thrust a hand through my hair, trying to process this information. It all sounds crazy. "Okay, so…magical creatures are popping up. But why now? And what does it have to do with me?"

Efrica fixes me with a piercing stare. "Ye're not from this time, Joseph Finnegan. Yer very presence here has caused ripples in the fabric of reality. 'Tis a fact we only fathomed recently. That's why we didnae tell you about it. We hoped to find answers first, but that plan never came to fruition."

Everything inside me freezes. "Are you saying this is my fault?"

Rachel steps closer to me, her hand finding mine again. "Nay, Joey. 'Tis not your fault. But yer arrival may have…hastened things."

Perfect. I might be the catalyst for evil magics that could destroy these people I've come to think of as friends—or more, in Rachel's case. But I might destroy their futures.

That's just my luck.

Chapter Sixteen

Rachel

*E*ver since the *beithir* incident a few days ago, we have been searching for more information, scouring old books we have ne'er read before, poring over texts and studying drawings. Thus far, we have not
found anything that might explain the appearance of the *beithir*. It had
revealed itself at the precise moment when Joey and I were in the throes. But
that cannae be what triggered the creature's appearance.

Yesterday, all of us gathered in the solar to discuss the problem, though
none of us wished to talk about the dire consequences Joey might suffer
if either his former associates or shadowy dark forces attempt to infiltrate
the castle. We have all been going about our business as usual—if the term
"usual" even applies. We have all experienced magics at one time or another. Mayhap it's time for Joey to explain about his past. But that is not
my decision to make.

While my parents engage in a hushed conversation, sitting side by side
in a most romantic manner, the great-aunts are busy preparing spiced wine
for us. Joey and I take two chairs near the windows and await whatever
news they wish to impart to us.

My father smiles at Great-Aunt Efrica, his eyes glimmering with mischief. "What have you brought us this eve, gràidh? A keg of whisky,
perhaps?"

My mother elbows him in the side. "Behave, Kieran."

Efrica carefully carries a mug toward the laird, as if she worries she might
spill the contents. When she hands the mug to my father, he accepts it—and

sniffs the liquid. His brows rise. "Spiced wine? I havenae drunk this in years." He takes a sip and smiles. "*Iontach*, Efrica. You lasses are gifted at more than magics. You also excel at blending spirits and, of course, baking."

Once Mother and the aunts have taken their seats—and their cups—Joey and I finally indulge in our spiced wine treat.

"This is damn good," he declares. "Mind if I ask what's in it?"

Lachina smiles. "Not at all, dearie. We included ginger, pepper, cloves, galangal, and black peppercorn. Do ye like it?"

"I love it. But what does *iontach* mean? I feel like I need a Gaelic dictionary so I won't need to ask you guys for translations all the time."

"*Iontach* means 'wonderful.'"

The next morning, we all rise early. Father ensures we will awaken at the same time by bellowing, "Rise and shine, women! We have guests today! Dress appropriately, please!"

He then clangs a cow bell. We have no cow, so I cannae imagine from whence he got that thing.

Today, we have other things to concern ourselves with, namely, the arrival of the MacLeod clan. The *beithir* hovers in the back of my mind. Yet I am currently more worried about the MacLeods. Alisdair wants to marry me, and he has made that clear on many occasions. *Bod an Donais*, I'd rather marry the *beithir*.

The arrival of the MacLeod clan triggers a flurry of activity throughout our already bustling castle. I can't help but feel a twinge of anxiety as I watch the procession of kilted warriors and their families file through the gates. My gaze darts nervously to Joey, who stands tall beside me, his jaw clenched, demeanor resolute.

"Breathe, Rach," he whispers, his warm breath tickling my ear. "Considering our magical problems, a rival clan seems like a piece of cake."

"Aye, that's true." I wince. "Now I'm craving cake."

Joey chuckles. "Sorry, I shouldn't have mentioned desserts. Promise I'll bake a cake for you later."

"You bake?"

He shrugs. "My last foster mom forced me to cook, bake, and do all the cleaning."

I snuggle up to him. "Poor Joey. I'll gladly cook for ye."

Try as I might, I cannae suppress the butterflies in my stomach. It's not just the MacLeods that worry me, but the growing tension concerning Alisdair. As if summoned by my thoughts, the warrior himself materializes from the crowd, his dark eyes fixed on me. A shiver slides down my spine, and I instinctively lean closer to Joey. The air crackles with an unseen energy, and I can't help but wonder if it's the result of the mounting tension or something more…magical.

Joey's hand finds mine, his fingers intertwining with my own. The simple gesture grounds me, a reminder that I'm not alone in this increasingly complex web of clan politics and supernatural forces.

"Rachel," Alisdair's voice cuts through the din of the arriving clan. He approaches us, his eyes never leaving mine. "Your father requests your presence in the great hall. The MacLeod chieftain wishes to greet you."

Och, must I endure more MacLeod nonsense? But I must do what Father wants. He is not the clan chieftain or even the clan chief—except in my eyes. The laird of Dùndubhan presides over our wee corner of the MacTaggart world. "Of course, Alisdair. I'll be there shortly."

As Alisdair turns to leave, his gaze flicks to Joey, a flash of barely concealed hostility passing between them. The moment feels taut as a bowstring, until Alisdair strides away.

"I don't like this," Joey snarls, his grip on my hand tightening. "Something feels off."

I've felt a similar sensation, unable to shake the feeling that we're walking into a trap. But what choice do we have? To refuse would be an insult to both clans.

"Come with me," I say, tugging Joey towards the great hall. "I'd rather face whatever awaits us with you by my side."

"This is a friendly gathering, not a battleground. Right?"

I am less than convinced that it won't become just that.

As we make our way through the throng of MacLeods and MacTaggarts, I catch glimpses of unfamiliar faces. One in particular stands out—a tall, imposing figure shrouded in shadows. I take half a step toward him. But then he vanishes, and I'm left to ponder whether I'd seen the figure at all or simply imagined it.

As we enter the great hall, the space is a cacophony of voices and laughter when we enter. My father stands at the far end of the room, deep in conversation with a man I assume to be the MacLeod chieftain. I had only seen the MacLeod twice in my life before this moment. As we approach, I feel Joey tense beside me.

"Ah, Rachel, mo nighean," my father says, his voice carrying over the din. "Come, greet Chieftain MacLeod."

I paste on my most diplomatic smile, squeezing Joey's hand before releasing it to step forward. The MacLeod is a bear of a man, his wild red beard streaked with gray, his eyes sharp and calculating beneath bushy brows.

"So, this is the famous Rachel MacTaggart," he rumbles, his gaze sweeping over me in a way that makes my skin crawl. "I've heard tales of your beauty, lass, but they dinnae do you justice."

I force a laugh, falling back on years of training in clan etiquette. "You're too kind, Chieftain MacLeod. Welcome to Dùndubhan Castle. We're honored by your presence."

"Aye, I'm sure you are." The chieftain squints at Joey. "And who might this strapping lad be?"

He jerks his chin towards Joey, who stands rigid at my side.

Before I can think of anything to say, Joey steps forward, extending his hand to the chieftain. "Joey Finnegan, sir. I'm…a guest of the MacTaggarts."

MacLeod's bushy eyebrows shoot up, his gaze darting between Joey and me. "A guest, ye say? Interesting. I wasn't aware the MacTaggarts were in the habit of entertaining outsiders at Dùndubhan."

My father steps in, pushing between me and Joey to face the MacLeod chieftain. "You are in the MacTaggarts' domain, Chieftain MacLeod. As laird of Dùndubhan, I may invite whomever I choose to visit our family."

"The lad speaks strangely."

"He is English," Father tells the chieftain smoothly. "How many Sassenachs have you encountered? I encountered many of them during my travels, before I took over as laird of the castle."

"I reckon I'll accept that explanation—for now." MacLeod's lips curl into a smirk. "But we have come for a specific reason, namely my son's desire to wed Rachel. We have brought a dowry to seal the arrangement."

Joey glowers at MacLeod, his jaw set and his hands fisted. "Rachel will decide for herself who she marries, and I guarantee it won't be your son."

MacLeod's voice is dangerously soft. "And what authority does an English guest have to make guarantees about a Highland lass's future?"

Before I can speak up for myself, a commotion near the entrance draws everyone's attention. The crowd parts, revealing a familiar face. I'm shocked to see him here, but we MacTaggarts will all be delighted.

Guarin Abadie is sauntering toward us.

"Forgive my late arrival," he says, his lush French accent a welcome sound we've not heard for some time. "I'm afraid I got a bit lost in your lovely Highlands. It has been a long while since I visited Dùndubhan."

Guarin's arrival is like a breath of fresh air, momentarily dispelling the tension. His charming smile and easy manner work their magic on everyone in the room, even the gruff Chieftain MacLeod.

"Ah, Monsieur Abadie!" my father exclaims, clearly relieved by the distraction. "We weren't expecting you, but what a pleasant surprise you've given us."

I seize the opportunity to step away from the MacLeod chieftain, tugging Joey along with me. We make our way to Guarin, who greets us both with warm embraces despite the fact he has never met Joey before.

"Rachel, *ma chérie*," he says, kissing both my cheeks. "And who might you be, *jeune homme?*"

Joey proffers his hand to the Frenchman. "Joey Finnegan, sir."

Guarin chuckles. "Never call me 'sir.' I am no knight, and I never stand on ceremony. It is a pleasure to meet you, Joey. You are indeed a young man, as I said a moment ago in my native tongue."

As Guarin and Joey exchange pleasantries, I can't help but notice the subtle shift in the room's atmosphere. The MacLeod chieftain's piercing gaze flits between us, his brow furrowed in what I can only assume is suspicion or curiosity. I silently thank the heavens for Guarin's timely arrival, providing a much-needed buffer against the mounting tension.

"Monsieur Abadie," the MacLeod chieftain's gruff voice cuts through the chatter. "I wasn't aware the MacTaggarts were expecting French visitors. What brings you to our wild Highlands?"

Guarin turns to face the chieftain, his easy smile never faltering. "Ah, *mon ami*, I am here on matters of commerce and friendship. The MacTaggarts and I have long been allies."

I watch as Guarin works his charm on everyone in the room, defusing the tension with his easy manner and lilting accent. Even the MacLeod chieftain seems momentarily disarmed by Guarin's infectious humor.

Eventually, Guarin reveals his true motive for this visit. "I wouldn't dream of coming to the grand castle of Dùndubhan empty-handed." He slaps my father's arm and grins. "In fact, I've brought a special vintage from the vineyards of Bordeaux that I believe everyone will find quite intriguing. Naturally, I have brought a dozen bottles, enough for all to taste."

Our moment of respite is short-lived, however, as Alisdair barges through the crowd to install himself at my side. Joey takes umbrage at Alisdair's hubris, and I sense trouble coming.

The increasing tension of this situation has me biting my lip.

Alisdair's hand settles on my shoulder, heavy and possessive. "Rachel, my father wishes to discuss the arrangements for our wedding."

Joey sidles closer to me, his shoulder pressing against mine in a protective stance. "Funny, I don't recall Rachel agreeing to any wedding."

Alisdair's feral smile gives me a shiver. "This is clan business, Sassenach. It doesn't concern you."

Joey pulls his arm back and punches Alisdair squarely in the face. While my would-be suitor bleeds from the nose and stumbles backward a step, Joey slams his knee into Alisdair's groin, making the cacan shout and stagger backward even further. He bumps into a small table and loses his balance, plummeting to the floor.

Chieftain MacLeod stomps up to Joey, jabbing an accusing finger at him. Spittle sprays from his lips as declares, "Ye'll pay for what ye did to my son, ye English bastard!"

Father and Guarin come up beside me and Joey. But the Laird of Dùndubhan takes the lead. He stabs a finger at the MacLeod chieftain. "You came to our home to stabilize our alliance. But instead, ye've used this day as an opportunity to insult and harass us." Father thrusts an arm out, pointing one finger. "Get out of my house, MacLeod. Do it now, or we will do it for you."

The MacLeod chieftain's face darkens to a shade of crimson that rivals his beard. For a moment, I fear he might explode right there in our great hall, scattering bits of angry Highlander across our tapestries.

"Ye dare order me about, Kieran MacTaggart?" The MacLeod chieftain plants his feet wide, his hand moving to the dirk at his belt. "After yer English pet assaults my son?"

The hall falls silent save for Alisdair's pained groaning as he struggles to rise from the floor. I can feel the tension in Joey, his body coiled like a spring ready to unleash. *A mhic an damnaidh*, I how did this day devolve into anger and recriminations.

"I dare," Father replies, his voice dangerously quiet, "because this is my home, and my daughter is not chattel to be bartered for."

Chieftain MacLeod pivots on his heels and barks orders to his fellow clansmen, ordering them to vacate the premises. My family, and Joey, all march outside to make certain the MacLeods have truly gone. Once they've traveled beyond our sight, Father shuts the gates. Have we just earned an enemy in the MacLeod clan? And will they seek vengeance? Alisdair still wants me as his wife, and I cannae help wondering what he might do next, especially after Joey shamed him.

A Dhia, save us from the wrath of the MacLeods.

Chapter Seventeen

Joey

After the crazy shit that went down the other day when the MacLeods came for a visit, we all needed to decompress. I punched Alisdair in the face. He totally deserved it, but ever since, I've been worrying about the consequences of my act of defiance. What if I've accidentally triggered a clan war?

I'll think about that later.

Today, I have different plans. They involve a beautiful Scots lass, nudity, and orgasms galore. Since I plan to make Rachel scream in ecstasy, I intend to whisk her away to a secluded location that's also conveniently near the castle. I told Big Daddy that I'd be taking his daughter out for a picnic along the river. He might've guessed that I'm a horny goat, but if he did, Kieran didn't seem to mind.

The ladies of the house whipped up a sumptuous picnic for us that includes a bottle of Guarin's wine. The Frenchman left Dùndubhan yesterday, and we were all sorry to see him go. Guarin is a great guy and lots of fun.

Rachel and I walk hand in hand as we make our way down the river to a waterfall Alyssa had suggested might be a good spot for a picnic.

"This is lovely," Rachel says. Her golden-brown hair catches the breeze, and I'm momentarily distracted by how the sunlight turns the edges to liquid amber. "Just us. No clan politics, no mysterious portals, no one trying to kill you."

"Yet," I add with a wink. "The day is young, and I tend to attract trouble like an industrial magnet."

She bumps her hip against mine. "Don't jinx it, *mo leannan*."

I've learned that the phrase mo *leannan* means "my sweetheart." That's what Rachel has become to me too. She also told me "*A Dhia*" means "oh God."

"It's just down this way," Rachel says, now tugging me along the winding path.

Yeah, I'm pretty sure she knows exactly what kind of "picnic" I have in mind.

The pounding rush of water intensifies as we draw nearer to the falls. It's not massive—no more than fifteen feet high—but it creates a perfect curtain of crystal droplets that cascade into a deep, clear pool below. It's like something from a damn fairy tale, which is fitting since my entire life has become one since I fell through that portal. The surrounding rocks form a natural enclosure, sheltered by ancient pines that provide privacy from prying eyes.

"Alyssa wasn't kidding," I say, setting down our basket on a flat rock. "This place is perfect."

I drop to one knee, pretending to arrange our picnic while stealing glances at Rachel. She stands at the pool's edge, her reflection rippling on the water's surface. My chest tightens at the sight.

"The locals call it *Abhainn Na Daoine Maithe*," Rachel says, slipping off her shoes. "The River of the Good Folk. It's a reference to the legends of the fairies that supposedly live here."

"Does that mean the river is enchanted?" I ask, only half-joking. With everything I've experienced in the seventeenth century, magical waterfalls aren't exactly outside the realm of possibility.

Rachel's cheeks dimple in a mischievous smile. "They say couples who swim here together are blessed with eternal passion of the Ashrays."

"Uh, what's an Ashray? Is it some kind of fish?"

"Nay. The Ashrays are a type of fairy folk that love the water. And they are said to inhabit this part of the river."

I gaze into the water more deeply, intrigued by Rachel's explanation of the Ashray. "I wonder if an Ashray will bless us while we're getting it on like wild animals."

She begins unlacing her bodice with deliberate slowness. "Would ye care to find out?"

Her question makes my dick start to firm up. "Sure, yeah. For science, naturally."

"Of course," she agrees with a wink.

The laces of her bodice come undone, and Rachel lets the fabric fall away. I'm still not used to the complicated layers of a Scottish woman's clothing. It's like unwrapping the world's sexiest present, with about fifteen more ribbons and ties than seems necessary.

"Need some help there?" I ask, stepping closer.

"Are ye offering your services as a lady's maid now?" She raises an eyebrow, but her fingers pause on the ties of her skirt.

"I prefer 'gentleman undresser.' It's a more dignified title."

Rachel grins.

As I help her with the remaining layers, my fingers brush against her warm skin, sending electricity racing through my body. Rachel shivers despite the summer warmth.

"Got a chill?" I whisper against her ear.

"Nay," she whispers back. "Just eager to have you inside me again."

When she finally stands before me in nothing but her shift, I almost forget to breathe. The thin fabric clings to her curves, virtually transparent wherever the sunlight catches it just right.

"Your turn," she announces, tugging at my leather jacket.

I shrug it off quickly, nearly tripping over my own feet in my haste to undress. Rachel laughs, the sweet sound echoing across the ravine like music. She helps me get rid of my clothes, fingers dancing across my chest as she pushes my shirt up and over my head.

"You know," I say, my voice husky as her palms press against my bare skin, "I'm starting to think Scotland's greatest magic isn't in your witches or your portals."

"Do ye now?" She gazes up at me through those impossibly long lashes. "And what would ye say the greatest magic is?"

"You." I capture her lips with mine, tasting the sweetness of her lips, feeling her smile against me. "I need to fuck you right now, baby."

"I was hoping you'd say that." Rachel brushes her lips against mine, her fingers already working at the fastenings of my trews. "Though we Scots prefer a more poetic turn of phrase."

"What would a proper Highlander say, then?" I ask while I help her push my trews down my legs. My cock springs free, now so stiff that it's almost painful. That's how much I crave this woman.

Her eyes darken as she leans in close, her lips grazing my ear. "I want to feel ye move inside me until I canna remember my own name."

The way her accent thickened just now makes my cock twitch against her thigh. *Hold on, little buddy.* We'll get what we want soon, but her pleasure comes first.

I cough into my fist. "That's...definitely more poetic."

We stumble toward the water's edge, neither of us willing to break contact long enough to walk properly, kissing all the while. Rachel's shift is the last barrier between us, and I tug at the thin fabric until she raises her arms, allowing me to pull it over her head. Fortunately, I'd already laid out the picnic blanket for us.

The sight of her naked body steals my breath away. The dappled sunlight filtering through the trees plays across her skin, highlighting the gentle curves of her breasts and hips. Her nipples harden in the cool air, and I can't resist touching them, circling one with my thumb while my mouth finds the other. Rachel moans, her fingers tangling in my hair as she arches against me.

"Joey," she whispers, my name sounding like a prayer on her lips.

I lose myself in the taste of her skin, trailing kisses down her neck, across her collarbone, between her breasts. Every kiss elicits another sigh, another shudder that courses through her body and straight into mine.

"The water," she reminds me breathlessly. "We should—oh!"

My hand has found its way between her thighs, fingers sliding through her slick heat.

"Ye waste no time," she says, laughing softly, but the laughter turns to a soft whimper as I circle her glistening clit. Her hips move in rhythm with my touch, and I feel so drunk on her desire that I can't think straight. The scent of her cream intoxicates me, and I groan as she grinds herself against my hand. Damn, I need to devour that little nub.

We're so close to the water that the spray from the falls mists over us like rain. Before I can lose myself completely, Rachel flips me onto my back with surprising strength and straddles my waist. The magic of this place has definitely given her some extra energy. I love her enthusiasm for sex. It means I'll be able to give Rachel multiple orgasms before I come inside her slick channel.

She drags herself along the length of my cock, already slick and ready for me.

"Let's make sure both of us are blessed with great pleasure," she breathes, guiding me to her entrance and slowly lowering herself onto me.

The sensation of her body enveloping me and her juices dribbling down my flesh has my chest heaving. I've never known another woman who got so wet so quickly. I grit my teeth against the blissful tightness. "Oh fuck, Rachel…"

Her head tilts back as I fill her inch by inch. "It's even better than I remember."

Those words resonate through me, amping up my hunger for Rachel's body. I need to experience every quiver and cry she unleashes and the slick heat of her channel surrounding me.

Before I can respond to her statement, she begins to move, a slow roll of her hips that nearly undoes me right then and there. The water sprays around us, catching the sunlight in rainbow arcs as she rides me with increasing urgency. It sends rivulets down her hair and skin. She is a mermaid queen, bending so that her breasts graze my chest as her lips steal my breath away.

The rush of the waterfall echoes like our own pulses pounding. Her movements grow frantic above me, and she moans into my mouth as she clenches tight around my cock.

"Rachel," I rasp, losing myself completely to the fervid magic of her body. I take hold of her waist, needing more of her, all of her. My thrusts match her wild rhythm, each one driving her gasps louder, quicker, until it feels we're both moments from breaking apart in ecstasy.

"Joey!" Her sudden scream pierces the air, and water crashes around us as a wave of pleasure overtakes her.

She digs her nails into my shoulders like she needs something solid to cling to. Pulse after pulse grips me until I can't hold back anymore. I'm helpless against the onslaught of her inner muscles milking me. The world collapses to a single point of light. Stars blaze behind my eyes as I come harder than I ever thought possible.

When we float back down from the heights together, Rachel collapses against me. We're both panting hard, catching our breaths where we still lie tangled on the blanket.

"We might have scared off the Ashrays," I finally manage to say.

Rachel snickers wickedly. "Or they got jealous and told all the other water spirits how the American made a Highland witch scream."

She knows the power she has over me and relishes it.

"Damn right I did that," I say, kissing the top of her head where it rests on my chest. My cock is still throbbing, still half-hard inside her from that incredible orgasm. Even better, I'm pretty sure she's ready for another round.

Rachel adjusts her hips a little, reminding me just how perfectly our bodies fit together. "You're ready to go again already? Ye spoil me, Joey."

I briefly wonder if she hit me with some of her magics. But no, Rachel didn't need supernatural assistance to turn me on. I'm helpless to stop her from riding me again despite the fact it's only been a minute or two since our first round.

"Guess I've got some work ahead of me," I murmur, letting her set the pace as my cock swells even more. "Keeping you satisfied might become a full-time job."

"What are ye waiting for, then?" She angles her hips so each thrust dives deep, and my cock nudges her inner walls.

The velvety texture of her channel feels so fucking incredible that I can't stop myself from pounding into her harder, faster, wilder until I swear my eyes might roll back in my head. I grip her thighs, overwhelmed by the power and urgency in every movement of her body. The mist shrouds us. The rocks are distant shadows beyond the river, and our gasps become wild cries. Every time I buck my hips up into her, Rachel's moans magnify into throaty shouts, and I can think of nothing but how close she is to falling into spams of ecstasy again—and how much I want that to happen.

As Rachel rides me like a bucking bronco, her body gleams with water droplets, and something shifts in the air. The mist from the falls seems to coalesce, swirling in patterns too deliberate to be natural. For a split second, I swear I see faces in the water—beautiful, otherworldly faces with eyes that shimmer like the surface of the pool.

"Joey," Rachel gasps, her rhythm faltering. "Do you feel that?"

I do. It's like electricity dancing across my skin, making every nerve ending hypersensitive. The pleasure intensifies tenfold, spiraling through my body in waves that match the ripples in the water.

"The Ashrays," she cries out, her tone strained. Her eyes are wide with wonder and lust. "They're here."

Whether it's magic or just the most intense sex of my life, I don't care. Rachel's movements become more fluid, almost otherworldly, as if she's being guided by something beyond herself. The water churns around us, splashing higher up the rocks than should be possible given how still the pool had been.

"Rachel," I gasp, feeling something profound and spellbinding that grips us both. My entire body tingles with an energy I can't explain, every touch magnified until it's almost unbearable.

Rachel's eyes lock onto mine, and I see something ancient and knowing flash behind her gaze. Her fall open, but instead of words, a sound like rushing water escapes. The mist thickens around us, forming a cocoon that blocks out the world beyond our intertwined bodies.

I flip us over so I'm on top, taking control as the magics overtake us. We both come, so swiftly and powerfully that our cries become hoarse and weak, barely whispers. She sprawls over me while sweat beads on her skin—and mine too. I feel the magics dissipating little by little and hold her close as the tremors of our lovemaking gradually fade.

What we just did…I have no idea what it means. All I'm sure of is that something has radically changed between us.

Suddenly, a wave of dizziness overtakes me—and I pass out.

Chapter Eighteen

Rachel

I shake Joey hard, so hard in fact that I fear I've jostled all the brain cells out of his head, and soon they'll come tumbling out of his ears. My first response is to panic, but I take a deep breath and urge myself to relax. Mayhap Ashray-inspired sex was simply too much for Joey. But no, he's a strong lad. Only Joey Finnegan would have dared to punch Alisdair MacLeod.

He will come through. He must.

Since I cannae wake him with any amount of shaking or slapping, I have just one option. I must somehow drag him back to the castle. But I dinnae dare leave him here alone and unconscious. So, I grasp him under the arms and attempt to heave him up. Sweet Mary, the man is heavy as a boulder—all that muscle weighs more than it seems. With a mighty struggle, I manage to get him half-upright before my arms begin to shake with the effort.

"Joey Finnegan, I swear by all the witches of the Highlands, if ye dinnae wake up this instant, I'll hex ye into the next century," I holler, though my threat lacks conviction.

I resolve to get us both dressed before I attempt to drag him home. By the time I've finished my task, I'm out of breath and speckled with dirt. Joey is also filthy. I'll wash his clothes for him later. Right now, I need to find a method of getting him home.

I let him slide back down gently, cradling his head so it doesn't thump against the ground. His face is remarkably peaceful in unconsciousness, those whisky brown eyes hidden beneath closed lids. I explore the area, hunting for anything I might use as a litter. After what feels like hours, but couldn't have been more than a few moments, I find two branches lying on the ground and a few smaller ones that I use as crosspieces. Then, I stretch my shift across the entire framework.

Aye, this might work.

I take a wee break to eat some of the food in our picnic basket. I'll need energy to haul Joey back to the castle. The sustenance helps, and I feel strong enough to undertake my journey. Fortunately, the waterfall isn't far from home. I allow myself only a few breaks to rest along the way, arriving at the rear of the castle just as the sun is beginning its descent. The bakehouse is attached to the rear, and it's closer than the garden door. So, I drag Joey into the bakehouse and set the litter down on the floor as gently as I can.

Once I've caught my breath, I fling the bakehouse door open and shout, "Help! Help!"

My parents are in the courtyard. They race toward me, reaching me swiftly.

"What's happened to Joey?" Father asks. "He seems pale."

"And not well at all," Mother interjects. "Let's get him into the house, Rachel's explanation can wait until later."

"Aye, it can." Father lifts Joey off the floor and throws the laddie over his shoulder. "Alyssa, go and get the aunts."

She races away, following his orders.

My father carries Joey out of the bakehouse and marches straight into the house. As he stomps up the staircase, heading for Joey's room on the third floor, my mother and my great-aunts emerge from downstairs wearing anxious expressions. I'm worried also, but I cannae think about what has happened to Joey. He will be all right? Or won't he? Aye, of course he will. He must.

But what if someone has poisoned him with dark magics? I'm being ridiculous. The aunts would know if such a thing had been done to him.

Father stalks into Joey's chambers and lays him down on the bed. Then he turns to me. "You lasses can take care of him now."

Kieran MacTaggart departs the bedroom, his footfalls growing softer and softer until I can't hear them at all. He didnae even ask why Joey was naked, thank goodness. I dinnae care to explain that.

My mother and the aunts set about working on Joey. I know I should help, but I cannae tear my gaze away from his limp form and his pale complexion. I stand frozen, my heart pounding in my chest as I watch the women fuss over Joey. His face is ashen, his breathing shallow. What if he doesn't wake up? What if I've lost him forever? The thought sends a shiver down my spine.

"Rachel, *leannan*," Great-Aunt Lachina says in a gentle tone that disperses my panic. "Fetch us clean cloths and water, will ye?"

I nod curtly, grateful for something to do. As I hurry to gather the supplies, I can hear the hushed whispers of my mother and the aunts, though I can't make out their words. They're speaking in Gaelic, that's all I can tell.

When I return, Morna is holding her hands over Joey's chest, her eyes closed in concentration. A faint blue light emanates from her palms, pulsing in rhythm with Joey's shallow breaths. I hand the cloths and water to my mother, who begins to dab at Joey's forehead with a damp cloth.

I wring my hands. "What's wrong with him?"

Efrica glances at me. "It's not poison, dearie. But there's a darkness clinging to him, like a shadow that doesn't belong."

"Is it...because of me? Because I brought him into the castle? Mayhap those dark forces are after Joey because they know I care for him."

My mother pulls me into a firm hug. "Hush now, sweetie. This is not your doing. Something far more sinister is at work here."

I watch as Morna continues her ministrations, the blue light growing stronger. Joey's chest rises and falls more steadily now, but his eyes remain closed.

"There's a battle raging within him," Morna declares, her eyes still closed. "Something is trying to take hold, to claim his very soul."

"Can ye help him?"

"We're doing what we can, gràidh," Lachina assures me, placing a comforting hand on my shoulder. "But this is unlike anything we've encountered before."

Joey's body suddenly goes rigid. His back arches off the bed, and a pained groan escapes his lips. I rush to his side, my pulse pounding in my ears.

"Joey!" I reach for his hand. But as soon as my fingers brush his skin, a jolt of energy courses through me, and I stumble backward.

"Rachel!" My mother exclaims, steadying me with her hands on my shoulders. "What's wrong, sweetie?"

I lean down, clasping Joey's face with my hands. "Please come back to me, please. I cannae lose you."

His eyes dart back and forth behind his lids.

As I gaze at his impassive face, desperate to help him, I suddenly understand what I must do.

I crush my lips to his mouth.

A faint moan escapes his lips—along with a single word. "Rachel..."

I pull him into my arms, clutching him to my breast. A rush of power courses through my veins. It's unlike anything I've ever experienced before—-raw, primal, and ancient. The magic of my ancestors, passed down through generations, pours out me in a torrent that threatens to overwhelm my senses. I cling to Joey, anchoring myself to him as the energy builds. The shadows writhe and shriek around us, their inky tendrils recoiling from the growing light that emanates from our embrace.

I gasp, and my eyes fly open, but my lips still pressed against Joey's. His eyes snap open too, wide and disoriented. We stare at each other wide-eyed, both panting heavily.

"Rachel?" Joey whispers, his voice hoarse. "What just happened?"

"Ahmno sure. But it seems like dark magics got hold of you."

"Was it the Ashrays?"

I shake my head. "That cannae be. The Ashrays are good folk—fairies—not demonic forces."

Joey's grip on my hand tightens. "I remember…darkness. And cold. So much cold."

He shivers, and I instinctively move closer to him, offering my warmth. I grab another blanket too, draping it over him.

"Ye fought it, Joey," I assure him. "Ye didn't let it take ye."

"Because of you. Your presence was a white light in the darkness." He pushes up into a sitting position. "I can't explain it, but while I was unconscious, I felt a presence hovering around me. Something dark and dangerous. It wanted me, sure, but also you and everyone else here at Dùndubhan."

I sweep a lock of hair away from his eye. "We will figure this out together."

"There's something else." He pushes up on his elbows. "When I was out of my head, I saw things. A dark place. Visions, maybe? Flashes of the past and…things that haven't happened yet."

The room falls silent, all eyes fixed on Joey. Even my great-aunts, usually unflappable, exchange worried glances.

"What sort of visions?" Great-Aunt Lachina asks.

Joey's brow furrows as he tries to recall. "It's all jumbled, but I saw… battles. Ancient ones, with men in kilts wielding claymores. But also, modern warfare with guns and explosions. And I saw…us. Me and the whole family, fighting against something dark and terrible."

"There's more," Joey continues, his voice growing stronger. "I saw a figure, shrouded in darkness. It was controlling everything, pulling strings across time itself. And I heard a name…but I can't remember it now."

Lachina grows pale. "*An Bodach. Tha e tighinn.*"

I stare at Efrica, unable to believe what Lachina has said.

Joey's gaze flicks to me. "Is she speaking Gaelic?"

"Aye. Lachina said 'The Old Man is coming.'"

"What old man?"

"He is a malevolent spirit from ancient folklore." I glance at my great-aunt again, just as she seems to come out of her trance. "What did you see, Lachina?"

Her eyes refocus, her gaze sharp as she studies Joey and me. "I beheld what your laddie saw—darkness stretching across time, threatening to engulf us all. The Old Man, *An Bodach*, he's more than simply folklore, Rachel. He is an ancient evil that has slumbered for centuries."

Joey shifts uneasily on the bed. "And now he's waking up? Why?"

Efrica steps forward, her face grim. "The barriers between centuries, between worlds might be weakening."

"Cracks that *An Bodach* might exploit," Morna adds.

A shiver ripples down my spine, raising the hairs at my nape. "So, what do we do? How do we stop him?"

Lachina shakes her head slowly, her gaze distant. "It won't be easy, *leannan. An Bodach* is cunning and powerful, according to the folk tales. You and Joey might be the twin poles around which everything turns. He'll seek to divide us, to turn us against each other with his trickery."

Joey's hand tightens around mine. "We won't let that happen."

I give him a reassuring smile, but a flicker of doubt gnaws at me. How can we fight something so ancient and terrible?

"First things first," my mother interjects, her practical nature asserting itself. "Joey needs to regain his strength. Rachel, that broth, if you please. We can deal with ancient, unseen evil another day."

I reluctantly disentangle myself from Joey and head for the door, but his voice stops me.

"Rachel," he calls softly. When I turn, his eyes are intense, filled with an emotion I can't quite name. "Thank you. For saving me—again."

I flash him a tight smile, then walk out of the room. But the vision Lachina's dà-shealladh showed her haunts me. I pause in the corridor, leaning against the cold stone wall to steady myself. The weight of what's happening bears down on me like a physical force. *An Bodach.* The Old Man. I've heard whispers of him since childhood, tales meant to frighten wee bairns into obedience. But now...

The kitchen is empty when I enter, and the hearth fire still burns at a low level. The smell of burning wood and simmering broth wafts around me, a comforting scent that contrasts with the fear and uncertainty swimming in my mind. I ladle broth into a wooden bowl, trying not to focus on the dire news we've learned tonight. As I turn to leave, a chill passes through the room, causing the flames to flicker and dance. I freeze, my breath catching in my throat.

The moment passes, and I hurry to bring Joey the broth.

My rapid footsteps echo loudly in the stillness of the castle as I climb up to the third floor, halting at Joey's door. I knock gently.

Efrica opens the door. "Give me the broth, dearie. You should find Kieran and inform him of the laddie's condition."

Efrica shuts the door.

As I walk downstairs, I cannae help twisting my fingers in the folds of my skirt, a nervous gesture that's unlike me. Joey will be fine. I believe that in my heart and my soul.

How quickly our moment of passion had turned to terror.

When I enter the solar, my father is sitting in a big chair by the hearth, where a blazing fire crackles. The moment he looks at me, I fall to pieces and sob.

He pats his thigh, inviting me to sit on his lap. "Come, mo nighean, cry on my shoulder the way you would when you were but a wee lassie."

I rush to him, crawling onto his lap, and weep the tears I had struggled to hold back until this moment. My father makes shushing sounds and begins to stroke my hair.

Joey will recover. I know it to be true. And I am more grateful than words can express that my family loves and supports me.

Chapter Nineteen

Joey

An entire week goes by while nothing much happens. I recovered from my "injury" after two days of rest, during which Rachel insisted on staying by my side as if I were on my deathbed. But I get why she's anxious. A Scottish demon wants to…do something evil. That's all any of us knows.

At least my mafia buddies can't find me here in the past.

I'm trying not to let the tension get to me, but it's like waiting for a bomb to go off. Every creaking branch makes me jump, and I swear the shadows are moving when I'm not looking. Rachel's not much better, pacing back and forth like a caged tiger, constantly scanning for threats.

Today, we're walking round and round inside the castle walls. For safety's sake, nobody goes outside the fortress alone, and we only go out there unless there's a damn good reason for doing so.

As we round a corner, Rachel grabs my arm. "Joey, did ye hear that?"

I halt, swiveling my head as I strain to listen for the slightest sound. Then I relax. "No, there's nothing."

She frowns, shaking her head. "I could've sworn I heard…never mind. The fog is getting to me, I reckon."

At least I'm not the only one who's spooked.

We continue our stroll around the courtyard, but I can't shake the feeling that we're being watched. Maybe it's the tall keep or the gatehouse or…nothing at all that's set me on edge. The air feels oddly thick. The utter silence, broken only by the barely audible sound of our footfalls, makes the hairs on the back of my neck rise and stiffen. The pea-soup fog unnerves me, but I don't think that's the main cause of my anxiety. I might not have second sight, but even I can tell something's off. It's like the whole castle is holding its breath, waiting for something to happen. Ever since my bout with dark magics that nearly killed me, I've become hyperaware of pretty much everything weird that crops up.

A deafening crack of thunder splits the air and seems to shake the very foundations of Dùndubhan. Rachel and I stumble, grabbing onto each other for support as the castle walls themselves tremble.

She grips my arm. "That's no ordinary storm."

"Yeah, I know." I pull her closer. "Stay close to me. Don't want to lose you in this preternatural fog."

"Aye. Mayhap we should go inside."

Before I can respond to her suggestion, an unearthly howl pierces the air, infecting me with a chill that raises goosebumps on my skin. The torches lining the hallway flicker and die, plunging us into darkness.

I fumble for Rachel's hand as we start running, our footsteps echoing off the stone walls. The air grows colder with every step as an un-natural chill seeps into my bones. Rachel's hand tightens around mine as we race into the house and through the darkened corridors. I can still smell the lanterns that had been burning everywhere, but they've all snuffed out now.

"The great hall," Rachel pants. "We need to get to the others."

Another bone-rattling boom shakes the castle. I swear I hear wood cracking and stones falling. Nobody could've broken down the gates, could they? The wind howls through the halls, carrying with it the acrid scent of smoke and something else—something rotten and decayed.

We burst into the great hall to find chaos. Kieran stands at the center, shouting orders as Alyssa and the aunts rush here and there, arming them-selves with swords, bows, knives, and—bizarrely—modern guns. The aunts have linked hands as they chant in a language I don't understand, a faint blue glow emanating from within their circle.

A husky voice laughs. "Ye cannot escape me, Joseph Finnegan. I'm com-ing for yer lass, and ye cannae stop me. I shall ravage her and take her maid-enhead. She will become my bride."

The laughter turns maniacal, and suddenly, I know who spoke to me. It's *An Bodach.*

I spring upright, abruptly awakened from my nightmare. Cold sweat trickles down my skin as I gasp for air, my pulse racing. Rachel stirs beside me, her eyes fluttering open. We've been sharing the same bed lately, but I haven't made love to her since our encounter at the waterfall. Why didn't

An Bodach know that? He's supposed to be a badass at magical shit. I've wondered about that ever since.

"Joey? What's wrong?" she asks, her voice a touch slurred from sleepiness. After volunteering to help Efrica make breakfast for everyone, Rachel and I had both been ready for a mid-morning nap.

I rub my eyes, trying to clear the lingering tendrils of the nightmare. "Just a bad dream, baby. Go back to sleep."

But the words feel hollow even to my own ears.

Rachel sits up, her hair a tousled mess. She reaches out to touch my arm, and I flinch involuntarily. "It was him, wasn't it? *An Bodach.*"

I swallow hard, unable to meet her gaze. "The Old Man said he was coming for you. He must have sent the *beithir* to frighten us."

"Let him try," she says fiercely. "We're ready for the old man."

But are we? The question hangs unspoken between us as a wicked gale rattles the windowpanes. Rachel and I exchange a wary glance, both of us on edge.

"Maybe we should check on the others," I suggest, already swinging my legs out of bed.

"Nay, if anything were amiss, we would know by now." Her cheeks dimple. "Because we would have five women and my father kicking the door down."

"Good point." I swing my legs back onto the bed and roll onto my side, draping an arm over Rachel's naked body. "Since we're already awake..."

She springs into a sitting position and grins, her tits flapping. "Ye want to enjoy carnal relations again?"

Her excitement is adorable and sexy. So yeah, it turns me on big time.

I gently urge Rachel to lie down again, then roll on top of her, careful not to crush her beneath me. "Rach, I've been having dirty dreams about you every night, and they always get me hard. But I wasn't sure if you wanted to get it on again."

"Oh, aye, Joey, I want ye now." She wriggles her hips just enough to make me hiss in a breath. "Make love to me, please."

"Don't need to ask me twice."

I kiss her deeply, savoring the softness of her lips and the warmth of her body beneath mine. Rachel responds eagerly, her hands roaming over my back, pulling me closer. The lingering fear from my nightmare begins to fade, replaced by a growing heat that spreads through my body. Our kisses grow more passionate, more heated, as I trail my lips down her neck, relishing the soft sighs that escape her. My hand finds her breast, thumb brushing over her nipple as it hardens under my touch. Rachel arches into me, her fingers tangling in my hair.

The scent of her cream is driving me mad.

"Och, Joey," she breathes, her voice husky with desire. "I need ye inside me, buried as deep as possible. By God's bones, please fuck me like a demon and make me scream. No one will hear us. Our chambers are on the highest floor of the castle."

I position myself between her thighs, pausing to gaze into her eyes. The trust and love I see there nearly overwhelms me. Slowly, I push inside her, both of us gasping at the sensation. Rachel wraps her legs around my waist, pulling me deeper. I groan at the exquisite feeling of being buried inside her with her juices dribbling down my cock. For a moment, we're perfectly still, savoring our connection.

Then I start to move, slowly at first, building a steady rhythm. Rachel meets me thrust for thrust, her nails digging into my back. The room fills with the sound of our ragged breathing and soft moans.

"Harder," Rachel gasps. "Please, Joey."

I oblige, picking up the pace. The bed creaks beneath us as I drive into her with increasing force. Rachel throws her head back, her spine arching, her eyes closed in ecstasy. I trail kisses along her exposed throat, tasting the salt of her skin while the scent of her lust envelops me.

"Oh God, Joey!" she cries out. "Don't stop! I love your *acainn cungaidh*!"

"My what?!"

"Your cock."

I can feel her tightening around me, close to the edge. My own release is building, a white-hot pressure coiling in my core as I growl and grunt. Rachel rakes her nails down my back, her breath coming in short, desperate gasps. She can't even speak now, so close to exploding that her cheeks have turned a lovely shade of rosy pink, and she can barely breathe.

"Let go, Rach, I've got you."

With a cry that echoes off the stone walls, Rachel comes undone beneath me. Her body arches, trembling with the force of her release. The sight of her, lost in ecstasy, pushes me over the edge. I bury myself deep inside her as my own orgasm crashes over me, wave after intense wave of pleasure coursing through my body.

We collapse together, a tangle of sweaty limbs and ragged breaths. I roll to the side, pulling Rachel with me so she's nestled against my chest. For a long moment, we just lie here, basking in the afterglow and listening to each other's heartbeats slowly return to normal.

I'm still catching my breath when she hits me with a bombshell.

Rachel climbs on top of me, straddling my hips. "Let's do that again—at least three more times."

"Three?" I almost choke on the syllable. "I'm mere mortal, you know, not a Greek god. My dick needs time to recover."

She slants closer, her hands at either side of my head, with those luscious tits dangling right above me. "I could whip up a potion that will keep you hard all night long."

"Do we really want to resort to magic just so you can use my body for your own pleasure?"

She clasps my flaccid penis. "Are ye saying ye dinnae want me again?"

Of course I do. She knows that, and she's using my desire for her to get what she wants—me, inside her. Yeah, I want that too. I defy any man to turn down Rachel MacTaggart.

She begins to massage my dick.

A sharp grunt bursts out of me. "Fuck, yes, you know I want you every minute of every day."

"Are you saying…"

"Yeah, Rachel, hit me with any magics you want."

She grins and giggles. "Ye willnae regret it, Joey."

Rachel leaps off the bed with surprising agility, her naked form illuminated by the moonlight streaming through the window. She rummages through a small chest near the hearth, pulling out various bottles and pouches.

"What exactly are you concocting over there?" I ask, propping myself up on my elbows to watch her work.

She throws me a mischievous grin over her shoulder. "Just a wee something to keep ye going all night long, mo *leannan*, just as I promised."

I experience a mixture of excitement and stone-cold fear as she mixes ingredients in a small wooden bowl. The room fills with an earthy, spicy scent that makes my nostrils flare.

"Are you sure this is safe?" I ask, eyeing the mixture warily as she approaches the bed.

Rachel rolls her eyes. "Och, ye modern men and yer worries. Trust me, Joey. I've been studying these potions since I was a wee lass. This one's as safe as mother's milk."

"If you say so." I cast a wary glance at the murky concoction. "But if I end up with some kind of magical STD, I'm blaming you."

"STD?"

"That means sexually transmitted disease. We have those in the twenty-first century, so I'm guessing you've got them here too."

"Only if they *caith* inside a whore who hasn't washed herself in…ever."

"I see. What does *caith* mean?"

She smiles in a devilish way. "It's when a lad spills his seed inside a woman's body."

"Oh. I get it." My gaze flicks to the cup she's still holding out to me, and I wince. "What if this stuff makes my dick shrivel up?"

She laughs, a musical sound that never fails to make my heart skip. "Just drink it, ye silly gealtair."

"What did you just call me? A silly gelding?"

"No, Joey, you are not a eunuch. A gealtair is a coward. So, drink."

Taking a deep breath, I down the potion in one gulp. It tastes like cinnamon and something earthy I can't quite place. For a moment, nothing happens. Then a warm tingling spreads through my body, pooling in my groin. To my amazement, I feel myself hardening again as lust courses through me with renewed vigor.

She smirks. "See? I told ye it would work."

"Rach, I need you. Now."

She climbs back onto the bed. But this time, she lies on her back waiting for me to take control. "We have all night, remember?"

I don't need to be told twice. With a growl, I pounce on Rachel, claiming her lips in a ravenous kiss. The potion has set my blood on fire, every nerve ending hypersensitive to her touch. I trail kisses down her neck, nipping and sucking at the soft skin, relishing the little gasps and moans she makes.

"Joey," she breathes, arching into me. "Please, I need ye inside me."

I position myself between her legs, teasing her entrance with the tip of my cock. She's already wet and ready for me, her eyes dark with desire. In one smooth thrust, I bury myself to the hilt, both of us groaning at the sensation.

"Ye feel so good," Rachel pants, her nails digging into my shoulders. "Move, Joey. Take me hard."

"Yes, ma'am. You command, I serve."

Chapter Twenty

Rachel

Joey initiates a rough, irregular rhythm of thrusting, employing more and more force, but it feels as if he's holding back. I cannae say why. *A mhic an damnaidh.* "Son of damnation" has become my favorite expletive of late—in Gaelic and English. I have a voice, and I've never shied away from uncomfortable questions. Why, then, am I doing so now? *Baothaire.* Aye, I am an idiot for thinking Joey will balk at what I want him to do to me.

He freezes in mid thrust. "What's wrong, baby? If I'm being too rough—"

"Nay, nay, it's the opposite." I summon my courage and just say it. "Fuck me hard, Joey. Make the bed bounce and dinnae be shy about it. I want anything you want."

His frozen expression swiftly melts into a sly grin. "You got it, Rach. Prepare to scream so hard your voice goes hoarse."

Joey's face becomes a mask of lustful determination, and he pulls back slowly, teasingly. I shiver in anticipation, my body thrumming with need. Then, without warning, he slams into me with such force that the headboard bangs against the wall.

"Oh, God!" I cry out, my fingernails digging into his shoulders.

My cream-slick channel tightens around him, welcoming the savage rhythm he's finally unleashed. The restraint that held him back has vanished, replaced by raw, untamed hunger. Every punishing thrust drives me higher and higher toward a mind-altering climax. The bed creaks and groans and thumps beneath us while our heavy breaths and desperate moans fill the air. I wrap my legs tightly around his waist, pulling him even deeper inside me.

Joey growls through gritted teeth. "Is this what you wanted, baby?"

"Aye, please," I gasp, barely able to form words. "Dinnae stop, Joey. Please dinnae stop."

The room fills with the heady scent of our lovemaking, an intoxicating mix of sweat and my cream. I glide my hands down his back, feeling the strength coiled there, marveling at how perfectly we fit together. The bed creaks in protest beneath us as the wooden frame seems on the brink of collapsing. Joey pounds into me with abandon, unleashing a savage cry. His hands grip my hips, fingers digging into my flesh hard enough to leave marks—badges of passion I'll wear proudly tomorrow.

"Rachel, fuck, I'm about to blow my top. Come with me, baby, please come with me."

I can feel myself teetering on the edge, my climax just out of reach, so close I swear I can almost touch it. Joey must sense the same thing, because he shifts slightly, angling his hips to hit the magical spot inside me that will set me off.

"Oh, God!" I cry out, my back arching off the bed. "Right there, Joey. Don't stop!"

He rises slightly, just enough that he can kneel between my thighs. Then he pulls out of my body—but only so he can lift my legs above his head.

"Lock your ankles around my neck, Rach."

I comply without hesitation, despite having no idea what his intentions are.

Then he begins to thrust again in this strange new position. It grants him a sort of leverage he couldn't achieve in the usual position. He grunts and gasps and pummels me so wildly that the bed shakes and scrapes on the floor. The intensity of Joey's thrusts sends shockwaves of pleasure through my entire body. Every powerful stroke hits deeper than before, and I can feel myself stretching to accommodate him. The new angle allows him to reach places inside me I didn't even know existed.

But just when I can feel the orgasm rising inside me, he pulls his slat out of me. "Ready for the big finish?"

"Aye, please, hurry."

He rubs the red tip of his cock against my nub, over and over and over until I'm thrashing again and cannae shout because the pleasure is too intense. He keeps going, though, until he can tell I'm on the edge.

And he pulls out again.

My desperate noises echo through the room as I writhe, unable to think or see straight.

Then Joey wraps my ankles around his neck again, slamming into me like a wrecking ball. The wet sucking sound of our joining fills the room, and my ears begin to ring because I cannae take in a full breath. Dinnae give a shite.

"Joey!" I cry out, my voice raw with passion. "Never stop fucking me, never let me come until you want me to."

My hands fist in the sheets, desperately seeking something to anchor me as wave after wave of ecstasy washes over me. The pressure builds low in my belly, a coiling tension that threatens to snap at any moment.

Joey's face is a mask of concentration, his brows furrowed and jaw clenched as he drives into me relentlessly. Sweat glistens on his skin, high-lighting the flex and strain of his muscles. He's never looked more beautiful to me than in this moment of unbridled passion.

"Come for me, Rachel," Joey commands, his voice hoarse and strained. "Let go, baby. I want to feel you come around me."

His words are the final push I need. The tension that's been building inside me finally snaps, and I'm consumed by a tidal wave of pleasure so intense it steals my breath. My entire body convulses, muscles clenching and unclenching as the orgasm rips through me.

My Gaelic screams fill the room. My vision blurs, and for a moment, I can see sparks of magic dancing in the atmosphere. The intensity of my climax triggers something deep within me, and I feel a surge of power coursing through my veins, intertwining with the waves of pleasure.

Joey's rhythm falters as my inner walls clamp down on him one last time. With a guttural shout, he thrusts once, twice more before burying himself deep inside me. I feel the hot rush of his release, prolonging my own climax.

We stay locked together, panting and trembling, as the aftershocks roll through us. Slowly, Joey lowers my legs from his shoulders, pressing tender kisses to my ankles, calves, and knees as he does so. When he finally collapses beside me, I curl into him, relishing the warmth of his body and the steady thump of his heartbeat.

"Christ, Rach," Joey murmurs, his voice rough. "That was..."

"Aye," I agree, unable to find the words myself. I press a kiss to his chest, tasting the salt of his sweat on my lips. "It was perfect."

Joey's arms tighten around me, and I feel his chuckle rumbling through his chest. "Perfect, huh? I'll have to remember that for next time."

I smile against his skin, feeling utterly sated and content. But as the passion-induced haze begins to clear from my mind, I can't help but notice something... different. The air feels charged, alive with an energy I've never experienced before.

"Joey," I whisper, propping myself up on an elbow to look at him. "Did you...did you feel anything strange just now?"

He raises an eyebrow, a smirk playing at the corners of his mouth. "Besides mind-blowing sex? Can't say I did."

I roll my eyes, but I can't wipe the grin off my face. "I'm serious. When we...when I..." How can I explain the surge of magical energy I felt at the height of our passion? I cannae explain.

Joey's expression softens, his hand coming up to cup my cheek. "What is it, baby? You can tell me anything. I hope you know that."

"I do know, Joey." I lean into his touch, rubbing my cheek against his chest. "When I came, I felt a sort of...power. Like my magic was amplified somehow. Did you not notice anything unusual?"

Joey's brow furrows in concentration as he thinks back. "Now that you mention it, there was this moment where everything felt...heightened. Like the air was crackling with electricity." His eyes widen. "Wait, are you saying our lovemaking triggered some kind of magical surge?"

"I think might have, but I cannae be sure. It's never happened before, but then again, I've never felt quite like this before." I pause, biting my lip as I consider the implications. "Joey, what if this is something to do with the time portal? With our connection?"

"You mean, like our bond is somehow amplifying your magic?"

"Aye, or mayhap..." I trail off, a wild idea forming in my mind. "What if it's not just my magic? What if it's yours too?"

Joey's expression turns skeptical. "Baby, I'm no witch. I don't have any magical abilities."

"But you've traveled through time," I argue, sitting up to straddle his hips. "You've been exposed to a portal's energy. What if that's awakened something in you?"

Joey sits up too, running a hand through his tousled hair. "I don't know, Rach. It seems pretty far-fetched."

"More far-fetched than time travel?" I lean down to stare into his eyes. "Think about it, Joey. After everything we've been through, is it really so hard to believe?"

He chuckles, shaking his head. "Fair point. All right, let's say you're onto something here. What does it mean for us?"

"Ahmno sure yet." I pause to gather my thoughts, unsure of how to explain what I believe. "If our intimate moments can amplify magical energy, it could be a powerful tool against *An Bodach*. Mayhap he was the one who nearly killed you at the waterfall."

"That could be." Joey lifts his brows. "Wait, are you suggesting we use sex magic to fight the bad guys?"

I grin at his incredulous expression. "Well, when you put it that way, it does sound a bit daft. But think about it. If we can harness this energy, channel it somehow..."

"It could give us an edge." Joey nods slowly, his expression thoughtful. "You're right. We need every advantage we can get against that evil bastard." He pulls me close, pressing a tender kiss to my forehead. "But we need to be careful. If this power is as strong as you say, it could be dangerous if we can't control it."

I snuggle into his embrace, reveling in the warmth of his skin against mine. "Aye, you're right. We'll need to experiment, figure out how to harness it safely."

A naughty grin spreads across Joey's face. "Well, if we need to practice, I'm more than willing to volunteer my services."

I swat his chest playfully but can't suppress my own grin. "And I thought you might need some convincing."

"Oh, I think you'll find I need very little convincing when it comes to you, Rachel MacTaggart."

His lips capture mine in a searing kiss that steals my breath away. As passion reignites between us, I feel that familiar tingle of magic stirring beneath my skin. This time, I focus on the sensation, trying to understand and channel it.

Joey must sense the change in me because he pulls back slightly, his gaze questioning. "Are you feeling it again?"

I nod my head, not trusting my voice. The energy is building, pulsing in time with my rapidly beating heart. Joey skims his hands down my sides, leaving behind a tingling trail.

"Tell me what you need," he murmurs against my neck.

"Och, touch me, please," I gasp. "Everywhere. I need to feel you."

A knock at the door makes us both pause.

Joey groans, shutting his eyes briefly. We both know we must answer the door—or else whoever is out there will grow more insistent.

I sigh, reluctantly pulling away from Joey. "Just a moment!"

We scramble to make ourselves presentable, Joey tossing me my discarded dress while he pulls on his trews and tunic. I run a hand through my tangled hair, trying to smooth it into some semblance of order.

"Ready?" Joey asks, his hand on the doorknob.

I take a deep breath to compose myself. Then Joey opens the door, revealing a flustered-looking Morna.

"I'm sorry to interrupt ye," she says, her eyes darting between us. "But there's been a disturbance at the edge of the property. Kieran sent me to fetch ye both."

My heart races, all thoughts of our magical discovery momentarily forgotten. "What sort of disturbance?"

Great-Aunt Morna's eyes dart nervously between Joey and me. "It's Alisdair MacLeod. He's determined to see you."

Joey and I exchange worried glances.

"Do ye think he means to abduct me?" I ask.

Morna shrugs. "I was told to fetch ye, that's all. We're gathering on the green."

"We'll be right there," I assure Morna. "Tell Father we're on our way."

Chapter Twenty-One

Joey

As soon as Morna hurries away, Rachel and I spring into action, hastily pulling the rest of our clothes on. When we reach the great hall, the others have already grabbed weapons—even the ladies. Alyssa wields a sword, though it's smaller than Kieran's claymore. Rachel and I select weapons as well, with me opting for a dirk which is basically a really big knife, or you could call it a small sword.

What's up with all the weaponry? Is everybody worried the MacLeods might be coming to kidnap Rachel? Honestly, I can't swear I haven't thought of that too. But if that cretin so much as looks at Rachel cross-eyed, I'll kill him.

"You don't think this is because of us, do you?" I ask Rachel in a hushed voice as we rush down the corridor. "Alisdair couldn't know that we've been, ah, enjoying each other's company."

She shakes her head. "I don't know. It seems unlikely, but considering the sinister events of late, I cannae say for certain."

As we rush out of the house and toward the garden doorway, Rachel's entire family follows behind us—with all their weapons, of course. We burst out of the castle into the crisp night air, holding each other's hands tightly. Amid the light fog, I see a single torch held up by…Alisdair's hand, naturally. Damn, I want to beat that jerk until he's nothing but a pile of bloody entrails.

We hurry across the green with Kieran in the lead. The damp grass soaks the hem of Rachel's skirts, but she doesn't seem to notice. There's something eerie about the whole scene, like it's straight out of a Dracula movie or something.

Then it hits me. This is eerily similar to that creepy dream I had, the one that involved *An Bodach*.

As we approach Alisdair, I can make out his smug expression in the flickering torchlight. The flames break through the mist just enough. My grip on Rachel's hand tightens, and I feel her squeeze back reassuringly. The rest of the MacTaggarts fan out behind us, weapons at the ready. Even Efrica, the oldest person in our group, wields a small sword.

I come up beside Kieran, dirk in hand. He nods his approval.

"Well, well," Alisdair drawls, his gaze raking over Rachel. "What a warm welcome for a late-night visitor."

"State your business, MacLeod," Kieran snarls, stepping forward with his claymore raised.

Alisdair chuckles, a sound that makes me want to crack his spine just for the hell of it. "I've come to claim what's rightfully mine. Rachel, *mo ciad-bhean*, it's time you fulfilled your duty to our clans."

Rachel stiffens beside me. "I am not your wife and never will be. Not your first, second, third or twenty-seventh wife."

"You were trothed to me at birth."

Kieran jabs his claymore toward Alisdair. "Neither I nor my wife ever pledged our daughter to you, ye *baltan*."

My free hand balls into a fist, while I keep my sword hand at the ready. If the bastard doesn't shut up and scurry back to his cave straightaway, I'll make sure he walks away with a limp and no dick. "What the hell is a *baltan*?"

"I'll never be yours, Alisdair," Rachel spits. Yeah, she literally spat at him. The spittle is visible on his cheek. "My heart belongs to another." Then she hisses to me, "It's an insult."

Alisdair's eyes narrow, his attention flicking back and forth between Rachel and me. A cruel smile twists his lips. "Ah, I see. The Sassenach thinks he can claim what's mine." The bastard takes one menacing step forward. "Yer meddling in affairs that have nothing to do with ye, laddie."

I bristle at his words, but Rachel's grip on my hand keeps me from lunging at him. I do growl, however. "I'm not claiming anyone, you jackass. Rachel makes her own choices."

"Aye," the woman in question adds, her voice hard as steel. "And I choose Joey Finnegan."

"He's a fucking Irishman?" Alisdair's face contorts with rage, and he spits his words at Rachel. "You dare reject me for this…this outlander?"

"Go home, Alisdair," Kieran snarls. "Ye'll never wed my daughter, so leave before I toss you into the moat with rocks tied to your ankles."

Alisdair studies our little army for a moment, then his shoulders flag. "I'll be back for Rachel, mark my words."

Our entire group follows the jackass as he makes his way through the castle and out the gates, onto the drawbridge. He keeps going, headed back to his own clan I assume.

Kieran invites me to go up the tower steps with him to check things out from a higher vantage point. I'm not ashamed to admit the long staircase leaves me a bit winded by the time we come out of the stairway and onto the walkway.

Kieran chuckles softly, seeing my condition. "Thievery hasn't made your body stronger, eh?"

"Guess not. I'm hardly a wimp, though. Just not as wicked strong as you are."

"That can be remedied—with enough training. I recommend sword-play."

As we prowl the walkway, searching for enemies beyond the gates, Kieran explains the architecture. "These are crenellations—solid blocks between slits in the wall, which allow archers to fire off arrows while hiding behind the blocks."

"That's cool. I never knew castles had features like that."

"Warfare in this time is different than the sort waged in the twenty-first century, or so my wife has told me."

"Yeah, it's very different. You don't even need men to fight for you. Machines do it for us."

Kieran shakes his head slowly. "I ne'er could've imagined such things before I met Alyssa."

As we continue our surveillance along the walkway, I start to hear odd little noises that almost sound like…footsteps crunching on the dirt path that ends at the drawbridge. I halt, smacking Kieran's arm. "Hey, do you hear that?"

He stops and swivels his head side to side. "Aye, I hear it too. Someone is coming this way." He whips his claymore out of its scabbard. "Go, warn the others."

I rush down the walkway to the top of the staircase, taking the steps two at a time. As I burst into the great hall, my heart pounding, I find Rachel and the others huddled around the fireplace. Their heads snap up at my abrupt entrance.

"Someone's coming," I gasp, gripping the doorframe. "Kieran's on the walkway. He sent me to warn you."

Rachel's eyes widen, and she's at my side in an instant. "How many? Did you see them?"

I shake my head. "Just heard footsteps. Sounded like one person, so it could be Alisdair again."

Alyssa's expression hardens as she hefts her dirk. "That dirtbag never knows when to quit."

"We need to prepare," Rachel says. "Morna, Efrica, start preparing for a confrontation. You ladies know how to handle an invasion. Use magic if necessary."

The two older women nod grimly and hurry off, their skirts swishing as they move with surprising speed for their age. Lachina has stayed behind.

Rachel turns to me. "Joey, we need to get back up there with my father. If it is Alisdair, he won't be alone this time. Warriors know how to be stealthy, and they could easily trick us into believing there's only one man."

"Good point." I grip my dirk tightly. "I'm right behind you."

"I'm coming too," says Dale Vescovi, Alyssa's dad. "Maybe I'm old, but I'm not incapable. Traveling back to medieval days has forced me to get buff. Who says senior citizens can't be badasses?"

Norma Vescovi, Alyssa's mom, expresses her desire to help too. "I was an Olympic archer back in the day. That means I can help too."

After I hand out the weapons, we're ready to go.

We all race back up the tower steps, our footfalls echoing in the narrow stairwell. As we emerge onto the walkway, I see Kieran crouched behind one of the crenellations, his massive frame barely concealed by the stone block.

"What do you see, Father?" Rachel whispers as we approach.

"A group of men, at least a dozen. They're trying to be stealthy, but I can hear them crunching twigs under their feet—softly, but aye. The sound is audible."

My heart races as I peer over the crenellation. Sure enough, dark shapes move through the woods, their outlines barely visible in the misty night.

"Alisdair, that riatach," Rachel hisses. "He's brought reinforcements."

I grip my dirk tighter as adrenaline burns through my veins. Don't need a translation to understand what Rachel said. Her nasty tone tells me that Scot must be a real bastard. "What's the plan?"

Kieran's face is grim as he surveys the approaching threat. "We need to bottleneck them at the gate. Rachel, go with your great-aunts and your mother, Norma too. Hide as best you can. Joey, you and I will take the lead at the gates. Fight only as a last resort—and no magics. These are mundane men, not monsters."

Alyssa gives her husband a quick kiss, then dashes down the stairs while issuing orders to the other women.

Rachel hesitates, and there's worry in her eyes. "Be careful, Joey, please."

I pull her close for a quick, fierce kiss. "You be careful too."

She squeezes my hand and rushes after the other women.

Kieran and I take up positions on either side of the gate, our weapons at the ready.

"Remember," Kieran says, "aim for the weak spots—neck, groin, behind the knees. And dinnae hesitate."

I nod grimly, tightening my grip on the dirk.

We wait, every muscle coiled and ready to spring into action. The crunching of twigs and leaves grows louder, and I can make out hushed whispers carried on the breeze. My pulse pounds in my ears, but I force myself to breathe slowly, steadying my nerves. Alyssa's dad has joined us in our fight, and whatever I'd assumed about him previously has just flown out the window. Dale Vescovi is way tougher than I expected.

Movement catches my eye and, like a ghostly specter, Alisdair emerges from the mist followed closely by several others. His smug face comes into view, illuminated by the torchlight that casts flickering shadows across his face. He's flanked by burly men.

"MacTaggart!" Alisdair bellows. "I've come to claim what's mine. Send the lass out, and we'll leave peacefully."

Kieran's voice booms across the courtyard. "Ye'll never have her, ye spineless *cacan*. Leave now or face the consequences."

Alisdair's laughter echoes through the night. "Consequences? You're outnumbered, old man. I'll give you one last chance to surrender the lass."

I glance at Kieran, whose jaw is set. He gives me a subtle nod, and I know it's time to act.

"Hey, dickwad!" I shout, stepping out from behind the gate. "Rachel's not a prize to be claimed. She's made her choice, and it's not your sorry ass."

Alisdair's gaze zeroes in on me like a sniper targeting his quarry. "So, the Sassenach speaks. Tell me, laddie, do you think you can protect her from me and my men?"

"Don't need to," I retort, feeling braver than I probably should. "Rachel can protect herself. And she's got a whole clan behind her."

A deafening war cry erupts from behind us. I whirl around to see Rachel leading a charge of MacTaggart clanswomen brandishing swords, dirks, axes, and even flaming torches. The sight is both terrifying and awe-inspiring. They've taken up positions at either side of the gates.

Seeing Rachel this way makes me so horny.

Alisdair's smug expression falters for a moment before he regains his composure, sneering at me. "Ye think your ragtag bunch can stand against my trained warriors?"

Rachel steps forward, her eyes blazing with fury. "We are MacTaggarts, ye numpty. We've defended this land for generations against far worse than the likes of you. And Kieran MacTaggart is the most powerful warrior in all of Scotland."

Kieran's brow lifts faintly, his lip twitching upward into an almost-smile. Yeah, Rachel is a badass in disguise

Big Daddy raises his claymore, the blade glinting in the torchlight. "This is your last warning, MacLeod."

For a moment, no one moves or speaks. We all simply glower at each other, wearing various types of angry expressions. Alisdair's smug grin falters as he takes in the determined faces of the MacTaggart clan.

But then Alisdair's jaw clenches, and he bellows, "Take them!"

The battle has begun.

Chapter Twenty-Two

Rachel

As the MacLeods race toward us, aiming to take the drawbridge and all of Dùndubhan, I suddenly realize there might be a less violent solution to Alisdair's challenge. If they cannae get close enough to seize us—or me, that is—then mayhap they will give up on this moronic attempt to abduct me.

I rush to the nearest spot where I can still see Joey up on the walkway. And I shout to gain his attention. "I've got an idea. Follow my lead."

He leans over to stare down at me. "Rachel, what—"

Without waiting for his response, I dash toward the gatehouse, my skirts flapping wildly in the wind.

"Rachel, what in the Sam Hill are you doing down there?"

The approaching thunder of hoofbeats threatens to drown out anything I might. But I have a wee window in which to shout, "We're going to give them a wee surprise! Well, a large one, actually."

Joey shakes his head, then returns to helping my father.

As I reach the winch that controls the drawbridge, I grab the handle and attempt to give it a mighty heave. But I cannae do it. My father always manned the drawbridge, and I never bothered to learn how to operate it.

Joey emerges from the inside the castle, coming up beside me. "Need a hand, Your Highness?"

"Aye, please. The drawbridge is bloody hard to maneuver."

Joey manhandles the mechanism, forcing the ancient gears to function. They groan in protest, but gradually, the bridge begins to move. It creaks and groans as it rises, the ancient wood protesting against the sudden movement. I watch with bated breath as the gap between us and the approaching MacLeods widens.

"Faster, Joey!" I urge. The thundering hoofbeats grow louder, and I can see the glint of steel in the sunlight as Alisdair's men draw their swords.

Joey grunts with his effort, his muscles straining as he works the winch. "I'm…trying…Rachel. This thing…weighs…a fucking ton!"

Just as the MacLeod clansmen reach the edge of the moat, the drawbridge slams shut with a resounding boom. I hear shouts of surprise and anger from the other side, followed by the splashing of several men falling into the water. Their mates fish them out but nearly drown one man in the process.

"Hah!" With a triumphant grin, I spin round to plant a quick kiss on Joey's cheek. The exertion of outsmarting the MacLeod clan has left me both exhilarated and exhausted. "That'll teach them to mess with the MacTaggarts of Dùndubhan!"

Joey doubles over, hands on his knees, sucking in deep breaths. "Holy shit, woman…You almost…gave me…a heart attack!"

I sober quickly and race to his side, my victory dimmed by the toll our narrow escape had taken on him. I rest a hand on his back. "Och, Joey, I'm so sorry. Are you injured? Ye dinnae look well."

Straightening up, he flashes me a crooked grin and waves a dismissive hand. "Nah, I'm fine, just out of shape. Guess hauling ancient drawbridges should've been part of my workout routine back in New York City."

A laugh splutters out of me. "Dinnae worry. We'll make a proper Scotsman of you yet."

Joey's retort is cut short by a booming voice from beyond the walls. "Rachel MacTaggart! You cannae hide forever! Open this bridge at once, or we'll find another way in!"

I roll my eyes, recognizing Alisdair's pompous tone. "That numpty never knows when to quit."

Joey raises an eyebrow. "Numpty?"

"Idiot," I clarify, then turn back to the wall. "Alisdair MacLeod, you bloody stupid pillock!" I take a deep breath, summoning all the bravado I can muster. "Ye can huff and puff all ye like, but this castle has stood for centuries against far worse threats than a sorry lad with delusions of grandeur!"

Joey snorts beside me, clearly enjoying the spectacle.

I flash him a quick grin before continuing my tirade. "If ye think ye can take Dùndubhan by force, then by all means, give it yer best shot. But I warn ye, the MacTaggart clan doesnae take kindly to uninvited guests!"

There's a moment of stunned silence from the other side of the wall. Then, Alisdair's voice rings out again, this time with a hint of uncertainty. "Rachel, be reasonable!"

I snort at Alisdair's plea. "Reasonable? You're the one who came charging at our gates with a band of armed men!"

Joey steps up beside me, his voice carrying over the wall. "Yeah, pal. Where I come from, we call that breaking and entering. Or possibly attempted kidnapping. Take your pick."

I give Joey an appreciative glance, warmth blooming in my chest at his unwavering support. Turning back to the wall, I call out, "Ye heard the man, Alisdair. Now take yer wee army and go home before ye embarrass yerself further."

A commotion erupts on the other side of the wall as muffled voices argue amongst themselves. I strain to hear, catching snippets of "…not worth it" and "…her father will have our hides."

Finally, Alisdair's voice rings out once more, this time tinged with frustration and a wee bit of defeat. "This isn't over, Rachel MacTaggart! You may have won this battle, but the war is far from finished!"

I roll my eyes at his dramatic declaration. "Away and boil yer head, Alisdair! There's no prize to be won here, only a fool's war!"

We listen as the sounds of hoofbeats gradually fade into the distance. When silence settles over Dùndubhan once more, I turn to Joey. "Well, that was a bit of excitement for the day, wasn't it?"

Joey pulls me into his arms and kisses me. "You Scots sure know how to keep things interesting."

"It's our way. Sometimes it's even more exciting 'round here."

Joey's eyebrows shoot up. "More exciting? What, do you have dragons hiding in the loch or something?"

"No dragons." I wrap my arms around his neck. "But we do have a resident kelpie or two. They're much more troublesome than dragons, if ye ask me."

Joey opens his mouth, likely to ask what in the world a kelpie is, when a shout from the courtyard interrupts us.

"Rachel! Joey! Are ye alright?"

I turn to see my father striding toward us, his claymore still firmly in his hand. Behind him, a small crowd has gathered, consisting of my great-aunts, my mother, and my grandparents.

"We're fine, *Athairich*," I say, waving reassuringly. "Alisdair will rue the day he tried to assault Dùndubhan."

As the Laird of Dùndubhan approaches, his grim expression slides into a smug smile. He visually scans every one of us for injuries. Finding none, his demeanor relaxes slightly. "Ye did well, lass. But what in the name of all that's holy possessed you and Joey to take on the MacLeods by yerselves?"

I shrug. "It was either that or let them waltz right in and snatch me away. I chose the more entertaining option."

Joey chuckles beside me. "Yeah, 'entertaining' is one word for it."

Now that the MacLeods are scurrying away to lick their wounds, we return to our normal daily chores and whatever else we might like to do. I still want to know more about Joey's past. He's been reluctant to tell me much, probably because he fears I might disapprove—or that my father might put him through another test of his mettle. But I approve of Joey wholeheartedly, and I dinnae believe my father will require more tests. He knows I have deep feelings for Joseph Finnegan.

After the evening meal, I excuse myself and Joey. He doesn't mind if I speak for him. I know that because he winked at me and smirked. My father and mother wish for me to remain inside the castle compound. I agree to the limitation, mostly because I have no wish to cause my family any further anxiety. We will be safe within these walls. The drawbridge remains closed, after all, and the sun won't set for a while yet.

Joey and I go into the garden for a private discussion.

I settle onto a bench, patting the empty space beside me. "Come, Joey, please do sit with me."

He cautiously rests his taut arse on the bench, mere inches from my thigh. "Should I be worried about why you brought me here? You've got that serious look in your eyes again."

I shake my head, brushing my fingers over his lips. "Nay, mo *leannan*. I simply…want to ken ye better. Ye've been through so much since ye arrived here, and I feel like there's still so much about ye I dinnae understand."

Joey's shoulders tense slightly, but he doesn't pull away. "Rachel, I…well, my past isn't exactly something I'm proud of. I'm not sure you'd want to hear all the seedy details."

I reach out to Joey, gently taking his hand in mine. "Joey, I care for ye. Whatever ye've done, whatever ye've been through, it's made ye the man ye are now. The man I…"

My thought trails off, and I'm feeling strangely shy.

"The man you what, Rachel?"

I take a deep breath, releasing it as I gather my courage. Speaking the truth has never been difficult for me. But this is the first time I've felt this way. I clear my throat and simply say it. "The man I've fallen in love with, Joey—you."

For a moment, he doesn't speak, his eyes wide with surprise. Then, little by little, a smile spreads across his face, lighting him up in a way I've never seen before. "Rachel, I love you too. God help me, I've tried not to, but I can't fight it anymore."

He leans in, cupping my face with his free hand, and presses his lips to mine. The kiss is tender at first, then grows more passionate as we both pour our pent-up emotions into it. When we finally break apart, we're breathing hard.

"*Bod an Donais*," I say, a bit dazed, "that was certainly worth waiting for."

Joey chuckles, resting his forehead against mine.

I smooth my skirts and clear my throat. "Now that we've got that settled, will ye tell me more about your past, Joey? I want to know everything."

He exhales a long sigh, leaning back slightly but keeping his hand entwined with mine. "It's not a pretty story, Rachel. I've done things I'm not proud of."

"Dinnae care," I reassure him. "I'm asking for honesty, not perfection."

"Yeah, I know." He scratches his head, twisting his lips into an odd expression. "Okay, you deserve the whole truth. Back in New York City, I... worked for some dangerous people. You know that already, since I told you about Damiano and Fulvio. But there's more. I started out just running errands and sneaking into pawn shops to steal a few things. But before I knew it, I was in deep."

I fold my hands around his, hoping the gesture will ease his anxiety.

"There was this one job," he continues. "It was supposed to be a simple break-in, just grab some documents and get out. But things went sideways fast."

I move closer. "What happened?"

Joey's eyes cloud with a sort of pain I've never seen in him before. "The owner was there. He wasn't supposed to be, but...We fought. I didn't mean to hurt him, Rachel, I swear it. But in the scuffle, he fell. Hit his head on the corner of his desk. There was so much blood..."

I feel a stab of shock at his confession. But rather than pulling away, I squeeze his hand tighter. "Oh, Joey..."

"The guy lived," he says quickly. "And he was only in the hospital for one night. I sneaked into his room and slipped some money into his wallet, as if that made up for my horrible mistake. But that's when I knew I had to get out. I couldn't do that kind of work anymore. But you don't just walk away from people like Damiano and Fulvio. They don't take kindly to deserters."

My heart aches for Joey, for the pain I see in eyes. But at last, I understand why he behaved the way he did when we first met. "So that's why ye came to Scotland? To escape from that den of savages."

Joey gives a hollow laugh. "Yeah, you could say that. Fulvio kept hounding me, so I figured putting an ocean between us might help. Jumped on the first plane out of the US, which got me to Scotland. Never imagined I'd end up traveling through time too."

I cup his cheek gently. "Ye didnae know about the portal when ye came here—and to me."

Chapter Twenty-Three

Joey

Rachel gazes at me with pure love in her eyes. How can she behave that way? As if I told her wasn't horrific? I injured an innocent man—by accident, but still. I don't deserve the love she's given me, yet I can't walk away from her. I need Rachel. That's not a good enough reason to stick around. We might have chased the MacLeods away, but the dark forces aligning against us won't be so easy to get rid of.

"Joey," she whispers, her lilting accent softening the edges of my name. "Ye canna blame yerself for what happened. 'Twas an accident, pure and simple."

I shake my head, unable to look her in the eye. The weight of guilt presses down on my chest, making it hard to breathe. "But Rachel, you don't understand. Where I come from, injuring someone like that…it's not just brushed off. I should've gone to jail for that."

She glides her fingers over my cheek. The touch affects me like a shock of static electricity, a stark contrast to the turmoil in my mind.

Rachel clasps my hands. "Aye, 'tis not something to brush off, but ye don't live in that world any longer, do ye? Yer here, in the Highlands, where a man's worth is measured by his intentions, not only his actions."

I finally glance up to gaze into those striking blue eyes. They're filled with fierce determination that both comforts and unsettles me.

"What about *An Bodach*," I ask, "and whatever other dark forces might be gathering against us? We can't keep ignoring them, Rachel. They're coming for us, and I don't know if I'm strong enough to face them."

Rachel's lips curve into a smile that's equal parts impishness and steely re-solve. "Bloody hell, ye must stop underestimating yerself, Joey Finnegan. And ye forget that ye've got me by yer side." She slides closer, her breath warm against my ear. "We've got magic in our blood, you and I. The old ways, the power of the Highlands—it's all around us."

A faint shiver passes over me at her fervent words, and I feel a crackle of energy in the air. It's like the very earth beneath our feet is alive with ancient power. But I struggle to sense it the way Rachel seems to. For a second, I do feel…something. A faint pulse, like a heartbeat thrumming through the stones and soil.

"Holy cow, I think I can sense it," I confirm, opening my eyes to find Rachel beaming at me.

"Aye, that's it. Ye've got the gift, Joey. It simply needs a wee bit of coaxing."

I shake my head, still skeptical. "But how can this magic help us fight against whatever's coming? I'm not exactly Merlin, Rachel."

"Ye dinnae need to be a sorcerer, ye daft man." She kisses my cheek. "Ye just need to be willing to accept that you have dormant powers within you and that I can teach you how to access them."

I rub my eyes, feeling a headache trying to blossom. "I don't know, Rach. Not sure I have it in me to wield supernatural powers. I'm a thief, not a hero. Besides, I'm more concerned with what *An Bodach* has up his sleeve. If other dark forces are working with him…we're royally screwed."

Rachel sets her hands on her hips, defiantly lifting her chin. "Ye listen to me, Joey Finnegan. Ye may have been a thief in your past life, but here, now, yer so much more. As for *An Bodach* and whomever else he brings with him, they'll ne'er know what hit them when we're through."

I can't help but smile at her fiery spirit, even as doubt gnaws at me. "And how exactly are we going to take on a centuries-old evil sorcerer? With your second sight and my ability to pick pockets?"

"Mayhap." She kisses me again, harder than before. "But ye've got more than that up your sleeve, Joey. Ye just havenae discovered it yet." She claims my hand. "Come with me. I want to show ye something."

Rachel tugs on my hand until I give in and let her lead me away.

She guides me through the winding stone corridors of Dùndubhan, her steps sure and purposeful. I shuffle after her, too consumed by my own thoughts to pay much attention to anything else. As we descend a narrow staircase, the air grows damper and warmer with every step.

"Where are we going?" I whisper, but Rachel just shakes her head, hold-ing a finger to her lips.

Up ahead, I see a wooden door.

Rachel halts there, her hand resting on the doorknob. "You've earned wee bit of relaxation, or as my mother would say, a mini spa vacation."

"What are you talking about? This isn't the garderobe, so I'm totally confused."

Her smile is enigmatic. "Close your eyes, m'eudail. I have a wonderful surprise for you."And to prevent confusion, m'eudail is the Gaelic version of 'my dear.'"

At last, she pulls the door open—and a wave of steamy air washes over me.

I gape at the room she's revealed. "Is this a steam room?"

"Aye, that's what my mother calls it. She swears that spending time in the steam room will cure all your ills and revitalize you in body and soul." She winks. "And it will, most likely, make us both very aroused."

"Steam room sex? Hell yeah, I'm on board for that."

The little sanctuary is composed of darker stones than the ones that make up the walls of the castle and the other buildings within the complex. Here, I find an oblong wooden tub and a chair as well as, of course, a hearth with a brass pot hanging above it that keeps the water steamy.

"This is incredible," I say, watching as Rachel latches the door behind us.

The stones beneath my feet radiate just enough heat that our feet won't get cold. I realize they must be connected somehow to the hearth. The air is thick with moisture and fragrant herbs—rosemary, lavender, and something else I can't quite place.

"My great-aunts created this chamber not long after I was born," Rachel explains, her fingers already working at the laces of her bodice. "The stones are from the sacred circle atop the mountain called Beinn Mhòr. They hold memories, Joey, and the wisdom of the MacTaggart witches who came before us."

I stand transfixed as she sheds her clothing with practiced ease, her hair cascading down her back. Steam curls around her naked body, lending her the appearance of a mythical creature—half woman, half mist. "How can the floor be so warm?"

She wags her eyebrows. "A bit of ceò-draoidh conjured by the daoine maithe, mayhap."

"You're claiming invisible faires were involved?" I lift my brows. "That other phrase you spoke is Greek to me."

"No, it's Gaelic. Ceò-draoidh means 'magic mist.'"

"You don't need magic, baby. I've been entranced by you since the moment we met, no spells required."

"Are you simply going to stand there staring like a wee bairn?" she teases, stepping forward to help me with the fastenings of my own clothing. "The magic works better when we're both bare beneath the mist."

I let her undress me, her fingers deftly working the unfamiliar clasps and ties of my medieval garb. I hiss in a breath as her knuckles brush against my skin. Then we both climb into the tub.

"I still don't understand how this is supposed to help us fight against *An Bodach*," I say, but I'm already distracted by the sight of her naked body and those gorgeous tits, glowing in the light from the hearth.

"The steam room isn't just for pleasure, Joey," she explains, though the gleam in her eye suggests that pleasure is definitely on the agenda. "The sacred stones amplify our connection to the old magic. In here, the veil between worlds grows thin. The heat and the herbs open our senses to what lies beyond ordinary sight."

As she speaks, she moves behind me, her hands sliding up my back to my shoulders. Her touch sends ripples of awareness through my body. I can feel the warmth of her breasts against my back, the softness of her belly against my spine.

"Relax," she demands, her breath tickling my ear. "Let the steam enter your lungs. Feel it coursing through your blood."

I let my lids drift shut and try to follow her instructions. The scented mist envelops us and infiltrates our senses. For a moment, I feel ridiculous—a modern man participating in some ancient ritual. But then something shifts.

It begins as a tingling at the base of my spine, spreading outward like ripples in a pond. The sensation climbs upward, vertebra by vertebra, until it reaches the nape of my neck and explodes into a thousand pinpricks of light behind my eyelids.

"What the hell?" I gasp, my eyes flying open.

Rachel's hands continue their steady rhythm on my shoulders. "That's it. Ye feel it now, aye? The old magic."

The steam around us seems to thicken, taking on shapes that dance at the edges of my vision. When I turn my head to follow them, they slip away like ghosts. But I can feel something stirring within me, a power I've never known before.

"I feel...different," I admit, my voice barely audible over the soft hiss of steam.

Rachel moves around to face me, water rippling around her waist as she straddles my lap in the wooden tub. Her blue eyes are luminous in the dim light, holding mine with a sensual intensity.

"The MacTaggart witches have used this chamber for centuries to awaken dormant powers," she explains, tracing the contours of my face with her fingertips. "Some call it da-shealladh—the second sight. But it's more than just seeing visions, Joey. It's about connecting with the very essence of the Highlands."

I want to dismiss it as superstition, but the energy humming through my veins tells a different story. The sensation is alien to me, unlike anything I've experienced before. It's as if my body is a tuning fork that's been struck against the bedrock of Scotland itself.

"And this will help us against *An Bodach*?" I ask. "It sounds too good to be true."

"But it is true, mo chridhe." Her wet hair clings to her shoulders, but beads of the warm dampness drizzle down my chest.

"The Old Man is powerful, aye, but his power comes from darkness—from taking, not giving. Our magic flows from the land itself, from centuries of MacTaggart witches who've loved and protected these hills."

She rolls her hips slightly, adjusting her position, but the movement wakes up my dick.

"Jesus," I whisper as my hands find her waist beneath the water.

"The old ones believed that pleasure and power were two sides of the same coin," she explains, leaning closer until her lips brush against mine. "That in moments of ecstasy, our spirits are most open to the magic that surrounds us."

Her kiss deepens, and I feel myself responding with an intensity that startles me. The steam swirls around us like a living thing, caressing our skin, heightening every sensation. When we break apart, I'm breathing hard, and not just from the heat of the room.

"So, this is part of my training?" I ask. "Getting naked in a medieval hot tub with the most beautiful woman in Scotland?"

Rachel laughs, the sound echoing off the stone walls. "Aye, though I'd call it a ritual rather than training. The joining of our bodies creates a channel for the power to flow between us."

Her fingers trace the contour of my collarbone, leaving behind remnants of heat that have nothing to do with the steam. My arousal grows by the second, and I feel a kind of lust that I've never known before, something deeper mere lust.

Rachel abruptly becomes serious. "*An Bodach* knows that together, we are a threat to him. That's why he's tried to separate us ever since the day you arrived."

Chapter Twenty-Four

Rachel

I awaken in the morning feeling so contented that I dinnae want to get out of bed. Joey lies beside me, his arm draped over my belly, his breaths whispering over my skin. For a moment, I simply lie here enjoying the serenity and the quiet joy of sharing a bed with the man I love. My father hasn't even threatened to murder Joey in at least…two days. I call that progress. But then I remember what we must endure today and that a disaster will most certainly occur.

The gathering of the clans begins today.

I sigh, reluctantly stirring from my cozy nest. Joey's arm tightens around me, and I feel his lips graze my shoulder.

"Mornin', gorgeous," he slurs in his New York accent. He's only half awake—until he yawns and stretches, aiming a sweet smile at me. "Why the heavy sigh, Rach? Regretting your life choices already?"

"Not completely." I turn to face him and find myself smiling too, even as anxiety gnaws at my insides. "My only regret is that I must get out of bed."

"Then stay right here with me under the covers." He pulls me closer. "To hell with the clans."

Briefly, I'm tempted to agree with him. But the weight of responsibility settles over me like a cloak, and I moan pitifully. "We can't, Joey. As much as I'd love to, I have duties to attend to."

Joey groans, burying his face in my hair. "Can't we just pretend the whole world doesn't exist for one more hour?"

I laugh softly, running my fingers through his tousled locks. "I wish we could, mo chridhe. But if we don't show up, my father will likely burst in here with his claymore drawn."

"Point taken," Joey reluctantly releases me. "I'd rather not start the day with a sword at my throat. Kieran loves to sneak up behind me and threaten to behead me."

"Aye, but he likes you."

Joey snorts, trying not to laugh. "He has a funny way of showing it."

"Do ye think Father would let me sleep with you if he didn't have a soft spot for ye?"

"Maybe he's just waiting for a good time to toss me down the garderobe channel."

As we rise and begin to dress, I'm amazed at how seamlessly Joey has adapted to life in medieval Scotland. His leather jacket hangs beside my tartan, a strange but oddly fitting juxtaposition.

"So, what should I expect from this clan gathering?" Joey asks, pulling on his boots. "Lots of kilts, bagpipes, and haggis, I'm guessing?"

I roll my eyes but cannae stop myself from smiling at his cheeky grin. "Aye, and don't forget the caber tossing and sheep shearing contests."

"Wait, really?" His eyes widen comically. "Dear God, I'd better polish up on my Catholic schoolboy manners or else I'll be burned at the stake."

"No, ye daft man," I laugh, swatting his arm playfully. "Though there will be some traditional games. But mostly, it's a time for the clans to come together, discuss alliances, settle disputes, and…well, drink a fair bit of whisky."

Joey's expression turns thoughtful. "Sounds like a powder keg waiting to explode. Rival clans, alcohol, and sharp objects. What could possibly go wrong?"

I can't help but grimace at Joey's astute observation. "Aye, that's why I'm a wee bit anxious. These gatherings can turn volatile faster than ye can say 'slàinte mhath.'"

Joey raises an eyebrow. "Slawn-ge what now?"

"It means 'good health' in Gaelic," I explain, fastening my cloak. "Ye'll be hearing it a lot today, so ye might want to practice."

"Slan-ge va," Joey attempts, his accent mangling the words. "Close enough?"

I try not to laugh, but I fail miserably. "We'll work on it, mo chridhe."

Joey has just finished dressing, but now he gazes at me with his brows wrinkled. "You've said those words before, but I have no idea what they mean."

Should I tell him the truth? I hadn't intentionally called him *mo chridhe*—my heart—but I realize that is what he's become to me.

Joey rushes toward me, grasping my arms. "What's wrong, Rachel? Your eyes have teared up."

"I know. It's just that I suddenly understood how much I feel those words."

"What do they mean?"

I gnaw on my lip for a moment, then I tell him. "The phrase *mo chridhe* means 'my heart.' And that is precisely what you've become for me. I love you, Joey."

He brushes hair away from my face and smiles in the sweetest manner. "I love you too, Rachel. And if I could pronounce that Gaelic phrase without mangling it, I'd say it right now."

I touch his cheek. "After the gathering, I'll teach it to you."

As we amble into the great hall hand in hand, the castle is already buzzing with activity. The aunts are scurrying about, trying to decide what to wear. My mother does the same and keeps asking me if her outfit is good enough for a clan gathering or if she should "fix up" her hair differently. Dale and Norma will be attending the event along with our little group of Mac-Taggarts—and Joey, naturally. My grandparents have lived in the medieval world for almost as long as Mother has.

We must bring gifts, of course, to show the other clans how civilized we've become despite the fact we live in a castle in the middle of nowhere. The clan gathering provides an opportunity to reconnect with friends and to meet new ones. By the time we leave Dùndubhan, I've become genuinely excited about this event. The journey to the gathering takes time since Dùndubhan is situated deep in the wilderness. The sun has just begun to rise, and we carry lanterns to guide our way.

As we hike through the misty forest, the lantern light casting eerie shadows among the ancient trees, I can feel Joey's tension radiating off him in waves. He's trying to hide it, but his grip on my hand is a bit too tight, his eyes darting from shadow to shadow.

"Relax, mo chridhe," I whisper, giving his hand a reassuring squeeze. "The forest won't bite."

"Easy for you to say," he mutters back. "You didn't grow up watching horror movies where the creepy forest is always full of ax murderers and werewolves."

I can't help but giggle. "Werewolves? Really, Joey?"

"Hey, after being thrown back in time and living in a castle with honest-to-God witches, I'm not ruling anything out."

As if on cue, a twig snaps in the darkness, and Joey nearly jumps out of his skin. I stifle a laugh as he whirls around, eyes wide and fists raised.

"Easy there, warrior," I tease gently. "It's probably just a deer."

Joey relaxes slightly, but I can see he's still on edge. "Right. A deer. Not a kilt-wearing psychopath with an ax."

"I thought ye were worried about werewolves?"

"And wolves of all kinds. My range of potential forest-dwelling murderers keeps expanding."

I'm about to reassure him again when I catch sight of my father's face. Kieran MacTaggart's golden eyes are narrowed, his jaw set in a grim line as he scans the tree line. A chill runs down my spine. If my father is worried, mayhap Joey's paranoia isn't entirely unfounded.

"Father?" I whisper, moving closer to him. "Is everything alright?"

His eyes flick to mine, then back to the shadows between the trees. "Aye, lass. Ahm simply keeping watch. These woods can be treacherous, especially with so many clans converging."

Joey sidles up beside me, his earlier bravado replaced by genuine concern. "Treacherous how, exactly?"

My father's lip curls in a humorless smile. "Rival clans, old grudges, new alliances...It's not unheard of for some to take advantage of the chaos to settle scores."

I feel Joey tense beside me. "And here I thought the werewolves were the biggest threat."

"Werewolves?" Father's brows lift. "No, I'd assume your worst enemy will be Alisdair MacLeod."

Joey has his dirk on his lip, sheathed in a scabbard, and he gives it a pat. "I'll be ready for that dirtbag this time."

As we continue our trek through the misty forest, Joey's hand remains firmly clasped in mine. His fingers twitch toward the dirk at his hip at every rustle of leaves. It's amazing how quickly he has adapted to our ways, even as worry gnaws at my insides.

"Alisdair MacLeod," I say with a grumbling sigh. The name tastes bitter on my tongue. "I'd hoped we'd seen the last of him."

"No such luck, I'm afraid," Father growls, while still scanning the tree line. "I'm certain that snake's been whispering in the ears of the other clan chieftains, stirring up old resentments."

Joey shakes his head. "What's that jerk's endgame? Besides being a general pain in the ass, I mean."

I can't help but snort at Joey's colorful description, even as Father shoots him a disapproving look.

"Alisdair's always had his eye on power," I explain, keeping my voice low. "He believes the MacLeods should rule over all the clans, and he'll do whatever it takes to make that happen."

Joey grunts. "Including trying to murder us."

Father nods grimly. "Aye, and worse. The man's as cunning as he is cruel. We'll need to watch our backs at this gathering."

As if summoned by our hushed conversation, a chill wind whips through the trees, causing the lantern flames to flicker ominously. I shiver, drawing my cloak tighter around me.

"Rachel, look." Joey points at my face. "Your eyes..."

I blink, realizing with a start that my vision has gone hazy around the edges, a telltale sign of my second sight kicking in. Lachina has been teaching me how to invoke my powers. The world around me blurs and shifts, ghostly images overlaying the misty forest.

"What do ye see, lass?" Father asks urgently, his hand on my shoulder.

I squeeze my eyes shut, trying to make sense of the visions that swirl behind my lids. "I see...flames. A great bonfire, but it's not celebratory. There's shouting, the clash of steel..." My breath catches in my throat. "Blood on the ground, mingling with spilled whisky."

Joey's grip on my hand tightens. "That doesn't sound good. Any chance your magical powers can tell us how to avoid that specific future?"

I shake my head. "It doesn't work like that. The visions are...fragments, possibilities. Nothing's set in stone."

As my sight clears, I notice the worried looks on Joey and Father's faces. Mother and the aunts rush forward to fuss over me, but I dinnae need to be fussed about. I'm not ill. But still, I give them a reassuring smile.

"We'll be all right," I say, trying to convince myself as much as them. "We just need to stay alert and stick together."

"Absolutely," Joey agrees. "No wandering off alone, no accepting food from strangers, and definitely no getting into drinking contests with rival clansmen."

Father grunts in approval. "Aye, that's sound advice. And keep yer wits about ye. There'll be more than swords and dirks to watch out for at this gathering."

As we continue our journey, the forest gradually thins, giving way to rolling hills dotted with heather. A wee bit further away, the dark waters of Loch Fairbairn spread far and wide. In the distance, I can see smoke rising from multiple campfires, and the faint sound of bagpipes drifts on the breeze. The clan gathering is nearly upon us.

Joey whistles softly. "Wow, this is quite the turnout. How many clans do you think are here? It reminds me of an outdoor rock festival I went to back in high school."

"At least a dozen clans have gathered here," I reply, scanning the colorful array of tartans in the distance. "Mayhap more. It's been years since we've had a gathering this large."

"Aye, and that's what worries me," the laird says. "The more clans, the more potential for conflict." Father gives Joey a baffled look. "*Pit air iteig*! What is an outdoor rock festival?"

"Explain pit air iteig to me, and I'll explain rock festivals to you."

"'Tis a fair exchange. The Gaelic phrase means 'flying vagina,' a common, if not polite, oath." Father tilts his head to the side. "A rock festival involves men hurling boulders, I presume."

Joey tries not to laugh but winds up snorting loudly. "Uh, not quite, Kieran. A rock festival is a gathering where people sit or stand outdoors and listen to music. Loud music. And the instruments are electric guitars, electric keyboards, and other stuff like that."

Father's expression has gone blank. "I...see."

But clearly, he doesn't. I do, but only because Joey described such things to me. None of that matters now, though. We have a horde of clans from all round the Highlands who might not take kindly to us if they realize we are witches.

Chapter Twenty-Five

Joey

Alyssa kisses her husband's cheek. "I'll explain rock concerts to you later, when we're alone in our chambers at home. Sex is the best teaching tool for you, honey. But we shouldn't talk about that during the clan gathering, hmm?"

Kieran smirks. "Aye, 'tis good advice. And I greatly enjoy your sort of instruction."

As we crest the final hill, the full scope of the gathering comes into view. A sea of tents and pavilions stretches across the valley, each flying the colors and crests of their respective clans. I survey the area as we draw closer, noting the diverse array of tents on display—marquees of varying sizes, simple wall tents, wedge-shaped ones, and so much more.

In the center of the gathering, a massive bonfire roars. Long tables laden with food and drink encircle the area. The air is filled with the scent of roasting meat, wood smoke, and hundreds of bodies packed together. The cacophony of bagpipes, drums, and raucous laughter grows louder by the minute.

"Holy crap," I say under my breath, suddenly feeling small and out of place, like I had all those years ago during my foster-child days. "What I'm seeing seems like Braveheart meets Coachella."

Rachel shoots me a quizzical look. "Coachella? Is that some sort of American clan gathering?"

"Kinda like that," I reply, not wanting to get into the complexities of explaining modern music festivals to a medieval witch. Kieran was baffled, so Rachel probably will be too. So, I tell Rachel, "Let's just say it's a lot to take in."

As we make our way down the hill, I swear I can feel eyes turning in our direction. The chatter dims slightly, replaced by hushed whispers and pointed fingers. I try to stand a little taller, channeling some of Kieran's intimidating presence. But I can't shake the feeling that I'm a walking anachronism, a neon sign flashing "NOT FROM THIS TIMELINE" in bold letters.

Rachel squeezes my hand reassuringly. "Don't worry. Stay close to me and follow my lead. Remember, you are a MacTaggart now, in spirit if not in name. Hold your head high."

"Thanks, baby. That's good advice."

As we approach the outskirts of the gathering, a group of burly men in kilts steps forward to greet us. Their leader, a giant of a man with a fiery red beard, breaks into a wide grin.

"Kieran MacTaggart!" he booms, his voice carrying across the field. "Ye've finally decided to grace us with yer presence, ye great *buamastair*!"

"Ye dare call me a dolt?" Kieran's stern facade cracks, and he embraces the man with a hearty laugh. "Angus Campbell, ye overgrown ginger root! I see ye've managed to drag yerself away from the ale tent long enough to greet us properly."

I whisper into Rachel's ear, "What's a boo-muh-stead?"

"A dolt," she explains, speaking in a hushed tone. "In this case, 'tis a friendly insult."

Guy talk, medieval style? Hmm, I might fit in around here after all.

The two Scots clap each other on the back with enough force to make me wince. As they pull apart, Angus's attention falls on me, and his bushy eyebrows shoot up in surprise.

"And who might this wee laddie be?" he asks, his gaze flickering between Kieran and me.

I open my mouth to introduce myself, but Rachel beats me to it. "This is Joey, a friend of the MacTaggart clan. He's come a long way to join us for the gathering."

Angus nails his gaze to me, squinting slightly. "A long way, ye say? From where precisely?"

A bead of sweat trickles down my spine as Angus scrutinizes me. Rachel clamps her hand around mine, almost painfully so.

"From across the sea," I blurt out, remembering our hastily concocted cover story. "I'm a trader. From Europe."

Angus's bushy eyebrows knit together. "Europe, ye say? Ye don't sound like any trader I've ever met."

"Well, I've been traveling for quite some time. Picked up all sorts of accents along the way."

Kieran steps forward, his imposing presence drawing Angus's attention away from me. "Aye, and Joey's acquired some valuable skills as well. He has a keen eye for strategy and a quick mind. He'll be a fine addition to our clan during the games."

Angus strokes his beard, watching me intently. "Well then, we'll be sure to put those skills to the test. Welcome to the gathering, Joey from across the sea. I hope ye're ready for some Highland hospitality."

"Looking forward to it."

Kieran inserts himself between me and the big guy. "It's been good to see you, Angus. But we wish to meet with Clan Grant right now. I'm sure you understand."

Without another word, we march deeper into the gathering, and the crowd parts before us like the Red Sea. I can feel the weight of hundreds of curious stares boring into me. Snippets of whispered conversations reach my ears.

"Who's the stranger?"

"Never seen him before..."

"Doesn't look like he belongs..."

"What an unusual accent he has..."

I do my best to ignore them, focusing instead on the sights and sounds around me. This gathering is so large that I bet I could hike for miles without seeing the same people twice. Kieran informs me that Clan Grant is quite a bit smaller than many of the other families, and that's why the MacTaggarts have become trading partners and even allies with the Grants.

But before we meet up with that clan, first we will spend time with another branch of the MacTaggarts—the ones who had banished Kieran a long time ago. I guess the Big Daddy wants to mend fences.

When I tell Kieran that, he chuckles. "Ahmno needing to mend anything. My banishment was lifted long ago. When Rachel was born, the chieftain of all the MacTaggarts visited us at Dùndubhan to inform us that we may attend clan gatherings if we wish. We haven't done so, however—not until now."

"Why did you wait so long?"

"Because my aunts were not invited. Their witchcraft unsettles some." He scratches the back of his neck. "But that edict is unfair. I do witchcraft as well. If my whole family cannae attend, then none of us will."

"But you are attending this clan gathering."

"Aye, 'twas time to do so and show our clan, and others, that we mean them no harm."

As we approach the MacTaggart section of the gathering, the tension in the air becomes almost palpable, like an electric charge crackling around us. Kieran's jaw is firmly clenched, a clear sign of his resolve, while he sweeps his gaze over the crowd with a blend of cautious vigilance and steely determination. The atmosphere feels laden with unease. Rachel threads her fingers between mine in a silent promise of support.

"Remember," she whispers, "you're with us. You belong here."

"Yeah, I know." Despite my best efforts to believe my own words, I can't quite do it.

The MacTaggart encampment is a sea of blue and green tartan with slender threads of orange too, and a proud stag emblazoned on their banners. As we draw closer, conversations die down, and all eyes turn to us. I can see the recognition dawning on their faces as Kieran scans the crowd.

An older man with a salt-and-pepper beard steps forward, his gaze narrowing as he regards our small group. "Kieran Aulay MacTaggart, we didnae expect to see ye here."

Kieran draws himself up to his full height, towering over the older man. "Uncle Hamish, it's been many years."

Hamish's attention flickers between Kieran, Rachel, and me. "Aye, it has indeed been a long time. And who might this lad and lass be?"

"This is my daughter, Rachel," Kieran says, placing a hand on her shoulder. "And this is Joey, a friend of our family from across the sea."

I try to smile, but it feels more like a grimace. Hamish's piercing gaze makes me want to shrink into my boots. His focus lingers on me for a moment longer before he swerves his attention back to Kieran. "A friend from across the sea, ye say? Would that be France? Or mayhap fairy land?"

The skepticism in his voice is clear, and I can feel the tension ratcheting up another notch. Kieran's jaw clenches, but before he can respond, Rachel steps forward.

"Uncle Hamish," she says, her voice warm but firm. "We've come in peace and friendship. Is that not what these gatherings are for? To strengthen bonds between clans and families?"

Hamish's expression relaxes as he looks at Rachel. "Ye have yer father's stubbornness, I'd wager. It's a family trait." He gestures toward the center of the MacTaggart camp. "Come then. Ye might as well join us for a drink."

I follow Kieran, Rachel, and Hamish into the heart of the MacTaggart camp, trying not to gawk at the sea of men and woman who surround us. The scent of peat smoke and roasting meat wafts around us, making my stomach growl audibly. Rachel gives me an amused glance.

As we approach a large central tent, a hush falls over the gathered MacTaggarts. Whispers ripple through the crowd, aimed at Kieran, but also me. I've never liked being the center of attention—that's how a thief operates—but the scrutiny I'm getting from these folks is unnerving.

I do my best to keep my expression neutral, channeling Kieran's stoic demeanor. Inside the tent, a group of older men and women are seated around a long table. They all fall silent as we enter, their eyes widening at the sight of Kieran. The tension in the tent is palpable as we walk inside. I can feel the weight of their stares and a mix of curiosity and suspicion about the mysterious MacTaggarts of Dùndubhan. Kieran stands tall, scanning the faces of his clansmen.

An elderly woman with silver hair and pale blue eyes rises from her seat at the head of the table. Her gaze locks onto Kieran. For a moment, I swear I can see a flicker of something—recognition or possibly affection—cross her weathered features.

"Kieran," she says, her voice strong despite her age. "Ye've finally come home."

He briefly bows his head in deference. "Morag, it's been too long. I was sorry to hear of Roddy's passing."

"My husband lived a long and fruitful life." Her eyes drift to Rachel and me. "And who might these young ones be?"

Rachel steps forward, her chin held high. "I'm Rachel MacTaggart, Kieran's daughter, and this is Joey Finnegan."

I wave awkwardly, feeling completely out of place among these imposing Highlanders. Morag sweeps her gaze over me, and I have the distinct impression she can see right through our flimsy cover story.

"A friend, ye say?" Morag arches an eyebrow. "From whence do ye hail, laddie?"

"From across the sea. I'm a trader who's traveled far and wide."

Morag squints at me. "Is that so? And what brings ye to our gathering? 'Tis for clan members only."

Before I can fumble through a response, Kieran intervenes. "Joey has skills that will be valuable in the games. He's quick-witted and observant, with a knack for strategy, and he's quite strong."

Morag studies me for a moment longer before she nods sharply. "Very well. We shall see how he fares in the trials ahead." She turns her attention back to Kieran. "Ye've been away for many years. There's much to discuss."

"Aye, there is."

Whispers ripple through the gathered MacTaggarts. I catch snippets of hushed conversations, but I can't decipher any of the words because they're all speaking Gaelic.

Morag raises a hand, silencing the crowd. "Ye speak of friendship, Kieran, but ye've brought a stranger into our midst. How can we trust your intentions?"

Kieran's jaw tightens, but he keeps his voice level. "I understand your caution, Morag. But I assure you, Joey poses no threat. He's here to learn our ways and participate in the games, nothing more."

Another MacTaggart pushes through the crowd to glare at Kieran. "Your new mate is no Scot. He must be a Sassenach, but his accent doesnae sound English."

Kieran's nostrils flare, and his eyes narrow to slits. "I vouch for Joey, and that should be enough for my own clansmen."

If this gathering were in modern times, it might turn into a cage match that leaves both men bloodied and bruised. No cages here in Scotland, though. They have fists, swords, and maces instead.

Someone might die today. And it will probably be me.

Chapter Twenty—Six

Rachel

Tam MacTaggart is still glowering at my father, and everyone still seems afeard and confused by the altercation between my father and Tam. Despite all the bravado on display today, I doubt any blood will be shed. And finally, the two men give up their staring match. No more flaring nostrils. No more squinted eyes. Neither man has audibly conceded, yet everyone can these two warriors have settled their differences.

My father raises his brows.

Tam seizes his arm at the elbow, and Father does the same. It's the MacTaggart handshake. Aye, the tension has evaporated. All those in attendance blow out a collective breath and relax.

"Let the games begin!" Tam shouts while grinning and now shakes hands with my father, who smiles in return.

The MacTaggarts and the Grants have been allies for as long as anyone can remember. Aye, my fellow MacTaggarts have given my father a hard time, but they dinnae hold any animosity toward our family. His banishment ended a long time ago. But according to my mother, strapping men occasionally need to insult and threaten each other to feel like masculine.

Aye, Alyssa Vescovi knows more about men than I do.

But as I watch the two clans face off, their hands hovering near their weapons, unease ripples through me. I and my aunts, my father as well, possess varying degrees and types of magic. I pray no one realizes that. Practicing witchcraft is still a capital offense in Scotland.

I edge closer to my mother, seeking her reassuring presence. And I whisper, "Are ye certain about this?"

She winks. "Don't worry, sweetie. This is just men being men. They'll be sharing a dram and laughing about old times before you know it."

I want to believe her, but something doesn't feel right. My fingers tingle with an unfamiliar energy, and I wonder if my own latent magical abilities are trying to tell me something. My fingers trace the outline of the small stone in my pocket—a gift from my great-aunts, imbued with protective spells. Its warmth reassures me, even as doubt gnaws at my insides.

"Rachel," my father's deep voice cuts through the din. "Come here, lass."

I make my way through the throng of kilted men who are participating in various feats of strength and cunning but pass by them without a glance. Then a wave of dizziness swamps me. I stop in my tracks, holding a hand to my forehead. What is happening? I struggle to focus my gaze, but the world has begun to spin around me.

Then the dizziness vanishes.

As I shake off the bizarre sensation, I begin to walk again, and as I approach, I catch a glimpse of a stranger standing beside my father. His clothes mark him as an outsider, but there's something in his eyes that speaks of familiarity. A shiver races down my spine as our gazes connect, and for a split second, the world seems to fade away.

"Rachel," my father says, his voice gruff but tinged with an undercurrent of worry, "I want ye to meet Joey Finnegan. He's...well, he's not from around here."

Joey extends his hand, a gesture that seems both foreign and strangely fitting. "It's a pleasure to meet you, Rachel."

But...I've met him before. I know the situation is not as it should be, yet my mind is clouded by images I cannae understand.

As I reach out to shake Joey's hand, a jolt of energy surges through me. The world tilts, and suddenly, I'm seeing double—Joey as he stands before me now, and another version of him, dressed in strange garb, standing in a place that looks like Dùndubhan, but is...different. Newer.

While my father and Joey go on conversing as if they have never met before, the scene around me shifts once more. I glance down at myself. I am wearing strange clothes that expose much of my arms and legs, and my hair is shorter. My shoes have strangely tall heels that make it difficult to maintain my balance. As for the castle before me...

It is Dùndubhan, but it also is not. People dressed as peculiarly as I am wander about the premises and even traipse inside the castle. And with a jolt, I ken what I'm seeing.

This is the future. The twenty-first century.

I wander toward the entrance of the modern version of Dùndubhan, growing more comfortable with my high-heeled shoes with every step. I seem to have arrived at the start of some sort of guided tour of the castle. I might as well go along with the crowd. It must be my dà-shealladh that's causing this to happen, though I cannae understand the purpose of it. All I can do is go with the flow, as my mother would say.

While I follow our tour guide, a chipper lass with pale blonde hair begins her spiel about the history of Dùndubhan. I find myself only half-listening, my gaze darting around the great hall as I struggle to understand the strange mix of ancient stone walls and modern amenities.

"And here, ladies and gentlemen, is where the infamous 'Witches' Confrontation' took place in 1621," our guide explains, gesturing to a spot near the massive hearth.

My heart skips a beat. That's where I'm standing right now—or where I was standing, back in my own time. I blink, trying to reconcile the two realities warring in my mind.

"Legend has it," the cheerful lass continues, "that a mysterious stranger appeared during a clan gathering, causing a rift between the MacTaggarts and the Grants. Some say he was a time traveler, others claim he was a witch himself. But what happened next changed the course of Highland history forever."

My breath catches in my throat. She's talking about Joey. About what's happening right now, back in my time. I strain to hear more, desperate for any clue about what's to come.

As if summoned by my thoughts, I spot a familiar figure lurking at the back of the tour group. It's Joey, but not the Joey I just met. This one looks older, more weathered, with a haunted look in his eyes that speaks of secrets and burdens.

Our gazes lock, and I see recognition flare in his eyes. He starts to push through the crowd toward me, but before he can reach me, the world shifts again.

Before the tour guide can resume her spiel, a commotion erupts near the entrance. A group of men in dark suits push their way into the hall, their eyes scanning the crowd with predatory intensity. My heart races as I spot a familiar face among them—Joey Finnegan, looking exactly as he did moments ago in 1621, but now dressed in modern attire.

He catches sight of me, his eyes widening in recognition. Without a word, he grabs my arm and pulls me toward a hidden alcove behind a tapestry. My heart pounds as he presses me against the cold stone wall, his body shielding mine from view.

"Rachel," he whispers urgently, his breath warm against my ear. "I need you to listen carefully. We don't have much time."

I want to ask a thousand questions, but the intensity in his eyes silences me.

"The men who just came in are dangerous," Joey continues. "They're after something hidden in Dùndubhan—something that could change everything if it falls into the wrong hands. We have to get back to 1621 and stop them before they find it."

"What are you talk..." I start to ask, but Joey cuts me off with a shake of his head.

"I know this is confusing, but I promise I'll explain everything later. Right now, I need you to trust me. Can you do that?"

"I reckon so," I reply slowly.

"Thanks, baby." Joey exhales a gusty breath, evident in every line of his body. "It's complicated. The short version is that we're caught in a temporal loop. The decisions we make here, now, will affect what happens in the past—your present."

My head feels as if it's literally spinning now. "I don't understand."

"Those men out there? They're after something hidden inside Dùndubhan. Something powerful. If they get their hands on it, it could change everything—not just the future, but the past as well. We have to stop them."

I take a deep breath, trying to process everything Joey's telling me. "So, what can we do?"

Joey's eyes dart around, checking our surroundings. "We need to get back to the past. But first..." He reaches into his pocket and pulls out a small, glowing stone. "Take this. It'll help amplify your dà-shealladh. You might need it."

As I take the stone, our fingers brush, and another jolt of energy courses through me. Suddenly, I'm seeing double again—the modern castle overlaid with its medieval counterpart. I can see the clan gathering, frozen in time, tension thick in the air.

"Joey," I whisper, "I can see them. My family, the clans—they're all there, waiting."

"I know. But you need to remember this—the book was hidden for a reason and may not even exist anymore."

Suddenly, the tapestry is ripped aside. One of the men in dark suits looms over us, a cruel smile twisting his lips. "Well, well. What do we have here, Joey boy? Ya shouldn't be screwing a girl right now, not when you've got explaining to do."

"Who is he?" I ask Joey, my voice barely a whisper.

"Fulvio Barbieri, the mob enforcer," he replies in an equally soft voice. But then Joey abruptly shoves me behind him as he faces the intruders. "Run, Rachel!"

I hesitate for a split second, torn between fear and the desire to help. But Joey's urgent command spurs me into action. I bolt from the alcove, ducking under the arm of another suit-clad man who tries to grab me. Adrenaline burns through my veins as I weave through the startled tour group, my unfamiliar high heels clicking against the stone floor.

"Stop her!" I hear Fulvio bellow behind me, followed by the sound of a scuffle.

I pray Joey can hold his own against them.

But as I race down a corridor, I search frantically for a way out or back to my own time. The stone in my hand pulses with energy, and suddenly the world around me flickers. For a moment, I see the medieval castle superimposed over the modern one. I clutch the stone tighter and concentrate on the image of the clan gathering, willing myself back to that moment.

But I'm abruptly hit with a dizzying wave of disorientation. The world around me flickers and shifts, medieval stone walls blending with modern fixtures. I stumble and nearly lose my footing on the uneven ground.

"Rachel!" I hear Joey's voice, distant yet urgent. "The stone! Use the stone!"

My fingers fumble in my pocket, closing around the small, warm object. As soon as I touch it, my vision clears. I'm back in 1621, standing amid the tense clan gathering. But now I can see more—shimmering threads of energy connecting people and objects, whispers of future events echoing in my mind. The stone has amplified my *dà-shealladh* beyond anything I've experienced before.

But the stone is no longer in my hand. It's vanished.

You need to remember this— the book was hidden where none would think to find it.

I frantically scan the area, searching for Joey. He's still by my father's side, but his eyes are darting around, alert and wary. Does he remember what just happened in the future? Before I can make my way to him, a commotion erupts near the castle entrance.

Three men push their way through the crowd, their strange attire marking them as outlanders of the most outland sort. With a jolt, I recognize them as the suited men from the future. Somehow, they've followed us back.

"Fulvio," I whisper, remembering the name Joey used. The burly man at the front must be him, his eyes cold and calculating as they sweep the area.

The clan members bristle at the intrusion, their hands moving to grasp their weapons, though they don't wield them yet. I can see the confusion and anger in their eyes, but also a flicker of fear at these strange outsiders.

"Who are ye, and what business do ye have here?" my father's voice booms across the hall, silencing the murmurs.

Fulvio steps forward, a predatory smile on his face. "We're here for something that doesn't belong to you, old man. Step aside, and no one gets hurt."

Joey tenses beside my father, his hand inching toward an unusual weapon I hadn't noticed before. It's black and L-shaped, bulky too. Our eyes meet briefly, and I see a flash of recognition. He remembers what I saw in the future.

"Rachel," my mother's urgent whisper catches my attention. "Rachel, stay close to me and the aunts."

I hesitate, torn between the desire to stay and help, and the knowledge that I need to find the book future Joey had mentioned. It might be the MacTaggart witches' book.

"Mum," I hiss, leaning close, "I need to go back to Dùndubhan immediately. It's urgent. No time to explain."

"You can't go anywhere by yourself, Rachel. Not with these thugs here who just showed up."

"I said step aside," Fulvio snarls, almost seeming to gnash his teeth like an angry animal.

My father stands his ground, drawing himself up to his full, imposing height. "I suggest ye leave now, before things get ugly."

Hamish and several other clan members gather round our wee family, encircling us in a protective manner. They bar their arms over their chests, just as Father and Joey also do.

If I were to search the entire castle from top to bottom, including the moat and the garderobe channel, then mayhap…No, it's impossible.

The book does not exist in this century.

Chapter Twenty-Seven

Joey

How the hell did Fulvio and his fellow goons find me here? In the frigging past? Oddly, I experience a brief sense of déjà vu as if I've seen things I couldn't have seen. Sure, that makes complete sense. You're losing your ever-loving mind, Finnegan.

Time travel will do that to a guy.

I have my arms strapped over my chest, just like all the Scots who've gathered around us. Kieran has a sword, and I have a dirk. I assume the other Scots have weapons as well. But Fulvio and his goons have firearms. They could mow us all down in one fell swoop without even breaking a sweat.

Guns trump swords. I'm sure of that.

I glance at Kieran, hoping his decades of battle experience might offer some insight into our current predicament. His eyes are narrowed as he assesses the situation with a warrior's calm that I can only envy.

"Ye best be dropping those strange weapons," Kieran growls, his deep voice carrying across the tense silence. "Ye've no business here in our lands."

Fulvio's lip curls into a sneer. "Oh, we have business all right. With him."

He jerks his chin in my direction.

Great. Just great. I've managed to drag my twenty-first-century mob problems into sixteenth-century Scotland. This is not how I pictured my day going when I woke up this morning. I figured I'd get razzed by a bunch of muscular Scots and maybe get dunked in the loch. But this...

"Listen, Fulvio," I begin, "I don't know how you got here, but this isn't the place for...whatever this is. These people have nothing to do with our beef."

Fulvio's eyes narrow, his grip tightening on his pistol. "You think I care about these savages? You owe us, Finnegan, and we're here to collect. No matter where—or when—you try to hide."

I feel Kieran tense beside me. He clearly does not appreciate being called a savage. I throw him a warning glance, silently pleading for him to stay calm. The last thing we need is for him to charge at the bad buys with nothing but a sword. The mob guys have guns.

"Okay, okay," I say, raising my hands slowly. "Let's talk about this. Just you and me. But first, I want to know how you got here."

Fulvio chuckles darkly. "*An Bodach* gave us a lift. He's got a major hard-on for destroying your girlfriend's daddy. And I've got one for slitting your throat, Joey boy."

Here I thought my number one enemy was Alisdair MacLeod.

"Yer in the midst of a clan gathering, ye olach," Kieran tells Fulvio. Yeah, that's the Gaelic word for a eunuch. "Go back to whence you came before the might of twelve clans rips you to shreds."

"Twelve clans, huh?" he scoffs. "And how many of them have guns, old man?"

I swear I can feel the tension in the air ratcheting up another notch. The Scots may not know exactly what guns are, but they can sense the danger. I hear the soft rasp of steel as more swords are drawn from their scabbards.

"Give it up," I say, trying to keep my voice calm. "You've made your point, Fulvio. You found me. But this isn't New York. You can't just start a firefight here without consequences."

"Oh yeah?" Fulvio challenges. "What consequences? These barbarians wouldn't know a Glock from an AK-47."

He and his buddies chuckle derisively. What jackasses.

More men from the twelve clans have joined our group, forming a wall of plaid and steel.

I feel a shift in the air, a sudden chill that has nothing to do with the Highland breeze. The hairs at my nape lift, and I catch a glimpse of movement from the corner of my eye. Rachel. She steps forward, her eyes blazing with an otherworldly light. The air seems to shimmer, and I swear I can hear the faint whisper of ancient words carried on the wind.

"Ye bring strange magic to our lands," she says, her voice resonating with power. "But ye forget, this is our home. Our magic runs deep in the very soil beneath yer feet."

Fulvio's smug expression falters for a moment as he takes in Rachel's appearance. I can see the doubt creeping into his eyes, the first flicker of uncertainty.

"What the hell is this?" he mutters, his gun wavering slightly.

The earth beneath me trembles beneath my feet. The ground seems to ripple, like waves on a loch, and a low rumble echoes through the glen. Fulvio and his goons stumble, struggling to keep their balance.

"What the fuck?" one of them shouts, his eyes wide with panic.

I watch in awe as tendrils of mist rise from the earth, coiling around the mobsters' legs. The fog thickens rapidly, obscuring their lower bodies and creeping upward. Fulvio fires his gun wildly, the shots echoing across the hills, but the bullets seem to dissolve into the mist harmlessly.

"Rachel," I whisper, "what are you doing?"

She doesn't answer, her eyes glowing an eerie blue as she continues to chant under her breath. The mist swirls higher, now reaching the mobsters' chests. They're shouting in panic, flailing their arms and trying to wade through the thick fog, but it's like quicksand, holding them in place.

"Finnegan!" Fulvio screams, his face contorted with rage and fear. "Make it stop!"

I wish I could, but I'm just as bewildered as he is. I observe while Rachel weaves her spell, her expression a mask of concentration. The air crackles with energy, and I swear I can see faint, glowing symbols swirling around her.

Kieran strides forward, his sword gleaming in the strange, misty light. "Ye've brought yer fight to the wrong place, laddies. Highlanders dinnae take kindly to intruders."

The mist continues to rise, now engulfing the mobsters completely. Their muffled shouts fade as they disappear into the swirling fog. I watch, transfixed, as the mist begins to coalesce, forming distinct shapes. To my astonishment, the fog transforms into towering, humanoid figures—misty giants looming over us all.

"Holy shit," I blurt out, unable to tear my focus away from the spectacle.

Rachel's voice rings out, clear and commanding. "Guardians of the glen, protectors of our people, I call upon ye to banish these intruders from our lands!"

"Wait!" I shout, as a sudden thought strikes me. "Rachel, we need to know how they got here! We can't just send them back without—"

Before I can finish that thought, the mist creatures evaporate.

The enforcer and his pals wear stark expressions. None of them has ever seen magic before, I'm sure. They still hold their guns, but they seem incapable of moving or speaking. Their shock wears off too quickly, though.

Fulvio nods to one of his goons.

While the rest of us are still reeling, he snatches Lachina away from her family and holds his gun to her temple. "Touch any of us and this old hag will get a bullet in her brain."

Old hag? Lachina is fifty-three. That might be old in the medieval world, but Fulvio's from the twenty-first century. Besides, Lachina is pretty and looks half her age.

I raise my dirk at Fulvio. "We've got more swords and knives than you've got guns. Twelve clans, remember?"

"Yeah, but you've got the joker card, and I've got the ace."

A swirling mass of darkness grows beside Fulvio, who doesn't seem perturbed at all, like he expected this to happen. He keeps his arm tight around Lachina's throat.

The dark mass resolves into…a grizzled, gray-haired man with huge biceps who must stand at least seven feet tall.

Fulvio smirks. "*An Bodach* is here, and he's very interested in the MacTaggart magics."

An Bodach glowers at Fulvio. "Silence, ye fool. A laddie with a wee bigealais is of no interest to me."

The creepy old coot glances down at Fulvio's groin. I'm guessing "*bigealais*" is another word for "dick."

Kieran snarls through gnashed teeth, "Release my aunt now, before the wrath of the clans is unleashed upon you."

An Bodach's gaze sweeps across our group, his eyes glowing with an eerie light. "The wrath of the clans? Ye have no idea what true wrath is, ye cacan. Did ye enjoy meeting my *beithir*? I conjured him just for you two."

I snort. "Gee, thanks, jackass. Your silly purple teddy bear was about as terrifying as a squirrel."

Can't let this evil bastard know that his *beithir* sent us running through the woods to escape from the magically created monster.

With a flick of his wrist, *An Bodach* sends a shockwave of energy rippling through the air. I feel it hit me like a punch to the gut, knocking the wind out of me. All around us, Highlanders now stumble and fall as their weapons clatter to the ground.

Rachel stands firm, her eyes blazing with defiance. "Ye may have power, old man, but this is our land. Our magic runs deep here."

An Bodach's lip curls into a cruel smile. "Aye, lass. And that's precisely why I'm here."

He turns his attention to Lachina, still held captive by Fulvio. "You, hag. You have the gift of the Two Sighs, do you not?"

Lachina's eyes widen, but she says nothing. Her gaze flicks to Rachel, a silent warning passing between them.

An Bodach chuckles darkly. "No need to play coy. I can sense the power within you. The MacTaggart line has always been strong in the ways of magic."

I glance at Rachel, hoping for some clue as to what's going on. Her face is a mask of determination, but I can see the fear in her eyes. Whatever this *An Bodach* character is after, it can't be good.

"What do you want with my aunt?" Kieran growls, his hand tightening on his sword hilt.

The old bastard ignores him, his attention fixed solely on Lachina. "You will show me the way to the ancient standing stones. The place where the veil between worlds is thinnest."

Lachina's eyes flash with defiance. "I'll do no such thing, ye demon."

An Bodach's face contorts with rage. He raises his hand, dark energy crackling around his fingers. "You'll cooperate, or I'll tear the knowledge from your mind piece by piece."

I feel utterly useless, my modern skills no match for this supernatural showdown. But I can't just stand here while this creep threatens Lachina.

"Hey, Old Man!" I shout, drawing *An Bodach*'s attention. "Why don't you pick on someone your own size?"

Okay, not my best taunt, but it does the trick.

An Bodach's eyes narrow as he turns to face me, his lips curling into a sneer. "Ah, the time-lost fool speaks. And what would ye know of power, small one?"

My first impulse is to spit an insult right back at him. But then I feel a chill slither down my spine as his gaze locks onto mine. I resolve to stand my ground—no matter what.

"Maybe not much," I admit, "but I know bullies when I see them. And you, grandpa, are nothing but a schoolyard thug with a fancy light show."

The old man's face contorts with rage, and I feel the atmosphere crackling with energy. Maybe antagonizing the evil wizard wasn't my smartest move.

"Joey, haud yer wheesht," Kieran hisses, but it's too late.

An Bodach raises his hand, dark tendrils of smoke coiling around his fingers. "Ye dare mock me, ye wee scunner? Well, it's time to prove who has the power. Hold on to your corsets, ladies."

Rachel steps forward. "Not so fast, ye auld devil. Ye forget where you're standing."

She raises her hands, and I feel the earth beneath my feet shift. The air grows thick with an energy I can't explain, like static electricity mixed with the smell of ozone before a storm.

An Bodach's eyes narrow. "Ye think yer wee tricks can stop me, lass?"

"They're not tricks," Rachel replies, her voice eerily calm. "This is the magic of the land itself. The magic ye seek to corrupt."

Suddenly, the earth erupts. Roots and vines burst from the earth, wrapping around *An Bodach*'s legs. He snarls, dark energy crackling around him as he tries to break free. Fulvio, momentarily distracted by the chaos, loosens his grip on Lachina. She seizes the opportunity, driving her elbow hard into his solar plexus. As he doubles over, gasping, she twists free and darts away.

"Lachina!" I shout, racing toward Fulvio. He's distracted by Rachel's chanting, and I seize Lachina easily, racing back to the others. But there's no time to celebrate.

An Bodach roars with fury as dark tendrils of energy slash through Rachel's vines. The air crackles with conflicting magics as he and Rachel face off.

"Ye cannae hope to match my power, girl," *An Bodach* snarls, hurling a bolt of shadowy energy at her.

Rachel deflects it with a shimmering barrier of light, her eyes blazing. "Perhaps not alone. But I'm far from alone."

For a moment, I don't understand what she means. Then it becomes clear. This battle will be like no other.

Magic. Steel. Twelve clans. Four mobsters.

This battle has just turned epic.

Chapter Twenty-Eight

Rachel

Icannae believe my magics are working so well, precisely when I need them the most. It's almost…unbelievable. But the being who calls himself *An Bodach* has been using dark magics for longer than I've been alive—or that my father or my great-aunts have lived. Do we have the power to stop *An Bodach*?

Joey clasps my hand, giving it a firm squeeze.

When I glance up at his face, I see love, trust, commitment, and so many other wonderful things. Joey Finnegan saved me from a life of boredom and solitude. He changed my world in ways I cannot even fully explain. I now realize I've loved him since the moment he fell from the sky and plunged into the depths of the moat.

'Twas magic that brought us together. But our love will stop the evil that threatens us today.

"Together, we're stronger than any dark magic," I whisper, not intending to speak but unable to silence my voice. Something inside me urges me to keep talking. "You, *An Bodach*, do not control the magics of all these good witches. You are of the darkness, but we are made of light."

"That's my girl," Joey says with a grin. "We've come too far to back down now."

I take a deep breath, drawing strength from his unwavering confidence. The air crackles with energy as my witchcraft responds to the intensity of the moment. Joey may not have magic of his own, but his presence amplifies mine in ways I never thought possible.

I square my shoulders and lift my chin. "Let's show this Bodach what happens when he messes with a coven of MacTaggart witches and my time-traveling lover."

Joey chuckles, the sound warming me despite the chill of anticipation. "Lover, huh? I like the sound of that, though I'd prefer 'dashing rogue' or 'strapping hero,' if you're taking suggestions."

"Dinna push your luck, Mr. Finnegan. We've got a battle to win first."

The air grows heavy, thick with malevolent energy. The shadows at the edge of the clearing begin to writhe and twist, taking on grotesque forms. *An Bodach*'s voice, cold and ancient, echoes through the trees.

"Foolish children," he hisses. "Your light is but a candle flame against the vast darkness I command."

I feel Joey stiffening beside me, but his grip on my hand remains steady. I draw upon our connection, feeling the magic surge within me, a crackling current of power that makes my skin tingle and my hair stand on end. I can feel Joey's strength flowing into me, his unwavering belief in us amplifying my abilities beyond anything I've ever experienced.

"A candle flame, ye say?" I call out, my voice ringing clear and strong. "Then prepare to be blinded, ye auld demon!"

With a flourishing gesture, I summon a blinding burst of light that cuts through the writhing shadows. *An Bodach* shrieks, a sound that chills me to the bone, but I stand my ground.

Joey's arm wraps around my waist, steadying me. "Go for it Rach. Show this creep what a MacTaggart witch can do."

The shadows retreat, but I know it's only temporary. *An Bodach*'s power is ancient and vast. But so is the legacy of the MacTaggart witches. I can feel the spirits of my ancestors stirring, lending me their strength.

"You think you can defeat me with parlor tricks?" *An Bodach*'s voice booms, shaking the very ground beneath our feet. The shadows surge forward once more, tendrils of darkness reaching for us like grasping fingers.

I raise my free hand, channeling every ounce of power I can muster. "These are no tricks, ye monster. This is the light of generations."

A blinding white light erupts from my palm, spreading outward in a dome that pushes back the encroaching darkness. Joey gasps beside me, his eyes wide with wonder.

"Holy shit, Rachel," he breathes. "You're like a supernova."

I can't help but grin, even as sweat beads on my brow and my chest is heaving.

An Bodach grins like the evil creature he is.

We do seem to be outdone in terms of magic. My parents' tale of a battle they won years ago taught me that what seems to be is not always so.

The mafia riatach, Fulvio, erupts into evil laughter as if he believes he's won—because *An Bodach* seems to be on his side. But I suspect the Old Man won't remain loyal to the mobsters for much longer.

"What are you thinking?" Joey asks, his voice hushed. "You've got the 'I have a plan' face."

I didnae realize I made a special face when I'm plotting something. But Joey knows me better than anyone else. I hiss out of the corner of my mouth, "Aye, you are correct. I have a plan. But I cannae guarantee it will work."

"How can I help?"

I glance at the mafia men. "Do you intend to live in the year 1621?"

Fulvio rolls his eyes. "Of course not. There's no percentage in living in ye olden days. I make a mint off crypto."

Whatever the word crypto means, I'm fair certain it's of no importance to me. I set my hands on my hips while my magics continue to swirl around me. "*An Bodach* is a trickster and a shapeshifter. His intentions are always malevolent and never benefit anyone but himself. You are a fool, Fulvio, if you believe he will protect you during the battle that will surely come."

The mafia moron wields his little gun, waving it about as if that will cow the Scots who have gathered here. "Four of us can mow down plenty of you hicks, especially with our friend here to provide a magical assist."

Joey has mentioned that guns can be deadly and faster than a sword. But with so many Scots from so many clans here with us, surely we can prevail.

My great-aunts gather round me, forming a circle within which I stand. The power of our magics crackles in the air like tiny golden sparks.

"Screw this," Fulvio snarls, as he and his friends pull out their weapons. "Old Man, get your ass in gear and take down these chumps."

An Bodach sniggers—softly, darkly, the sound imbued with the darkest intent. His voice reverberates with ancient, unyielding power as he taunts Fulvio. "Ye pitiful mortal. Did ye truly delude yourself into thinking I would conspire with such insignificant wretches?"

Fulvio's face contorts in confusion and anger. "What the hell are you talking about? We had a deal!"

"I trade only in chaos and suffering," *An Bodach* snarls, his form warping into an even more monstrous visage with every passing second. "And now, I shall gorge on the despair of all involved."

Dark, vicious tendrils of magic explode from *An Bodach*, striking out with relentless fury at both the mafia men and our group. I hear blood-curdling screams of terror from Fulvio and his cohorts as the shadows consume them. But there is no time to ponder their doom—the malevolent magic is surging towards us, poised to crush our defenses.

"Now, sisters!" I cry out to my great-aunts with desperate urgency.

In unison, we raise our hands, channeling our combined might into a blazing barrier of light. The darkness assaults it with the force of a raging storm against a cliff, yet our shield stands unwavering. Joey is at my side, his presence lending me strength too, even as his eyes widen in awe at the fierce magical battle erupting around us.

"Rachel, this is incredible," he breathes. "But how long can you keep this up?"

I grit my teeth, feeling the strain of maintaining such powerful magic. "Long enough, I hope. But we need to do more than just defend. We need to strike back."

Joey and my father raise their weapons—Joey's dirk and Father's claymore. Though fighting a demon with mundane weapons doesn't seem helpful, as I had realized earlier, this is only the first salvo. My great-aunts and I, working as one, can and will play a pivotal role.

All the men of all the twelve clans are swarming us, protecting us as best they can, for the real battle is about to commence.

As if in response to my words, *An Bodach*'s form shifts again, growing even more monstrous. His body stretches and twists, becoming a grotesque amalgamation of shadow and flesh. Tentacles of darkness lash out, seeking any weakness in our defenses.

"Rachel!" Great-Aunt Efrica calls out. "We must focus our attack!"

I nod curtly, instantly understanding what she means. The five of us—myself and the aunts—begin to move in a circular pattern, our steps in perfect synchronization. The men around us watch in awe as golden light begins to swirl at our feet, rising up to envelop us in a shimmering vortex.

The figure *An Bodach* melts into a seething cloud of black and purple that intensifies quickly as the air pulses with raw power. I feel the magic coursing through me, stronger than ever before. The combined strength of generations of MacTaggart witches flows through our circle, building to a crescendo.

"Now!" I holler, my voice ringing with authority. Och, is that my voice? Aye, it is.

As one, we thrust our hands forward. A blinding beam of pure light erupts from our circle, cutting through *An Bodach*'s dark cloud like a sword through mist. The demon shrieks, a sound of rage and pain that shakes the very earth.

His distorted voice reverberates through time stream and all of Scotland. "Noooo! You witches will suffer for this, and I shall have my vengeance!"

The whirlwind of black and purple rises high into the sky, blotting out the light. My great-aunts and I continue chanting as our voices gradually grow louder until the very air around us vibrates with the power of our words. The golden light emanating from our circle intensifies, pushing back against the swirling darkness above.

"Keep going!" I shout, my voice strained but determined. "We're weakening him!"

Joey steps closer, his presence bolstering my resolve as he shoves his dirk into its sheath, and his magics meld with mine. "You've got this, Rachel. Show the demon what a MacTaggart witch can really do."

Drawing strength from Joey's unwavering faith, I dig deeper, tapping into reserves of power I never knew I possessed. The light from our circle surges upward, piercing through *An Bodach*'s dark form like shafts of sunlight breaking through storm clouds.

The demon's screams grow more frantic, more desperate. "Impossible! You cannot defeat me! I am eternal!"

But I can feel the tide turning. *An Bodach*'s darkness is fragmenting, breaking apart under the onslaught of our combined light. "Ye may be eternal, but so is the light of the MacTaggart witches!"

With one final push, we channel every ounce of our power into a blinding explosion of golden energy. The light engulfs *An Bodach*'s writhing form, shattering his darkness into countless fragments that dissipate like smoke in the wind.

But he roars one last time, leaving us with these words: "I have multiplied your enemies, doideagan! They shall avenge me!"

As the last echoes of the demon's wailing fade away, an eerie silence falls over the battlefield. I sway on my feet, exhausted but exhilarated. Joey's strong arms wrap around me, steadying me.

"You did it, Rach," he whispers, his voice filled with awe and pride. "*An Bodach* is no more. From now on, he'll only be a bugaboo, a myth to scare naughty kids into behaving."

The aunts and I break away from our circle. Aye, we have won the magical battle and destroyed *An Bodach*. But he left behind enough monsters to do considerable damage. A battle must be fought now—a battle for the souls of the twelve clans.

"Oh, shit." Joey's eyes widen briefly as he realizes what has happened. Then a steely resolve hardens his features. "I wish I was hallucinating, and there aren't really an army of duplicate mobsters with guns ready to attack us."

My father sets a hand on Joey's shoulder. "Dinnae fash, laddie. Scots have fought worse battles than this, and our numbers are far greater."

"But guns can splatter your brains within a matter of seconds."

"Have ye lost yer faith in the clans?"

Joey raises his brows. "Did I say I was giving up? Hell no. It's time to show those mafia assholes what a bunch of Scots and one New Yorker can do."

I love his resolve, but I need to make sure all the men understand. "I'm afraid the members of our coven have depleted our magics—for not. We'll need time to replenish it. More time than this battle can handle."

My father grins like a feral beast. "Dinnae fash, Rachel. After all, *'s e Albannaich a th' annainn.*"

Joey's brows lift. "And that means…"

Father raises his sword high and shouts, loudly enough to hurt my years, "We are Scots!"

And just like that, battle begins.

Chapter Twenty-Nine

Joey

Fulvio and his duplicate minions have pulled out their weapons, and it's clear that *An Bodach* gifted them with one last helpful device—a Tommy gun. I really hate that bastard. Whatever it takes to rid the world of these jerk-offs, I'll do it. They wanted to kill me, after all, so I don't feel too bad about taking them out.

Kieran smiles with smug satisfaction as he winks at me, then hollers to the crowd. "We shall never concede to the enemy! Why? Because *'s e Albannaich a th' annainn!*"

Rachel presses her lips to my ear. "That means 'we are Scots.' It's a battle rallying cry."

"No shit. I wouldn't have guessed." I know she grasped my sarcasm. Rachel is wicked smart.

The Scots raise their weapons, shouting so loudly that I can't hear my own thoughts. I whip out my dirk, ready to go.

And the battle commences.

Chaos erupts as the Scots charge forward, their battle cries echoing across the glen. I'm swept up in the tide of kilts and claymores, and my dirk feels pathetically small compared to the massive broadswords around me. But hey, size isn't everything, right?

Fulvio's goons open fire with their handguns and a solitary Tommy gun, the rapid staccato of bullets cutting through the air. I duck and weave, thanking my lucky stars for all those hours spent playing Fortnite. Who knew virtual battle royales would prepare me for actual combat?

Rachel's by my side, her eyes blazing with a mix of fury and excitement. She mutters something in Gaelic that I'm pretty sure isn't appropriate for polite company, then hurls a fireball at the nearest gunman. The guy goes up like a roman candle, screaming and flailing.

"Nice trick," I shout over the din, my heart pounding like a jackhammer. "Got any more where that came from?"

Rachel grins wickedly, her hair whipping in the wind. "Aye, plenty. Watch and learn, outlander!"

She raises her hands, and suddenly the very earth trembles beneath our feet. The grass ripples like waves on a stormy sea, and several of Fulvio's men lose their footing, tumbling to the ground in a tangle of limbs and curses.

Kieran charges past us, his massive claymore cleaving through the air with deadly precision. He's like a force of nature, all raw power and Highland fury. I watch in awe as he takes on three goons at once, his blade singing a lethal melody.

"Don't just stand there gawking!" Rachel yells, snapping me back to reality. "Use that dirk of yours before someone mistakes you for a statue!"

Right, the dirk. I grip the handle tightly, my palms sweaty against the worn leather. A goon charges at me, his face twisted in a snarl. I dodge his wild swing and, before I can overthink it, plunge my dirk into his side. The blade slides in with sickening ease, and the man crumples to the ground with a gurgled cry.

My stomach lurches but I push through the nausea. Another attacker is already coming at me, this one wielding a wicked-looking knife. We dance around each other, feinting and jabbing. He's good, but I'm faster. I duck under his guard and slam the pommel of my dirk into his solar plexus. As he doubles over, gasping, I bring my knee up to connect with his face.

The goon drops like a sack of haggis, and I can't help but feel a surge of pride. Maybe I don't suck at this medieval combat thing after all.

But my moment of triumph is short-lived. A deafening crack splits the air, and I feel something whiz past my ear. The Tommy gun. I'd almost forgotten about that modern menace amid all this old-school sword swinging.

"Get down!" Rachel screams, tackling me to the ground just as another burst of gunfire tears through the space where I'd been standing. We roll together, like a human sandwich, and wind up with Rachel on top of me. For a split second, I forget we're in the middle of a life-or-death battle, distracted by the feel of her warm, soft body pressed to mine.

Rachel gives me a quick, hard kiss. Then she smirks and springs to her feet, dragging me up with her. "Focus, Joey, would you? The fight isn't over yet."

She's right, of course. The battle rages on around us, a chaotic symphony of clashing steel, gunfire, and magical explosions. I spot Fulvio near the edge of the fray, barking orders to his remaining men. His eyes meet mine, and a cruel smile twists his lips.

"Time to end this," I snarl, gripping my dirk tighter. "The mafia has no place in medieval Scotland."

Rachel nods, her face set with grim determination. "Then we must stop them, aye?"

"Absolutely." I glance around to get a better lay of the land, but the smoke from the guns and the deafening clash of swords make it difficult. "Listen, Rach, you should gather the women from as many clans as possible. Maybe they can help. They might even have some weapons, huh? The ones who don't have magic, that is."

"Oh, aye, Scots women are hardy. That was a brilliant idea, Joey."

While she races off to conscript the Scottish lasses, I charge toward Fulvio, weaving through the melee. The residual magics from Rachel's spells clear a path, sending enemies flying left and right. I deflect a sword strike with my dirk, feeling the shock reverberate up my arm. Damn, that hurt.

Fulvio sees me coming. He raises the Tommy gun, but before he can squeeze the trigger, a blur of tartan and fury barrels into him from the side. Kieran, his face splattered with blood and his eyes wild with battle rage, grapples with Fulvio for control of the weapon.

Is that Fulvio? Or one of his duplicates?

When Kieran thrusts his blade deep into the enforcer's gut, the guy disintegrates into a pile of black sludge. Okay, that must have been a duplicate.

I seize the opportunity, sprinting toward another fake Fulvio. The creep manages to wrench the gun free, but before he can bring it to bear, I'm on him. My dirk flashes in the fading light as I slash at his gun hand. He howls in pain, the Tommy gun clattering to the ground.

Kieran doesn't waste a second. He scoops up the fallen weapon. "I reckon you know what to do with this better than I do."

He tosses the Tommy gun to me, and I spray a volley of bullets at Fulvio's remaining men, knocking them down in quick succession, roaring like a wild man. The tables turned in an instant when the goons found themselves on the receiving end of their own firepower. All the fake mobsters are gone.

But where is the real one?

"Joey, look out!" Rachel's voice cuts through the chaos.

I spin around just in time to see the real Fulvio lunging at me, a wicked-looking dagger glinting in his hand. Time seems to slow as I raise the Tommy gun, but I know I won't be fast enough.

Suddenly, a blur of tartan and flashing steel intercepts him. Rachel, her expression the picture of defiant determination, parries Fulvio's strike with a sword she must have snatched from a fallen clansman. The clash of metal-on-metal rings out, but the hefty sword makes her stagger backward.

"I thought you were gathering the women, Rachel!"

She gives me a sloppy grin.

Fulvio pulls out his Glock, aiming the gun straight at the woman I love.

"Here, Joey!" Rachel cries out, tossing me her sword.

With a mighty battle cry, I leap in front of Rachel, claymore in my hand. I catch the sword in mid-air, its weight nearly pulling me off balance. But adrenaline surges through me, and I manage to bring the blade up just as Fulvio fires.

The bullet ricochets off the steel with a resounding clang, sparks flying, the impact vibrating through my bones. Fulvio's eyes widen in shock, and I seize opening. With a roar that would make Kieran proud, I charge forward, swinging the claymore in a wild arc.

Fulvio dodges, but he's not quite fast enough. The tip of the blade catches his arm, drawing a line of crimson. He hisses in pain, stumbling back.

"Not so tough without your goons, are you?" I taunt as a rush of confidence hits me. I think I'm getting the hang of this medieval warrior thing after all.

Abruptly, I notice that all the other warriors, and the witches too, are standing in a huge circle encompassing me and Fulvio. That bastard made my life hell, and he would've killed me if I hadn't been thrown back in time. But now he is the only bad guy left. The enforcer is going down. Right now.

Rachel appears at my side, her hands glowing with an eerie blue light. "Together, Joey, we do this together."

"Damn straight."

A sensation of raw power emanates from her, and the blue glow gradually spreads outward to encompass every single Scot, man or woman. We advance on Fulvio, who's now backed against a rocky outcropping, his eyes darting frantically between us and the circle of Scots who have surrounded the clearing.

"It's over, Fulvio," I growl, leveling the claymore at his chest. "You're a long way from Chicago, and your mafia tricks won't save you here."

He sneers, blood dripping from his wounded arm. "You think you've won? You're nothing but a punk kid playing dress-up in a kilt. I've survived worse than this."

Rachel's eyes narrow dangerously. "Aye, but you've never faced a Highland witch before."

She raises her glowing hands.

Fulvio's sneer falters as he glances nervously at the pulsing blue light. "What the hell is that?"

"This," Rachel says, her voice resonating with power, "is justice, Highland style."

The blue glow intensifies, spreading from Rachel to me, then rippling out to encompass the entire circle of Scots. I feel a surge of energy coursing through my body, making my hair stand on end. The claymore in my hands hums with an otherworldly vibration.

Fulvio raises his gun, but his hand is shaking. "Stay back! I'll blow you away, Finnegan, I swear!"

"Go ahead," I taunt, feeling invincible with Rachel's magic coursing through me. "Your bullets can't hurt us now."

Fulvio's eyes dart wildly as he aims the gun at my chest. He pulls the trigger, but the bullet dissolves into blue sparks before it reaches me. He gasps. "Impossible. This can't be real, I'm dreaming or…something."

He fires again and again with the same result.

I advance slowly, the claymore glowing with ethereal light. "This is for everyone you've ever hurt, you bastard."

With a primal yell, I swing the sword in a mighty arc. Fulvio tries to dodge, but he's too slow. The blade slices clean through him, and for a moment, everything goes still.

And Fulvio's body crumbles to ash, scattering on the wind.

The blue glow fades, and I slump to my knees, exhausted.

Rachel kneels beside me, wrapping her arms around my shoulders. "It's over, mo *leannan*. You did it, Joey. You saved us all."

I look up at her, my vision blurry with sweat. "We did it. Together. Every single person here today played a role."

"You are too humble, Joey. I still remember your arrogance when we first met, and I love that part of you too."

Rachel raises my hand high above us. "All hail the hero who vanquished Fulvio!"

The circle of Scots erupts in cheers, their voices echoing across the glen. Kieran strides over, his huge body casting a shadow over us. He extends a hand, pulling me to my feet with surprising gentleness.

"Well fought, laddie," Kieran declares, clapping me on the back hard enough to make me stagger. "You've proven yourself to be a true Highland warrior on this day."

Rachel's great-aunts trot over to us, beaming as if they know an amazing secret. Efrica speaks for the trio. "Dinnae ye realize what has transpired? Everyone who participated in this battle has become a part of history. On down the ages, from this moment onward, this day shall be known as the 'Witches' Confrontation' and 'twill be forever remembered."

"Thanks to our MacTaggart witches," Kieran says with a smile. "Rachel, Efrica, Lachina, and Morna. Your names might vanish from remembrance, but your valiant efforts on this day will never be forgotten."

Hamish thrusts his sword above his head. "All hail the valiant witches of Dùndubhan!"

A chorus of voices repeats the statement, expressing their appreciation for these amazing ladies.

Kieran claps a hand on my shoulder. "You are the hero of this day, Joey Finnegan, the man whose mysterious appearance at Dùndubhan heralded a true hero's arrival."

I pull off a weak smile. "Thanks, but I couldn't have done any of this without Rachel's magic. Or your claymore."

Big Daddy squeezes my shoulder. "*Macan*, I think it's time we forged a claymore specially for you."

I grin.

Chapter Thirty

Rachel

The clan gathering turned into something none of us could ever have imagined. I'm not talking about the Witches' Confrontation or the supernatural battle. No, I am referring to what transpired after that. The clans came together like never before, hashing out old grievances, discovering new friendships, and fundamentally altering the dynamics among the clans.

Aye, everything has changed. And it's wonderful.

Nine days after the Witches' Confrontation, Guarin Abadie comes to visit us again, and I look forward to hearing his tales of the other continent—Europe—and his travels through England as well as Scotland. The women in the family all agree with me that both countries reside on the same continent. However, the men—Joey included—disagree.

"Don't you girls have maps?" Joey asks with no small measure of sarcasm. "Britain is an island. Europe is a continent. Everybody knows that—except for Scottish women."

His smirk assures me he's being silly with his comment about Scottish women. He is entirely serious about the continent versus island debate, however. I roll my eyes at Joey's teasing, but I can't quash the smile that tugs at my lips.

"Aye, Joey, and I suppose you've sailed 'round the whole of Britain to prove it?" I retort, matching his sarcasm.

Guarin chuckles, his eyes twinkling with mirth. "Ah, mes amis, perhaps we should consult the spirits on this matter. They might have a unique perspective, non?"

"Don't you dare summon any spirits, Guarin," I warn, only half-joking. After the chaos of the Witches' Confrontation, I've had quite enough of supernatural meddling for a long while. Still, I haven't given up on my magics, and I never will.

Joey raises an eyebrow. "Wait, can Guarin actually do that?"

Before I have time to answer, a gust of wind sweeps through the room, rustling papers and causing the candles to flicker. I freeze, my eyes darting to Guarin. His expression has shifted from jovial to serious in an instant.

"I did not do that," he affirms. "I would have no idea how to create such a disturbance."

Joey's hand instinctively moves to his side, where I know he keeps a small dagger hidden ever since the calamity during the clan gathering. His New York street smarts have adapted well to our Highland ways. "Rachel, what's happening?"

I shake my head, my own magic stirring within me. "I don't know. Ne'er have I felt anything like this."

The whirls around us, forming a vortex in the center of the room. Papers and small objects fly through the air, and I'm forced to squint against the force of it. Through the maelstrom, I catch glimpses of something forming—shapes, shadows, figures that flicker in and out of existence.

As the wind howls, I experience a familiar tingling in my fingertips—my magic responding to the otherworldly energy swirling around us. I reach out, grasping Joey's hand while also gripping Guarin's. Their warmth grounds me as I focus my dà-shealladh, trying to puncture the mantle of chaos that swirls everywhere around us.

"It's a portal," I gasp, my voice barely audible above the din. "But like none I've ever seen before."

Joey grips my hand like a vise. "Another time jump?"

Before I can utter one syllable in response, the vortex unexpectedly contracts, collapses into a shimmering disc of swirling green fog. Through the haze, I catch glimpses of a world both familiar and alien—mist-shrouded mountains, ancient standing stones, and figures moving in the shadows. I can't believe what I'm seeing.

"The Otherworld," I whisper, awe and trepidation mingling in my voice. "We're looking into the realm of the *Daoine Maithe*."

Joey's eyes widen, but his New York skepticism kicks in, spurring him to become suspicious of the impossible sight before him. "*Daoine Maithe*? As in Scottish fairies? You've got to be kidding me."

But there's no denying the otherworldly beauty and danger emanating from the portal. The air sizzles with ancient magic, far older and wilder than anything I've encountered before.

Great-Aunt Efrica rushes to my side. "Rachel, we must close the portal. The veil between worlds is not meant to be pierced so carelessly."

I reach for my power, but before I can act, a figure emerges from the swirling green mist. Tall and ethereal, with skin like moonlight and eyes that shift colors like a kaleidoscope, the being steps into our world with preternatural grace. A lump forms in my throat as I recognize the unmistakable features of a member of the Daoine Maithe—the good folk.

"Children of the mortal realm, " the female fairy states, her melodious voice resonating with power. "It seems the winds of change have blown open doors long sealed."

Joey tenses beside me, his hand inching toward his concealed weapon. Mortal steel would be useless against such a being.

"My lady," I manage to say, dipping into a curtsy and pulling Joey down into an awkward bow. "We meant no disrespect by this…unexpected opening."

"Never mind that, child." The female steps closer, standing between me and Joey as she studies us with a slight smile on her lips. "I am Àille, Banrigh of the *Daoine Maithe*."

I am awed by her presence, barely able to speak. This radiant creature is Banrigh—or Queen of the Good Folk.

"The Witches' Confrontation has caused a rift in the time stream," the queen tells us. "You, Rachel and Joey, are the only ones who can fix it. But doing so requires you to go into the future—Joey's past—to find where the rift occurred."

"What will happen if we can't do that?" Joey asks.

"It's best if you do not know." The queen steps backward. "Now, it is time for you embark on a journey through time. But take care not to leave any traces that might affect the future or the past."

"Wait," I say, feeling foolish for speaking so boldly to the Banrigh. "What about the book? We searched for it but couldnae find it."

"All will become clear at the appropriate moment. Your minds are the only tools you shall need. Blessed be, my children."

"But I—"

The Banrigh waves her hand in a flourishing gesture—and vanishes.

"But she didnae send us—" My words are cut off as a vortex engulfs us, and we are hurled into the future. Bright light blinds me momentarily, then I turn to Joey. "We are inside Dùndubhan, in the long gallery."

"How do you know that? This is the modern version."

"I know because I have been here before, in a way. I told you that my *dà-shealladh* showed me visions of the past as well as the modern world."

"Oh, right. I almost forgot."

I pat his cheek. "Dinnae fash. It has been a whirlwind since the day you fell out of the sky and into my arms."

"We need to be careful. I don't see many people in here right now, but another tour might arrive any second."

Joey scans the long gallery, surveying the modern furnishings, the artwork that now adorns the ancient walls of Dùndubhan—and the glass cases filled with medieval weapons. "So, we're in the future? Or, I guess, my present?"

"Aye." My own gaze darts around the room as I search for any clues to our exact timeline. "It seems so. But when exactly, I cannae say."

As we cautiously explore the gallery, I can't help but marvel at how different yet familiar everything feels. The bones of the castle remain the same, but the trappings of modernity—electric lights, sleek furniture, and what I recognize as security cameras—create a jarring contrast to the Dùndubhan I know.

"Rachel," Joey's voice draws my attention. He stands in front of a large painting, his brows wrinkled. "Look at this."

I move closer to examine the painting Joey's fixated on. It's a grand portrait, ornate and clearly ancient, depicting a gathering of clan leaders. My breath catches as I recognize familiar faces—ancestors I've only known through stories and my own visions.

"That's Bróccin MacTaggart," I whisper, pointing to a stern-faced man in the center. "My great-great grandfather. And there, that's Gelis Campbell—she was said to be one of the most powerful witches of her time."

"What do we do now?"

Before I can answer, a noise from the hallway catches our attention. Footsteps, growing closer.

"Quick," I hiss, grabbing Joey's arm and pulling him behind a large display case. We crouch down to hide and wait for an opportunity to slip away.

"…and this is the Long Gallery," a crisp, professional voice announces. "Home to some of Dùndubhan's most precious historical artifacts."

I risk a peek around the edge of the display case, my heart racing. A small tour group enters the gallery, led by a smartly dressed woman in a blazer. Her polished accent marks her as English, and I assume she's a professional guide.

"As you can see," she continues, gesturing to the very painting we were just examining, "this portrait depicts a crucial moment in clan history. The Great Gathering of 1426, where alliances were forged that would shape the future of the Highlands."

Joey shifts beside me, his breath warm against my ear as he whispers, "The year 1426? Is that an important year in your family?"

"Aye, 'tis the year when the MacTaggart book of magics vanished. The story goes that a witch from our clan cast a spell that went awry, and that's how the book was lost."

"Then we need to find it, huh?"

"Aye, we do. But no one has ever been able to find it despite many attempts to do so." I cannae move, barely daring to breathe as the tour group moves closer to our hiding spot. The guide's voice drones on, explaining the significance of various artifacts, but my mind is whirling with the implications of what we've learned.

Suddenly, a small boy at the back of the tour group breaks away, darting toward our hiding spot with the reckless abandon only a child can muster. My heart leaps into my throat as his curious eyes scan the display case, inching ever closer to our concealment.

Joey tenses beside me, ready to spring into action if needed.

I squeeze his arm, silently willing him to stay still. The last thing we need is to cause a scene and alter the timeline even further.

Just as the boy's gaze is about to land on us, a stern voice cuts through the air. "Timothy! Get back here this instant!"

The child freezes, then reluctantly trudges back to his mother's side. I let out a breath I didn't realize I'd been holding.

As the tour group moves on, their voices fade down the corridor. Joey and I slowly emerge from our hiding place.

"That was close," Joey whispers, his eyes still darting toward the door. "But at least now we know when we need to go."

"Nay, my intuition urges me to avoid the year of The Great Gathering." I take a moment to consider the problem but cannae come up with any answers. "How do we get there? And more importantly, how do we fix whatever went wrong without making things worse?"

Joey runs a hand through his hair, a habit I've come to recognize as a sign of his frustration. "I don't suppose you have a time machine hidden away in this castle, do you?"

I can't help but smile despite the gravity of our situation. "No time machine, I'm afraid. But we do have magic."

"Right, of course," Joey mutters, still not entirely comfortable with the concept despite everything he's seen. "So, what? We cast a spell and…poof, we're in whatever time we need to be in?"

"Afraid it's not that simple," I reply, biting my lip as I consider our options. "Temporal magics are incredibly complex and dangerous. One wrong move could unravel the entire fabric of reality."

Joey's eyes widen. "Okay, let's avoid unraveling reality if we can. What do we need to do?"

"Find the book. We must invoke a spell that will guide us to it. That could be dangerous, if the book is protected by the witch or sorcerer who appropriated it."

He raises his brows. "Are you sure about this? Couldn't we potentially screw up the timeline if we layer more magics onto the problem?"

"Dinnae think so."

"You don't think so? That's awfully vague, Rach."

"It's our best chance," I say firmly. "Come, we need to move before someone else walks in."

As we slip out of the long gallery, the modern trappings of Dùndubhan feel surreal. Electric lights hum overhead, replacing the flickering torches I'm accustomed to. The stone floors are now covered with plush carpets that muffle our footsteps.

"This way," I whisper, tugging Joey's sleeve. My dà-shealladh will guide me through the familiar-yet-strange corridors and out of the castle. "We need to find a secluded place where I might cast the spell that will tell us where to go next."

Chapter Thirty-One

Joey

I know exactly where we should go," I tell Rachel. "Let's return to the place where I got sucked into a tornado and then tossed into the moat. You saved me then. The moat is where our origin story begins, and it would be fitting for the next chapter to start there too."

"But the moat does not exist in this time period."

"The location where it used to be is still there, though. The gates no longer exist, but the area where the moat was filled is right outside the castle walls."

She grasps my hand. "Aye, that's true. Let's walk to the spot where the moat would have been and see what happens."

As we make our way across the courtyard and through the gateway that has no gates anymore, I can't help but notice how different everything looks in this time. Where imposing gates once stood, and a drawbridge used to access a murky moat, all that's left now is open land with scattered wildflowers dancing in the Highland breeze and a modern gravel driveway. The castle behind us seems smaller somehow, less formidable than the fortress I'd tumbled into when I first arrived in the seventeenth century.

Rachel threads her fingers with mine. Her golden-brown hair catches the late afternoon sunlight, and for a moment, I'm distracted by how it frames her face.

She nudges my shoulder. "Joey, are ye even listening to me?"

"Sorry. It's just…weird being here but not here, you know?"

"Aye, time has a way of playing tricks on the mind." Rachel releases a wistful sigh, observing the landscape with almost reverent curiosity. "For me, this is all new history. But for you, it's where your adventure began."

We stop at roughly the spot where I'd once splashed down and nearly drowned. Now it's just a gentle depression on the earth, dotted with heather and wild grasses. The sun casts long shadows across the ground, painting everything in amber and gold.

"Do ye feel anything?" Rachel asks, her voice dropping to a whisper. "Tingling, mayhap?"

I close my eyes, trying to sense anything that might indicate the presence of magic. "Nothing yet. Maybe we need to—"

A powerful wind erupts around us, making it hard to speak. The wind seems unusually warm for the Highlands. Rachel's clutches my hand as the air shimmers, distorting the landscape around us like heat waves rising from summer pavement.

"Joey!" Rachel shouts over the sudden howl of wind. "I feel the magic stirring!"

The ground beneath our feet trembles, and I swear I can hear water—the phantom splash of a moat that hasn't existed for centuries. My skin prickles with goosebumps despite the unnatural warmth swirling around us. The sensation is familiar, reminiscent of that first disorienting plunge through time.

"Is this supposed to happen?" I yell, but my voice sounds distant even to my own ears.

Rachel flaps her head, clearly confused.

Without warning, my vision goes black, and I can't hear any of the normal sounds of nature. Not birds. Not even the distant chatter of tourists. What the hell? I reach for Rachel's hand but feel only a cold stillness. I start to shiver, but it isn't entirely from the freaky emptiness. Being alone, it evokes memories of my childhood, of the foster moms who only wanted me for the money the state would provide.

No, no, I won't go back there. I'm not that boy anymore.

Then I hear Rachel's voice, faint but unmistakable, calling my name through the darkness. "Joey! Joey, hold fast!"

And the fear vanishes. Because of her. Rachel is my anchor.

The world snaps back into focus with dizzying speed. I need a minute to reorient myself. We're still in the twenty-first century. An airliner soaring high above us proves that.

"Hot damn," I blurt out, grinning at Rachel. "We did it. Or rather, magics did something to us."

Then I finally realize where we are. "We're standing on Bow Bridge in Central Park. That's New York City, Rachel."

She stares at me, eyes wide. "You've come home again?"

"Yeah. But I never really had a home until I met you."

Rachel kisses my cheek. "Yer a MacTaggart now, Joey. We are your family."

My throat feels tight, and my eyes burn. I've rarely ever gotten this emotional about anything. But I can't help it now. My unwanted journey into the past has given me a home, a family, and a woman I love with all my heart.

I cough into my fist. "We, uh, should search for the book. It must be somewhere in the vicinity of Central Park. Why else would your magics drop us here?"

"Aye, that makes sense. The ancient magics wouldnae bring us here without purpose."

Rache surveys the sprawling green expanse of Central Park, noting the joggers, tourists, and street performers with undisguised wonder. For some-one from seventeenth-century Scotland, she's adapting amazingly well. I can only imagine what's racing through her mind.

"So many people," she says, her voice hushed. "And such strange garments they wear. The clothing reminds me of your attire when you arrived at Dùndubhan."

I give her hand a reassuring squeeze. "Just stick close to me. Your outfit might turn a few heads, but this is New York. People have seen weirder."

A rollerblader dressed as Darth Vader glides past us, complete with a portable speaker blasting the Imperial March. Rachel jumps back, her free hand instinctively reaching for the dirk that isn't there. She'd left it back in the medieval era.

"Just a costume," I explain quickly.

Rachel lowers her hand, embarrassment coloring her cheeks. "Of course. I should have realized."

As we start walking along the winding paths of Central Park, Rachel's wide-eyed wonder gives me a new perspective on the familiar landscape. Every fountain, every statue, every hot dog vendor becomes a marvel through her eyes.

"This place," she whispers, "it has a pulse of its own. I swear I can feel the city's heartbeat."

I sling an arm around her shoulders, tugging her closer, and peck a kiss on her forehead. I understand exactly what she means. New York has always had that effect, even on a jaded jerk like me.

"So, the book," I say, trying to focus on the task we came here to accom-plish. "Any witchy feelings about where we should look?"

Rachel closes her eyes momentarily, her brow furrowing in concentration. The wind picks up around us, tugging at her hair, almost as if it's responding to her silent inquiry.

"There," she announces, pointing toward the Metropolitan Museum of Art that looms at the edge of the park. "I feel it calling to us. The book is nearby, Joey."

"At the museum?" I squint at the massive stone building. "That makes sense, I guess. Lots of old stuff in there, dating back much further than the seventeenth century."

Rachel tilts her head, studying the grand entrance, its columns and steps crowded with tourists. "What manner of castle is that?"

"It's a museum—a place where they keep important artifacts and art from throughout history," I explain as we approach the imposing steps. "If your book ended up somewhere in this era, a museum would be a logical place to find it."

Rachel begins to shuffle her feet as we near the entrance, her head tilted back to study the structure, her eyes wide with both wonder and a hint of wariness. "These artifacts…they're kept behind glass, aye? Like precious jewels?"

"Exactly. But getting to anything in their collection that's not on display might be tricky." I knife a hand through my hair, mentally cataloging all the security measures we'd need to bypass. A cold realization washes over me. "I don't have my wallet. Or ID. Or money."

The cutest little dimple of confusion forms above her nose. "What is 'ID'?"

"Identification. In the twenty-first century, everybody needs to have some way of proving who they are. Driver's licenses are a common type of ID."

"I see." Rachel gives me a curious look, tipping her head slightly. "I understand money, but what need have we for coin? Can ye not simply explain our purpose in visiting this mew-zee-um?"

I can't help but laugh. "Things work differently here, Rachel. We can't just walk in and ask to see their ancient magical artifacts. Actually…" I pause, considering the problem. "Maybe that's exactly what we do. The direct approach."

Rachel grins. "Aye! The truth, or some version of it."

"Some very edited version," I agree, guiding her up the steps toward the museum entrance. "Follow my lead."

The massive entrance hall of the Met swallows us like a giant marble monster. Myriad voices echo in the hollow space. Rachel gasps beside me, her fingers tightening around mine as she takes in the soaring ceilings and imposing statues.

"Och, 'tis like a cathedral," she whispers.

I spot an information desk and make a beeline for it, Rachel trailing behind me with her eyes darting everywhere. The middle-aged woman behind the counter gives Rachel's medieval Scottish attire an appraising look.

"Shakespeare in the Park," I explain. "My fiancée is playing Cordelia in King Lear."

The woman lifts her brows briefly, then offers us a practiced smile. "Welcome to the Metropolitan Museum of Art. How can I help you today?"

I clear my throat, channeling the confident persona I'd perfected during my years of talking my way into places where I didn't belong. "I'm a professor at Edinburgh University, working on a project about Scottish artifacts in American collections. My fiancée is tagging along to help me. We're particularly interested in examining any medieval Scottish texts you might have, especially those related to Highland clans."

Rachel stands tall beside me, her posture shifting subtly into something more regal. "Aye. We're especially focused on clan histories from the Highlands, particularly texts that might contain…unusual illustrations or symbols."

The woman types something into her computer. "Most of our Scottish medieval manuscripts are in the European Collections. Some are on display in Gallery 304, but many are in our archives." She peers at us over her reading glasses. "Do you have an appointment with our curator?"

"Not yet," I say smoothly. "We just arrived in the city and wanted to see what was on public display before requesting a more formal consultation."

"I see." She hands us a museum map, circling an area with her pen. "The medieval European galleries are this way. If you'd like to arrange a viewing of the archived materials, you'll need to speak with Dr. Winters. His office is on the third floor, but he typically requires academic credentials and advance notice."

Fuck. Credentials? I'm not that good a thief. Snatching a necklace—no problem. Forging diplomas? That's way beyond my wheelhouse.

"Thank you kindly," Rachel says, her Scottish accent drawing an appreciative smile from the woman.

As we walk away, Rachel whispers, "What are these academic credentials?"

"Letters that say I'm a real professor," I mutter, steering her toward the medieval exhibits. "Which I'm definitely not. I dropped out of college after one semester."

Rachel's brow furrows. "But you speak with such authority. Surely that counts for something."

A laugh snorts out of me. "In my line of work—former line of work—sounding like you know what you're talking about is half the battle. But these museum types need paper proof."

We wander into a gallery that's filled with glass cases containing ancient manuscripts, armor, and ornate weapons. Rachel gasps, her fingers clenching around mine as she recognizes pieces similar to those she'd grown up seeing.

"Joey," she whispers, pressing her face close to a display containing a worn leather-bound book. "Look at this. The patterns along the binding—they're like the ones in my father's study."

I lean in, studying the intricate knotwork patterns etched into the leather. They do bear a striking resemblance to the designs I'd seen in Rachel's family castle.

"You're right, Rachel." I squint so I can read the small descriptive plaque. "Purported Scottish witchcraft manual, circa 1400s, acquired from the estate of Lord Loughty in 1932. Believed to contain herbal remedies and folklore from the western Highlands."

Rachel's breath catches. "Lord Loughty? That cannae be a coincidence. Clan Loughty were bitter enemies of the MacTaggarts for generations until they finally made peace. But the last Lord Loughty died in the nineteen forties with no children to carry on the line."

"But this Loughty guy might have stolen your family's book?" I keep my voice low as a security guard passes by.

"Or one very like it." Rachel presses closer to the glass, her fingers hovering just above the surface. "I can feel something…a faint pulse of energy."

The display case seems to shimmer, visible only to my eyes and Rachel's. A soft golden glow emanates from between the pages of the ancient tome, pulsing like a heartbeat.

"It's calling to you, isn't it?" I position myself to block the security camera's view of Rachel's hand. "Can you tell if it's the right one?"

Rachel closes her eyes, her fingers splayed just above the glass. "Aye, this is the one. I feel it in my bones, in my soul. This book belongs to the MacTaggarts. We must reclaim it."

"Okay then, that's what we'll do." I press my lips to her ear, whispering too softly for anyone to hear. "I'm going to steal the book tonight."

Chapter Thirty-Two

Rachel

Steal it?" I whisper. "Joey, couldnae ye be arrested for that? My mother has told me many things about the future, and I recall when she explained that criminals are sent to prison—often for years or even decades. Dinnae want that to happen to you."

"Don't worry, baby. Thievery is my forte."

"You were a petty thief, aye? You broke into small pawn shops, not museums. Correct?"

"Well, yeah. But stealing is stealing, right? The principle is the same." Joey's cocky grin falters a wee bit under my scrutiny. "Look, I'm not saying it'll be easy, but we need that artifact if we're going to close the portal for good."

I brush my fingers over the silver pendant at my throat, feeling the familiar tingle of magic that's been passed down through generations of MacTaggart witches. Though I've become more adept at using my *dà-shealladh*, I'm far from the level of my great-aunts. The second sight hasn't blessed me with any visions of how this ridiculous plan might unfold.

"The museum has guards," I remind him. "And those wee cameras ye told me about. The all-seeing eyes that never blink."

"Security cameras," Joey corrects. "And yeah, they have them. But I've cased the place enough to get the job done. Their system is outdated. Nothing I can't hack with a little finesse." He taps his temple with one finger, looking far too pleased with himself. "Besides, we aren't exactly swimming in options, are we?"

He's right, though I'm loath to admit it.

"Fine," I concede, pulling my cloak tighter. "But I'm coming with ye. My magic might be useful if things go awry."

"No way. This is a one-man job."

"Are ye certain of that? I'm the one with witchy powers, not you."

He twists his mouth into an expression that's half grimace, half pout. "Magic won't help if we're caught on camera. The cops don't exactly accept 'witchcraft' as a legal defense these days."

"And yet ye need the book that's written in a language only I can decipher." I cross my arms in a defiant gesture. The pendant at my throat warms against my skin, almost as if it's agreeing with me. "Unless ye've suddenly developed the ability to sense ancient Scottish enchantments?"

Joey thrusts a hand through his dark hair, disheveling it in a manner that makes my heart flutter traitorously. "Rachel, this isn't medieval Scotland where you can just wave your hands and make problems disappear. The twenty-first century has different rules."

"Aye, and I've been learning those rules since ye first stumbled through the portal. I am not a helpless lass who needs constant protection."

His mouth quirks into a half-smile. "Trust me, 'helpless' is the last word I'd ever use to describe you."

The warmth in his eyes nearly distracts me from standing my ground—nearly. "Then stop treating me like I'm made of glass. We're partners in this debacle, are we not?"

"Fine," he concedes, throwing his hands up. "But you follow my lead in there. We'll need a distraction of some sort to confuse the guards, but I don't know enough about security systems to figure out how to disable one."

"Allow me to handle that part of the plan."

He frowns. "It's more of a seat-of-your-pants idea than a full-fledged strategy."

"Whatever ye call it, I will provide the magical distraction while you do whatever is necessary to obtain the book."

"I love it when you get all spunky and determined. It's hot." Joey leads me away from the glass case that holds the book. He still has his arm around me. "Here's what I want you to do…"

His breaths tickle my ear as he outlines his hastily constructed scheme, and I find myself torn between wanting to slap him for his recklessness and kiss him for his fearlessness. But that's what I adore about him.

The pendant pulses against my skin, but I dinnae know if it's a warning or encouragement.

"So, I'm expected to create a wee bit of chaos to distract everyone while you sneak back to the glass case that contains the book?" I summarize, eyebrows raised. "That's your master plan?"

"Pretty much." Joey's grin is infectious. "Think you can manage it? Nothing too flashy. We don't want to hurt anyone."

I roll my eyes. "Dinnae worry about me, Joey Finnegan. I learned from the best—Alyssa Vescovi, my mother. The women in my family know how to cause a distraction."

We slip away to a secluded alcove.

I close my eyes and center myself as I've been taught by my great-aunts. The magic in my veins hums like a plucked harp string, eager to be released. When I open my eyes, Joey is staring at me.

"You're glowing a little around the edges," he whispers. "Is that normal?"

"Probably," I assure him, though in truth, I have no idea. The magics are different here—wilder somehow, less constrained by the natural laws that governed it in my own century. "Now, get ready. When the commotion begins, ye'll have exactly three minutes."

"Three minutes? I was hoping for a bit more time."

"Well then, ye should have found a witch with more experience," I retort, but I buffer it with a halfhearted smile. "Three minutes is all I can guarantee without risking something truly catastrophic."

"Define 'catastrophic', please."

I pat his head. "Best not to dwell on the details. Wait until you hear the screams, then move swiftly. Remember, at that point you will have only three minutes."

"Screams, huh?" He sighs. "Okay, then. Let's do this."

Joey sneaks out of the alcove, sauntering away as if he's doing nothing more hazardous than admiring ancient trinkets. No one seems to notice him, or if they do, they dinnae think anything of it.

I shut my eyes, feeling the energy surge within me, uncertain whether to embrace or resist it. The pendant, warm against my skin, serves as a reminder of the power of my great-aunts, the witches who taught me ancient Gaelic incantations. The magics course through my veins, and I'm torn between the thrill and the fear of what it might unleash.

As the magics crescendo, the words tumble from my lips, "*Sgàileadh na sùla, cleas an t-seallaidh, dìon ar slighe,*" a phrase that means "obscure the eyes, deceive the gaze, protect our way." With the biggest part of the spell complete, I hesitate, knowing I must step out of the alcove to create just enough chaos to protect Joey but unsure of the consequences.

A shimmer ripples through the air, originating from my fingertips and spreading outward in barely visible waves of magical energy. For a moment, I hold my breath, half-hoping nothing will happen. Then—chaos erupts.

Every light in the east wing of the museum flickers and dims, while the security cameras spin erratically, their red lights blinking like frantic eyes. In the distance, an alarm wails—not the main security system, fortunately, but something smaller, perhaps a fire alarm. People glance 'round in bewilderment, their faces lit by the eerie glow of emergency lights. The guards leap into action, their radios hissing with static and garbled words. I hadn't meant to disrupt their communications, but magic here has a will of its own, clinging to electronics like a moth to flame. Despite the turmoil I've unleashed, a small smile creeps onto my lips, echoing my mother's words about my magic's penchant for the dramatic, leaving me caught between pride and unease.

"Ladies and gentlemen," a voice announces over the intercom, which crackles intermittently, "we're experiencing a minor technical difficulty. Please remain calm and proceed to the nearest exit."

Perfect. I weave through the crowd, my cloak billowing around my ankles as I hurry away, narrowly avoiding a jostling elbow here and a trampling foot there. The chaos is escalating exactly as I'd hoped—not harmful, but disorienting enough to create the distraction Joey needs. I catch a glimpse of him from across the room, moving with surprising grace for a man his size, slipping behind the security guard who's frantically speaking into his radio, oblivious to Joey vanishing into the twilight within the museum.

I resume chanting my spell, letting the effervescent magics flow within me as I crisscross the throng of confused tourists, who are starting to panic.

A child points at me, tugging his mother's sleeve. "Mommy, that lady's glowing!"

His voice rises above the din, attracting unwanted attention.

The mother glances my way, her eyes narrowing suspiciously before she shakes her head. "Don't be ridiculous, Benji. It's only the emergency lights reflecting off her necklace."

Her dismissive tone does little to quell the growing unease around us.

I must be more careful. The magics are manifesting physically in ways I hadn't anticipated, drawing curious and wary eyes alike. I summon a cloaking spell, becoming instantly invisible, but the effect waivers under the stress of the situation. I'd waited to employ this final spell because it requires an enormous amount of energy. Joey will need all the help I can provide since he must be about to steal the book.

Now, all I can do is wait and pray that Joey succeeds before my magics fade completely. The pendant burns against my skin, a warning that I'm pushing the limits of what I can control in this strange modern world. I sidestep through the crowd toward the exhibit hall where the book sits in its glass prison. My cloaking spell flickers like a candle in a draft—now visible, now unseen—as the magics toil to maintain their hold. The museum visitors brush past me, bumping into my invisible form. Some startle and gasp when they glimpse me, since I seemingly appear from nowhere before vanishing again, causing a ripple of alarm through the crowd.

"Did you see that?" a woman gasps to her companion. "That woman just disappeared!"

"It's the power outage playing tricks on your eyes," her friend replies, though she sounds unconvinced.

Hurry, Joey, please hurry.

Chapter Thirty-Three

Joey

How hard is it to sprint through a museum while people are screaming, the lights flicker on and off repeatedly, and the patrons are frantically trying to flee the building? Well, picture the movie Jurassic Park—after the dinosaurs escaped—and you'll have a pretty good idea of what I'm going through right now.

I can't stop, not for anything. That book is the only weapon to prevent another vile monster like *An Bodach* from obliterating the past. Rachel has fulfilled her role. Now it's my turn to snatch that damn book.

"Joey! On your left!" Rachel's voice slices through the chaos, her Gaelic-tinged warning barely piercing the pandemonium engulfing us.

I whip around with a sharp pivot, narrowly evading a security guard whose eyes are wide with terror, more petrified by the supernatural chaos than intent on capturing me. The museum's grand hall unfolds before me like a twisted obstacle course from hell—display cases casting sinister glows in the stuttering lights, shadows writhing as if possessed by demons.

The MacTaggart book of magic lies tantalizingly close, just a few steps away. I smash my elbow through the glass case, shards flying bits of stars. But then I freeze, panting, transfixed by the ancient leather tome nestled among the wreckage. Its binding, worn by centuries, is exposed beneath the jagged glass. Whatever spell Rachel cast outside is working beautifully—if you can call this pandemonium "beautiful." The electricity surges erratically like a wild beast unleashed, as centuries-old artifacts quiver violently on their pedestals. Somewhere in the distance, the haunting wail of bagpipes echoes eerily, as if played by spectral hands.

A woman, her designer handbag clutched tightly like a lifeline, crashes into me. Her face is a mask of abject terror.

"The paintings! They're moving!" she shrieks, her voice slicing through the din before she bolts past me, a desperate blur heading for the exit.

She's right—the Highland landscapes on the walls have burst to life, clouds roiling across painted skies, heather dancing in an unseen tempest. In one particularly vivid battle scene, tiny warriors clash as their miniature swords ring out, their war cries a faint yet fierce undercurrent to the bedlam.

I seize the book, its leather radiating an odd warmth and throbbing in my grip like a heart torn from its chest. As I lift it from the shattered display case, the entire building seems to release a deep, collective sigh.

"I've got it!" I roar, though the tumult makes me question whether Rachel can hear my triumphant cry from wherever she is concealed.

Her voice fills my head rather than my ears: Run now, Joey. They're coming.

I don't need to ask who "they" are. The cops are after me.

As I race toward the main doors, I realize everyone has evacuated the museum—except for one beautiful, redheaded lass.

"Rachel, are you okay?" I ask while struggling to catch my breath. "I heard you shouting."

"Trying to get your attention, gràidh."

"Let's get out of here."

Rachel pulls me close and begins to chant in Gaelic.

The world spins around us, and the museum fades away. I feel like I might vomit from the high-speed whirling, but I squeeze my eyes shut in the vain hope I won't upchuck all over the woman I adore. The sounds of the city gradually return.

I open my eyes to see Rachel grinning. "You think my nausea is funny?"

"No, *leannan*. I'm smiling because we escaped unscathed." She tucks the book inside her cloak. "Would ye mind if we studied the book later? I would love for you to show me your world before we go home."

"How can I turn down an offer like that? I'd be honored to act as your tour guide. New York City is like nowhere else on earth."

"That's why I want to see it through your eyes, Joey."

"Let's get started, then."

Rachel's eyes light up with that infectious curiosity I've come to love. Even after all we've been through—medieval battles, time portals, and now museum heists—she still looks at everything like it's magical. Coming from an actual witch, that's saying something.

"Is that one of your steel dragons?" She teases, pointing at a yellow cab screeching around the corner.

"That's just a taxi. The steel dragons are much bigger and fly through the sky."

Her laughter bubbles up like champagne, melodic against the harsh city soundtrack. "You're teasing me again, Joey Finnegan."

"Only a little." I grab her hand as we merge into the crowd of pedestrians. "Stay close. New York has its own kind of magic—mostly the kind that makes your wallet disappear."

Nobody bats an eye at the Scottish hottie wearing medieval garb. A few guys give her salacious looks, but Rachel pays no attention to that. She has eyes only for me, and vice versa. I love watching her reactions—the wonder in her eyes, the thrill she gets from visiting the modern world.

We duck into a small coffee shop to catch our breath and take stock of our situation. The café's warmth envelops us like a shield against the chaos we've left behind.

"You're certain no one followed us?" Rachel whispers, her fingers still clutching the ancient tome beneath her cloak. The book seems to pulse between us, a living connection to her world—to our world now, I suppose.

"Reasonably certain," I reply, scanning the busy New York street through the steamy window. "The city's got millions of people. We're just two more faces in the crowd."

Rachel's eyes widen as a barista calls out an order with the theatrical volume unique to Manhattan service workers. "TRIPLE SHOT CARAMEL MACCHIATO FOR BRAD!"

"What manner of beverage requires such an announcement?" she asks, leaning closer to me.

I can't hold back my smile. "That's just coffee with extra stuff in it. Wait till you try it—it's like your morning tea, but if your tea could punch you in the face with energy."

Rachel's eyebrows arch with intrigue. "I should like to experience this face-punching beverage. Is it anything like a venti latte? My mother told me about that, but I have never tasted such a beverage."

"Let's get you one, then."

She grins.

While we wait in line, I notice her hand keeps drifting to where the book is hidden. The weight of it seems to tug at her, both physically and mentally. I lay my hand over hers, steadying her nervous fingers.

"It's safe," I whisper. "For now."

When we reach the counter, the barista—a guy with more piercings than I can count—barely glances at Rachel's medieval attire. This is New

York, after all. He probably assumes she's headed to a Renaissance fair or costume party.

"What can I get you guys?" he asks, his gaze flicking briefly to Rachel's cloak before returning to his screen with practiced indifference.

"Two vanilla venti lattes," I say, then glance at Rachel, whose eyes are fixed on the pastry display. "And...two chocolate croissants."

Rachel pastes herself to my side as we wait, her fingers still protectively curled around the book beneath her cloak. The café hums with the white noise of modern life—espresso machines hissing, phones chiming, dozens of conversations overlapping. To me, it's the soundtrack of normalcy. To Rachel, it's a symphony of wonders.

"Your world moves so quickly," she says in a hushed tone while watching a businessman juggle his coffee, phone, and briefcase while arguing with someone on his Bluetooth earpiece. "Everyone seems to be running from something or to something."

"That's New York, baby." I accept our drinks from the barista, holding them in one hand while using the other to give the guy a nice tip. "Everyone's chasing something—dreams, deadlines, dollars. Sometimes all three at once."

Rachel takes her first sip of latte, and her eyes widen in delight. "*Bod an Donais*! This is..."

Damn, she's adorable. I want to hug her, and fuck her, right now. But I don't care to get arrested.

Rachel searches for the right word, biting her lip while her eyes light up. "Magical. That's the word. But 'tis not like my magic. It's different."

"The magic of caffeine and sugar," I laugh, guiding her to a small table in the corner where we can keep our backs to the wall and our eyes on the door. Old habits die hard, even when you're thousands of miles—and several centuries—from the Scottish Highlands.

Rachel takes another sip, then leans forward conspiratorially. "The book is... restless," she whispers, her hand still pressed against her side. "I can feel it pulsing, like a heartbeat growing stronger. It wants us to return to the Highlands."

"Guess we better find a private place where you can decipher the magics." I lift her hand to my lips. "I'm ready to go home, Rach."

"So am I, mo chridhe. But I'm grateful I was able to experience a wee bit of your world."

I shake my head. "This isn't my world anymore. My life with you and your family, that's where I belong now."

Chapter Thirty-Four

Rachel

Though I cannae wait to go home, to my own time, I convince Joey to show me one last thing—his favorite place in all of New York City. The noise and the crush of people unsettle me. Still, I want to learn a wee bit more about Joey's past before I close the portal that brought us here and that should never have existed in the first place.

We've just left the cafe behind.

"My favorite place?" he says. "I know exactly where to take you."

I follow him through the maze of streets, flinching at the blaring horns and screeching brakes. The buildings tower overhead like mountains of glass and steel, reflecting the afternoon sun in blinding flashes. 'Tis a wonder anyone can breathe here.

"Almost there," Joey says, taking my hand. His touch is warm and reassuring. "You doing okay, Rachel?"

"Oh, aye. Just a wee bit...overwhelmed."

He chuckles. "That's New York for you. Even those of us who grew up here feel that way sometimes."

"Ye move like water through these throngs," I observe, clutching my cloak more securely.

"Years of practice, Rachel," he replies with that crooked smile, the one that still makes my heart flutter every time I see it. "When you grow up dodging foster parents and truancy officers, you learn to navigate crowds."

We board something called a "subway," a sinuous metal beast that roars beneath the city. The way these people trust such contraptions without a second thought! Joey stands protectively close as the carriage sways and rattles, his arm around my waist. I try not to show my anxiety as we're hurtled through darkness at speeds no horse could match.

"Almost there," he whispers, giving me a reassuring smile and an equally reassuring squeeze of my hand.

When we finally emerge from the underground, the air tastes sweeter. Joey leads me through quieter streets until we reach a vast expanse of green nestled amid the towering buildings.

"Central Park," he announces, pride evident in his voice. "Eight hundred and forty-three acres of sanity in this madness. You saw a small part of the park earlier when we popped out into the modern world on Bow Bridge."

"I remember that. It was a lovely location."

"Let me show you more of the park."

Joey kisses my cheek, then begins to lead me onward. I feel my shoulders relax as we walk beneath ancient oaks and maples, their leaves rustling in the gentle breeze. The din of the city fades to a distant hum.

"I used to come here when everything got too much," Joey says, guiding me to a rocky outcropping overlooking a serene pond. "It was the only place where I could breathe." Joey's voice grows softer, almost reverent, as he helps me onto the smooth stone. "Sometimes I'd spend whole days just sitting here, watching people live their lives, imagining what it would be like to have a real home."

The sun shimmers on his dark hair, highlighting strands of amber I've never noticed before. His whisky brown eyes seem far away, lost in memories I cannot touch.

"Did ye ever find it?" I ask, "A real home, I mean."

Joey turns to me, his expression unguarded in a way I've rarely seen. "'Til now? Not really."

I let those words settle between us, the weight of them making my heart ache and soar all at once. My fingers fidget with the small leather pouch of protection herbs my Great-Aunt Morna insisted I carry.

"Look there," he points to a couple rowing across the pond, their laughter drifting toward us on the breeze. "That's what I always wanted. Not just someone to love, but someone who'd choose this crazy world with me."

I watch the couple for a moment, feeling a strange tightening in my chest. "They look so happy."

"Yeah," Joey murmurs, his lips curling sweetly. "They do look that way. It's beautiful, wouldn't you say?"

"Absolutely beautiful."

We sit in companionable silence, our hands linked, my cheek on his shoulder. The park sprawls out around us like a fragment of the Highlands, though tamer, more sculpted by human hands. Still, 'tis a relief after the chaos of the city streets.

"I never belonged anywhere," Joey continues, picking up a small stone and turning it over in his palm. "Foster home to foster home, then the streets, then…well, you know the rest. The bad company I kept."

"The mafia, aye. Forget about that, *mo chridhe*. It's all in the past, literally." I nuzzle his cheek. "Are there any other spots you'd like to show me?"

"Sure thing. But first, feast your eyes on this view." Joey leads me away from the rocks, his arm encircling my waist as we gaze across the park's expanse. "This was my sanctuary when everything went sideways."

The tranquility stretches before us like a dream—families sprawled on blankets, children chasing squirrels, lovers walking hand in hand. 'Tis hard to reconcile this peaceful haven with the chaos just beyond its borders.

"I can see why ye loved it here," I say, resting my head on his shoulder. "Reminds me a wee bit of home—if ye squint hard enough and ignore all the strange contraptions."

Joey laughs, the sound vibrating against my side. "Come on, let's keep moving. There's more I want to show you."

Joey and I follow winding paths past street performers who conjure music from instruments I've never seen. One lad creates gigantic bubbles that float through the air like transparent spirits, delighting children who chase after them with squeals of joy.

"Witchcraft," I whisper to Joey with a wink.

"Just soap and water," he replies with a wink of his own. "Though I admit, some of the magic in your world makes more sense than the technology in mine."

He leads me deeper into the park, where the trees grow thicker and the paths less traveled. The late afternoon sun filters through the leaves, casting dappled shadows across Joey's face. I cannae resist studying his profile—the strong line of his jaw, the slight furrow between his brows when he's thinking, the way his eyes hold secrets I'm still discovering.

"This way," he says, pulling me gently off the main path.

We duck beneath low-hanging branches, following a barely visible trail. The overgrown path leads us to a secluded clearing encircled by ancient oak trees. A small, forgotten stone bench sits nestled against a moss-covered boulder.

"Not many people know about this spot," Joey says, brushing leaves from the bench before offering me a seat. "Found it by accident when I was running from some guys who weren't too happy about the results of a card game."

"Ye cheated them, did ye?" I ask playfully.

Joey grins. "They cheated first."

My laughter echoes through this private sanctuary. "I can see why ye'd hide here. 'Tis like a wee piece of the Highlands."

"That's what I thought when I found it," he admits, sitting beside me, our thighs touching. "It reminded me of something…something I couldn't quite name. Maybe I was remembering a place I hadn't been to yet."

"The Highlands," I whisper as a wee shiver runs through me. It has nothing to do with the gentle breeze. "Perhaps your soul knew where it belonged before you did."

Joey slips his finger between mine, his callused thumb tracing circles on my palm. "Maybe that's why I felt so at home when I landed there. Despite everything—the danger, the confusion, the fact that I was centuries out of place—something about it felt right."

I study his face, searching for the boy he must have been, seeking refuge in this hidden corner of the park. The thought of him alone makes my heart ache.

"Did ye come here often, then?" I inquire gently.

"All the time." His gaze goes distant, a slight smile playing on his lips. "Especially in winter. There's something about this place when it snows, like the whole world goes quiet. I'd sit right here and watch the flakes fall until my fingers went numb."

The image of a younger Joey, huddled alone on this bench while snow gathered on his shoulders, brings tears to my eyes. I blink them away before he notices.

"And what would ye think about?" I ask, "During those quiet moments?"

Joey's gaze drifts upward to the canopy of leaves. "Escape, mostly. Where I'd go if I could just…disappear." His lips quirk into a half smirk. "Never once imagined Scotland in the 1700s, though. Guess my imagination had limits."

"The universe had other plans for ye."

"I guess it did. And I'm grateful for that every single day."

A comfortable silence falls between us, broken only by birdsong and distant laughter. I close my eyes, breathing in the earthy scent of this place, committing it to memory. When I open them again, Joey is watching me with such tenderness that my heart aches—in the sweetest way.

Joey stands up, offering me his hand. "Time to go home, Rach. I miss my best buddy, the Laird of Dùndubhan. I'm feeling lonely without him threatening to run me through with his claymore and then rip out my entrails."

"Dinnae fash, Joey. I'm certain Father will be waiting for you to come home so he can murder you."

Aye, MacTaggarts are a strange, bloodthirsty lot. Joey fits into our miniature clan quite nicely.

This charming, cloistered spot seems like the best place for invoking magics without being caught in the act. Joey and I stand facing each other. I excavate the book from inside my cloak and hold it in my palm with one hand, then encourage Joey to do the same. Our palms are now sandwiched—a word Joey taught me—with the book in the middle.

I begin to chant in a hushed tone.

The words flow from my lips like water from Loch Fairbairn, ancient Gaelic phrases that my ancestors have whispered for generations. The air begins to shimmer, almost imperceptibly at first, then with growing intensity until it seems we stand within a veil of liquid light.

"Is it working?" Joey whispers.

"Shush," I hiss. "The spell requires intense concentration."

The book between our palms grows warm, then hot—not burning, but alive with energy that pulses in rhythm with my words. I feel the magic gathering, swirling around us like Highland mist, binding us together as it prepares to tear a hole through time itself.

Joey's fingers tighten around mine. His eyes never leave my face, and in them I see both excitement and a flicker of apprehension. This man who faced down mobsters without flinching is nervous about returning to my time—our time. It's disarmingly sweet.

He opens his mouth—to speak, undoubtedly.

But I give him a stern look. "Relax, Joey. My magic has never failed me."

Joey snaps his mouth shut, but his lips form an impish smile.

Sighing, I continue my working the magics. Wee sparks ignite, surrounding us as the spell magnifies. Small objects—leaves, twigs, even Joey's strange metal "keys" that he insists upon keeping in his pocket—begin to rise from his pocket, suspended in the swirling energies.

"Rachel," he whispers, ignoring my earlier directive for silence. "Your hair..."

I cannot see what's going on, but I can feel it. My hair is floating around my head as if I were underwater. The spell is working, gathering strength with each syllable I utter.

"A *Dhia*," I gasp as the book pulses with blue light, illuminating Joey's face in an ethereal glow.

"Rachel, your eyes—they're glowing," he whispers, awe replacing uncertainty. "Like actual blue fire."

I cannot break my concentration to respond, so I merely squeeze his fingers and continue the incantation. The words feel ancient on my tongue, each syllable vibrating with power as the veil between times grows thinner.

"Is it supposed to—" Joey begins, but his words cut off as a sudden gust of wind whips around us, bringing with it the scent of heather and peat smoke—aromas that don't belong in this modern park. The magic is working, pulling elements from my time through to this one.

The book between our palms flares with blinding light, and I hear Joey gasp. The pages flutter wildly. Then suddenly, the commotion snuffs out.

And we are standing in the solar at Dùndubhan.

My parents and the aunts rush to embrace us, smothering us with their excitement and love.

Aye, 'tis good to be home.

Chapter Thirty-Five

Joey

Once everybody stops trying to hug and kiss us, Rachel hands the book to Efrica. Okay, maybe Kieran didn't hug and kiss me—thank God—but I swear his eyes teared up just a little. Yeah, the Big Guy missed me. Ain't that sweet?

Kieran smacks my arm—hard. "Joey Finnegan, 'tis good to see you alive and well. I know Rachel would return, but you…well, we assumed the mafia would recapture you and drop your erse into a bottomless pit."

"Gee, thanks for the heartwarming welcome speech."

His smug smile proves he's razzing me.

"I missed that razor-sharp wit," Kieran says, the corner of his mouth quirking upward. "'Tis a wonder the mafia didnae kill ye just to silence your tongue."

I rub my arm where he smacked me. For a medieval guy, he's got a modern understanding of how to bruise without breaking bones.

Rachel stands beside her father, the smile on her face and in her eyes proving she's glad to be home. The Highland sun catches her golden-brown hair just right, giving her the aura of a fashion model who belongs on the cover of a "Visit Scotland" brochure—if they had those in the seventeenth century. Yeah, I kinda doubt those exist yet.

"The book, Father," Rachel says, nodding toward Efrica who's turning the ancient tome over in her hands. "The timeline has been restored, aye? No more interlopers can force their way into the wrong era?"

"Patience, child." Efrica's fingers trace the Celtic symbols embossed on the leather cover, then she flips the book open. The wrinkles around her eyes deepen as she squints at the text. Efrica mutters wordlessly, not bothering to glance up. "Ancient magic doesn't reveal its secrets to those who act hastily."

Rachel sidles closer to me. After everything we've been through—mobsters with guns, witches with grudges, time portals that fling us from one century to another like some demented carnival ride—I don't blame her for wanting reassurance.

I slip my arm around her waist, and she leans into me, fitting perfectly at my side. My brain still short-circuits a little when I remember that this gorgeous, fierce, time-traveling witch actually chose me, Joey Finnegan, former mob errand boy with a talent for getting into trouble.

"Well?" Kieran demands, his patience clearly wearing thin. "What does the book say, Efrica?"

His aunt throws him an annoyed glance. "The ancient ones didnae write their secrets for impatient warriors who cannae wait two minutes for an answer."

I bite back a laugh. Watching Kieran—all six-foot-something of Highland warrior—get scolded like a schoolboy by his plump, gray-haired aunt never gets old.

"The timeline…" Efrica says, her finger tracing the faded script. Her gaze flickers with something between relief and concern. "It has been mostly restored."

"Mostly?" Rachel and I blurt out in unison, our momentary comfort evaporating.

"What does 'mostly' mean?" I ask as I pull Rachel closer to me. "Because in my experience, 'mostly fixed' is like saying someone's 'mostly alive' or a bomb is 'mostly disarmed.' It's the kind of qualifier that ruins your whole day."

Efrica rolls her gaze up to mine without lifting her head. "The book shows that the major pathways between times have been sealed, but there are…ripples. Wee disturbances where the fabric hasn't fully mended."

"Ripples?" Rachel repeats. "Such as when a stone is cast into still water?"

"Aye," Efrica nods, her fingers dancing across the ancient text. "The magic recognizes your efforts. The book speaks of warriors who traveled the impossible path and returned victorious." She glances up at us, a hint of pride in her eyes, before bowing her head again to study the yellowed pages. "But magic that powerful leave scars."

"What you're saying," I suggest, "is that we patched the leak but there might still be a few drops getting through?"

Kieran crosses his arms over his broad chest. "I dinnae like the sound of that. We've had enough trouble with time-hoppers to last several lifetimes."

"The ripples are not permanent," Efrica says, closing the book with a decisive thump. "But they need time to heal properly. Like a wound that must be allowed to mend without being disturbed. Believe me when I tell you that neither *An Bodach* nor those mafia intruders will never again harass you, Rachel, or any of us."

"And until then?" Rachel asks. "Are we vulnerable to more…visitors of other sorts?"

"Not vulnerable precisely. But certain individuals—those with a connection to the original breach—might find passage easier than others would."

I groan. That's just awesome. "Anyone connected to the mafia guys we just dealt with could potentially pop through. Is that the gist of it?"

"There might be moments and places wherein the veil between centuries grows thin enough that small things might slip through."

I cross my arms over my chest. "Define 'small,' please. Are we talking squirrels and butterflies, or handguns and hitmen?"

Efrica's green eyes veer to me. "Information. Memories. Perhaps smaller objects. I dinnae see anything as substantial as a full-grown man passing through. But dreams, visions…those could filter between worlds for a time."

"Terrific," I mutter.

"Or warnings," Rachel suggests. "Perhaps 'tis not all bad, Joey."

I give her a sideways look. Only Rachel could find the silver lining in magical time-space tears. But then, that's one of the many reasons I'm crazy about her.

Kieran paces the stone floor, his boots echoing in the chamber. "How long will these…ripples persist?"

Efrica clutches the book to her chest, her fingers tapping rhythmically against the worn leather. "The next full moon should see the last of them sealed. Until then, we must be vigilant."

"Three weeks," Rachel calculates. "That's not so terrible."

I want to agree with her, but my experience with the MacTaggart clan has taught me that three weeks of "magical ripples" undoubtedly translates to three weeks of absolute chaos. "And what exactly does 'vigilant' mean in witch-speak? Because in my world, it usually involves guns and lookouts."

Kieran grunts. "Yer living with several witches, laddie. Have a wee bit of faith in their talents."

I turn toward Rachel—and smile. "Maybe having faith isn't that difficult after all."

Rachel's brow furrows. "How long were we gone in this timeline? Days? Weeks?"

"Oh, no, not that long," Alyssa confirms. Then she glances at her husband. "Isn't that right, Kieran?"

"Aye. 'Twas no more than a matter of hours." He turns to me. "When are ye planning to wed my daughter? She must be with child by now."

I hadn't even thought about that. With all the commotions we've experienced lately…well, I still should have guessed that our frequent love-making would result in a baby. Rachel can't be more than three or four weeks pregnant. And that realization leads to a question. "How could any-one know that Rachel is, uh, with child? We've known each other for barely a month."

Kieran smirks. "Yer living with witches, *mo macan*. Nothing is impossible."

I smack my forehead. "Duh. I should've guessed as much."

Big Daddy claps a hand on my shoulder. "Ye have an urgent task to complete, aye?"

"Urgent? No, I don't think…" Then his meaning finally hits me, and I give an exaggerated wink. "Oh, right, yeah. That thing I need to do."

Kieran smirks again, lines of humor crinkling around his eyes. "Best get to it, eh, laddie?"

I salute. "Yes, sir."

Then I seize Rachel's hand, hauling her out of the solar and out of the house. I don't stop dragging her along with me until we've left the castle grounds and are heading to a place that has come to mean a lot to us.

I stop and turn to face Rachel. "Remember this place?"

"Aye." She surveys the area, moving her head left and right. "It's the waterfall where the Ashrays live."

"And it where they imbued us with a sliver of their magics, giving us incredible sex."

Rachel blushes, the warmth spreading across her cheeks.

I wink.

"Joey!" she hisses, but there's no real indignation in her voice. "The Ashrays didnae give us 'incredible sex.' They merely…enhanced our connection."

"Enhanced. That's one way to put it." I wiggle my eyebrows at her, and she rolls her eyes, but I catch the smile she's trying to hide.

We settle on a flat rock overlooking the waterfall, its constant rush drowning out the rest of the world. Mist rises from where the water crashes against the stones below, creating a fine veil that catches rainbows in the afternoon sun. It feels like our own private sanctuary, this little corner of the Highlands where magic hums just beneath the surface.

"So," I say, trying to sound casual while my heart hammers against my ribs. "You're pregnant. Right?"

Rachel's hand instinctively shifts down to her still-flat stomach. "I reckon I am." Her voice is hushed, almost reverent. "The aunts would never lie about such things."

"Are you…okay with that?" I ask, suddenly uncertain. We've fought mafia hitmen and evil witches together, but somehow this conversation feels scarier than both combined.

She laughs, the sound mingling with the waterfall's rush. "Am I content to carry the child of the man I love with all my heart and soul? The man who crossed time itself to save the MacTaggart witches' sacred book?" Her eyes meet mine, blue as the Highland sky. "Aye, Joey Finnegan. I'm more than 'okay' with it."

The relief that floods through me is so intense I almost feel dizzy. I grab her hand, threading our fingers together like I'm afraid she might float away if I don't anchor her to me. "Well, I guess your dad was right about one thing. We should get married."

I tried for a casual tone, but my voice cracked embarrassingly on the last word.

Rachel tilts her head, the sunlight glistening on her hair. "Is that your idea of a proposal, Joey Finnegan?"

"What? No. I mean—" I stop, take a breath, and realize I'm messing this up spectacularly. Now for take two… "I had plans, you know. Before all the time-hopping and mafia-dodging. I was going to do this right."

The love in her eyes gives me a pang in my chest. "And what would 'right' entail?"

I gesture vaguely at our surroundings. "Not sitting on a rock after just finding out I'm going to be a father, for starters." I run my hand through my hair, feeling every bit the out-of-place modern guy I am. "Maybe dinner somewhere nice. That's what I would've said before I met you. Now…All I can say is this. I love you with all my heart and soul, and I'll go on loving you even after we've both shuffled off that old mortal coil. We'll be together for eternity."

She sniffles, wiping at her eyes. "Oh, Joey—"

"Not done yet." I dig an item out of my hip pocket and hold it out to her, lifting the lid from the tiny box. I tilt it toward her, so she can see the diamond ring. "Will you marry me, Rachel MacTaggart, good witch of the Highlands?"

Rachel's eyes widen, shimmering with unshed tears as she stares at the ring. "Joey, where did you…how did you…?"

I wince and scratch the back of my neck. "Well, I didn't have the dough to buy the kind of ring you deserve. While I was pinching that book for you at the Met, I kinda…stole a ring for you too."

Her eyes flare so wide they seem like they might pop out of their sockets. "You stole it? From the museum?"

"That ring was just sitting there in an unassuming case that nobody looked at, I'm sure. The plaque described it as 'unknown diamond ring, possibly circa 1600s, 1.50 ct., silver.'" I shrug. "Why let that poor little thing get dustier? It belongs on your finger, baby."

She stares at me, wide-eyed, not blinking.

My shoulders sag. "You hate it, don't you? I shouldn't have snatched the ring, I know. But you deserve the best of everything."

Rachel bursts into a fit of laughter. When she finally stops guffawing, she wipes her eyes. "Joey, mo chridhe, you are the sweetest thief. How could I reject the ring you stole for me? It's beautiful. Let me try it on."

I offer her the ring and wait with bated breath to see if the thing fits her finger.

She slips the ring on—and it fits perfectly, as if it had been waiting in that museum for me to find it and take it back to the past for Rachel.

The love of my life flings her entire body at me, smacking kisses all over my face.

Rachel is thrilled with the diamond ring. But how will Big Daddy Kieran feel about that?

Chapter Thirty-Six

Rachel

Yer giving our only child, our precious daughter, a secondhand ring ye stole from a…" my father looks to Mother. "Did ye call it a mew-zee-um, gràidh? That's a building that holds…artwork or some such rubbish. Aye?"

Mother struggles not to laugh but ends up spluttering instead. "Close enough, Kieran. I wish I'd had a dictionary in my purse that day when I was hurled into the past. Would've made translating twenty-first-century language into medieval Scottish-ese much easier."

Father rolls his eyes. "May I go on lambasting Joey Finnegan now, gràidh?"

"No lambasting of any kind, Kieran. Rachel and Joey are in love, the forever kind. And we will be supportive." Mother raises her brows, giving Father a reproving look. "Isn't that right, sweetie-pie?"

Oh dear. She called Father "sweetie-pie" strictly to prove who really wears the trews in their relationship. It's Alyssa Vescovi, of course. No man would dare claim otherwise.

Father growls out a sigh, then his shoulders sag. "Aye, all right, I will refrain from lambasting the laddie."

Mother pats his cheek. "Thank you, honey."

"We must begin the preparations for the wedding, aye?"

"Yep. Immediately"

The aunts and my mother drag me away from Joey and down to the great hall, which my mother has declared will from henceforth be known as "wedding central."

"Wedding central, is it? I dinnae remember agreeing to that." The voice belongs to Efrica, the eldest of my great-aunts

"Ye didnae have to agree," I say. "It's my wedding."

Mother winks at me as she pulls out a leather-bound journal that's already stuffed with fabric swatches and pressed flowers.

"When did you gather all that rubbish?" I ask her. "Is this my wedding or yours?"

Mother hugs me, for no apparent reason. "I'm sorry, Rachel. But I want you to have the wedding of your dreams, not like the kind your father and I had. We were in love, but we also had to worry about Simidh Gunn trying to kidnap me or kill me or both." She sets her hands on her hips. "I will murder anyone who gets in the way of your big day."

"Oh, Mother." I fling my arms around her. "That's the sweetest thing you've ever done for me. Or offered to do for me."

"Hopefully, murder won't be necessary."

Over the next four days, my mother and the aunts work together to create the perfect dress for me. I know Joey will approve of it. The gown has a lower bodice than the ones on the dresses I wear every day.

"Lower bodice?" Father's voice booms from the doorway, making us all jump. "Just how low, Rachel?"

Efrica shoos him away with a flick of her plump hands. "Away with ye, Kieran! 'Tis bad luck for the father to see the bride's dress before the ceremony."

"That's the groom, ye daft woman," Father grumbles, but he backs away nonetheless.

"Same principle," Efrica retorts, then turns to me with a gleam in her emerald eyes. "Now, dearie, let's discuss the enchantment for the veil."

"Enchantment? Dinnae want magic interfering with my wedding.

Mother pulls a delicate length of lace from her collection. "Just a small protection charm. Nothing that would interfere with the natural flow of things. Right, Morna?"

"Aye. 'Tis only a precaution."

While the aunts and Mother resume fussing with my wedding gown, I slip away to find my groom. Joey is in the courtyard—hurling a caber. By the looks of things, he must be on his tenth attempt.

"Joey!" I shout, lifting my skirts so I can run toward him. "Why are ye doing that, mo chridhe?"

He has the caber vertical, but he pauses to grin at me. "Hey, Rach. How's the wedding dress craziness going?"

"Well enough." I pore my gaze over the caber and the sweaty man in front of me. "Joey, you should have waited for me. You know I love to watch you hurl cabers. Your sweaty, glistening skin arouses me."

"Then you'll love what I'm about to do." He crooks a finger at me. "Come here, baby, and hold this thing up for a sec. All you have to do is put both hands on the caber. Piece of cake, right?"

I trust him completely, so I do as he suggested. A moment later, he rolls a caber toward me, and a moment after that, he has the log fully upright.

"Ye cannae toss two cabers at once, gràidh."

"No, but I can hurl one right after the other. Capisce?"

"Aye. But why must you fling two cabers?"

He grins and shrugs. "Just for the hell of it."

I shake my head, one hand on my hip. "What you mean is that you want to outdo my father."

"Well…maybe."

A woman must learn to accommodate her husband, I reckon. So, I nod my assent. "If your manly pride requires it, then go on and do what you must."

He kisses my cheek. "Thanks, Rach. Now, for caber number one…"

Joey lays the second caber on the ground, then takes the one I've been holding up. Surprisingly, I have no trouble keeping the log upright. Must be something to do with physics and laws of motion or some such thing.

I step back, watching as Joey positions himself, shoulders squared beneath the weight of the first caber. His gaze narrows, and his lips flatten, as he concentrates. Muscles flex beneath his linen shirt, now damp from exertion. There's something mesmerizing about watching him embrace our Highland traditions with fierce determination.

"Ready?" my fiancé hollers, his voice strained.

"Aye, ready to see ye make a fool of yerself," I tease, but my heart swells with pride. Joey has acclimated to the seventeenth century better than anyone, including myself, could ever have imagined.

Joey takes three powerful strides forward, hefts the massive log upward, and with a guttural roar that would make my father proud, launches it into the air. The caber spins perfectly, landing with a satisfying thud precisely as it should—twelve o'clock position.

I jump and down, shouting and whistling. "Go, Joey! The new king of the caber toss!"

He raises his arms, flexing his biceps.

And I pretend that I might faint.

Joey grins and laughs. "Let me toss the second caber before you act like that. Never know, I might tank this toss."

"You, Joey Finnegan? Never."

He walks the second caber into a vertical position. In one fluid motion, he takes it from me, his hands brushing mine in that deliberate way that always sends shivers down my spine. The caber must weigh twice what I do, yet Joey balances it with practiced ease now.

"This one's for your father," he winks, a bead of sweat trickling down his temple.

"He'll be spitting thistles when he hears about it," I laugh, backing away to give him space.

Joey's face transforms into the picture of intense concentration. His squints again, jaw clenched, as he positions his hands just so on the rough wood. Three deep breaths, then he's moving—one, two, three powerful strides before launching the massive timber skyward. For a breathless moment, the caber hangs suspended, then tumbles with perfect precision as it lands dead center at twelve o'clock, just like the first one had.

"Sweet Jesus, Mary, and Joseph!" I exclaim, rushing toward him. "Have ye been practicing in secret?"

Joey's chest heaves as he attempts to catch his breath, his triumphant smile lighting up his entire face. "Maybe a little. Your father's been giving me pointers when you weren't looking."

"My father?" I stop short, blinking in surprise. "The same man who threatened to use your bones for tent pegs when we first announced our betrothal?"

"The very same." Joey wipes his brow with his forearm, leaving a smudge of dirt across his forehead that somehow makes him even more appealing. "Turns out the fearsome Kieran MacTaggart has a soft spot for anyone willing to embarrass themselves repeatedly in pursuit of Highland traditions."

I throw my arms around Joey and pepper kisses all over his face. The tang of sweat on my tongue only heightens my lust.

Joey drags me into him for a deep, hot kiss that leaves me breathless. "Ready for the wedding tomorrow morning?"

"Oh, aye. Cannae wait to be your wife."

"Do you regret that we decided to abstain until our wedding night?"

"I could never regret anything we've done together."

But now it's time for me to become Joey Finnegan's wife.

We both agreed to sleep in separate rooms overnight, so I haven't laid eyes on my betrothed in precisely fourteen hours. I counted. Our bedroom has a clock on the mantel, after all. My mother helps me get into my gown while the aunts fuss with my hair, weaving tiny white flowers through the braided crown they've created.

"Hold still, lass," Morna chides, accidentally jabbing another pin into my scalp. "Beauty requires sacrifice."

Fortunately, those were only wee pricks—and I have thick skin.

"I'm not certain Joey cares about elaborate hairstyles," I say, wincing as another pin finds purchase.

Mother laughs, adjusting my bodice. "Maybe not, but he'll remember how you looked on this day for the rest of his life. Trust me."

The enchanted veil comes last, settling over my face like morning mist. It's so fine I can barely feel it, yet I sense the protection magic humming against my skin—gentle but unmistakable.

"There," Efrica declares, stepping back to admire their handiwork. "A vision of loveliness, just as your mother was on her wedding day."

Mother's eyes mist over as she adjusts the veil one final time. "Oh, Rachel. My little girl is getting married. Next will come babies—lots of them."

"Dinnae get ahead of yourself, *Màthair*," I reply, smoothing the delicate fabric of my gown. "We will have at least one babe, but after that...who knows."

"I predict a dozen babies."

My attempt to stop myself from laughing results in a loud snort.

A knock at the door interrupts us, and Father's gruff voice calls through the wood. "Are ye nearly ready? The guests are assembled, and your future husband looks like he might wear a hole in the stone floor with his pacing."

"Almost there!" Mother calls back, then turns to me with a smile that trembles at the edges. "Ready to become Mrs. Finnegan, my sweet baby girl?"

"I've been ready since the moment that infuriating man tumbled through a time portal and into my life." My voice remains steady, despite the butterflies in my stomach.

When the doors to the great hall open, I feel as though I'm floating. The room has been transformed with flowers and greenery, candles flickering in every alcove. Our guests—Guarin Abadie, as well as the chieftains of clans Grant and, surprisingly, MacLeod too—rise to their feet.

But I see only Joey.

He stands tall at the end of the aisle, his dark hair falling casually across his forehead. I've grown to love his goatee for the bad-boy flavor of it. His gaze is fixed on me with such intensity that I feel my knees weakening. He wears a MacTaggart kilt, specially made for him, and a white linen shirt that makes his tanned skin glow in the candlelight.

"Ye look bonnie, my sweet Rachel." Father clasps his hand over mine on his arm as we begin our walk up the aisle. His voice is rough with emotion. "I may have been hard on Joey, but know this—I couldnae have chosen a finer man for ye if I'd searched a thousand years."

I struggle not to cry as we walk down the aisle. Joey never looks away from me for even one second, and the smile spreading across his face makes me choke up a wee bit. How did I get so lucky? This man traveled through time itself to find me.

When we reach the altar, Father places my hand in Joey's, his own lingering for just a moment longer than necessary. A silent warning, mayhap, or simply reluctance to let his only daughter go.

"Take care of her, lad," Father murmurs, "She's our beloved daughter and our only child."

Joey's eyes never leave mine as he responds, "I'll protect her with my life, sir. That's a promise."

Father nods once, then steps back to join Mother, who immediately clutches his arm with tears streaming down her face.

The ceremony begins, but I barely hear the words. Joey caresses my hand with his thumbs in small, soothing circles. I feel the tremble in his fingers—my fearless, time-traveling warrior is nervous. And that makes me love him even more.

My parents wed in an irregular marriage. But Joey and I will have the usual sort with a minister.

"I, Joseph Anthony Finnegan, take thee, Rachel Morainn MacTaggart..." His voice is steady despite his trembling hands, each word pronounced with deliberate clarity as though he's been practicing for weeks. Mayhap he has.

The vows continue, beautiful Gaelic words binding us together for eternity. When it's my turn, I speak clearly, though my heart threatens to burst from my chest.

"I, Rachel Morainn MacTaggart, take thee, Joseph Anthony Finnegan..."

The minister nods approvingly as we exchange rings. Joey slides onto my finger the "borrowed" museum piece that caused such a stir with Father. I place a thick silver band on Joey's finger, one crafted by our clan's metalsmith specifically for this day.

"By the power vested in me," the minister intones, "I now pronounce you husband and wife."

Joey pulls me in for a deep, romantic, exquisite kiss that leaves me slightly woozy in the best manner. Then he sweeps me up in his arms and twirls us round and round while I giggle like a silly lassie. Once he sets me down, Joey gives me an odd look.

"Your middle name is Morainn?"

"Aye. 'Twas my grandmother's name. She was a Ross by birth, but once she met my grandfather Uilleam, she became a MacTaggart through and through."

"When did she die?"

"Oh, long before my father met my mother."

"I'd love to learn more about your family tree, but right now..." He sweeps me up in his arms once more. "It's time for the wedding night to begin."

Epilogue

Joey
Eight Months Later

Could anyone be happier than I am? Nope. I'm sitting on a settee in the solar with my wife—and our newborn son. Yeah, I'm a dad. Nobody who ever knew me before I got sucked into a time-travel vortex would believe I'd turn out this way. "Bad seed" was the phrase most often applied to me. But my new life in the medieval era has shown me that I was never that kind of kid.

Now I'm all grown up, and I can't wait to see how my son will turn out. Joey Finnegan, a former troublemaker who found himself unexpectedly transported to medieval Scotland, is now a proud father.

Yeah, I'm grinning from ear to ear these days.

I stroke the downy dark hair on my son's head, marveling at how tiny his fingers are as they curl around mine. Rachel leans against my shoulder, exhausted but radiant after bringing our little miracle into the world.

"He has your eyes," she whispers, "but thank heaven he has my nose."

"Hey, my nose has character."

"Aye, the character of someone who's been in too many brawls," she teases, but there's nothing but love in her voice.

Outside, a storm batters the stone walls of Dùndubhan, but in here, it's warm and safe. The fire crackles in the hearth, casting long shadows across the solar. We named our son William, after Rachel's grandfather who died before she was born. At my request, we Anglicized the Gaelic name Uilleam. Kieran didn't mind. He's so thrilled to have a grandson that I doubt he'd care if I suggested we call the kid "Fatso."

Okay, Kieran would mind that.

William is a much better name, anyway.

A soft knock interrupts our little cocoon of family bliss, and Kieran's massive frame fills the doorway. For such a badass warrior, he moves with surprising gentleness as he approaches us, his gaze fixed on the bundle in Rachel's arms.

"How fares my wee grandson?" he asks, his gruff voice softened to something almost tender.

"Sleeping like the dead," I reply, and then wince. "Bad choice of words."

Kieran chuckles. "The lad has good timing. Storms always bring change."

Rachel shifts slightly, making room for her father to sit beside us. "Father, would you like to hold him again?"

The fierce Highland warrior—a man I've seen cleave enemies in battle without blinking—now looks almost fearful as Rachel carefully transfers William into his massive arms. Once Kieran's done mooning over the baby, he turns to me.

"I was wrong about you, mo *macan*," Kieran admits. "From the beginning, I assumed you were the treacherous one who might wish to destroy my daughter. But 'twas the MacLeods, and later, *An Bodach* as well as your mafia mates who were the true menace. Their treachery escaped my notice. I regret my assumptions about you, and ahm honored to have ye in our family, Joey Finnegan."

"Thanks, Kieran."

"You are my son now, and I've no doubts you'll be a fine father."

Am I getting choked up? Kinda. Just a little. I have something I never thought I'd find—an extended family of grandparents, aunts-in-law, a father-in-law, a mother law, and a wife and child too. I'm still getting used to the whole dad thing. Me, Joey Finnegan, responsible for a tiny human. The kid's been out of the womb for less than a week, and already I'd fight a hundred Highland warriors for him.

"Do you think he has the gift of dà-shealladh?" I ask quietly, watching William's eyelids flutter in sleep. At least I finally figured out how to pronounce that Gaelic phrase, and some others too. My wife is determined to get me up to speed.

Rachel's gaze drifts to the window, where lightning sparks in the sky off and on. "It's too soon to tell. But with our bloodlines, there's a good chance."

Da-shealladh. The second sight. Just one more thing to worry about as a parent in medieval Scotland. As if a *beithir*, marauding clans, and the occasional time-traveling mafia goon weren't enough.

"He'll be a warrior," Kieran announces. "Look at those fists. Already prepared to hold a claymore."

"Father, he's three days old," Rachel says with a laugh. "Perhaps we can wait until he can hold his head up before we start weapons training."

I catch Kieran's eye and wink. "Don't worry. I'll sneak him some dagger lessons when his mother isn't looking."

Rachel swats at my arm, careful not to disturb William, who sleeps peacefully against her chest. It's still surreal to me—this tiny human we created. Every breath he takes feels like a miracle.

"Joey Finnegan, if you put a blade in my son's hand before he can walk, I'll show you exactly how fierce I can be."

Kieran sneaks out the door, only to return a moment later carrying something in his hand—a small bundle wrapped in a piece of tartan. He approaches with the careful steps of a warrior trying not to wake sleeping enemies. It's almost comical watching this bear of a man tiptoe across the stone floor.

"A gift for the wee laddie," he says, unwrapping the cloth to reveal a small wooden figure of a carved wolf. The detailing is intricate despite its small size.

"Father, it's beautiful," Rachel says.

"Did you carve it yourself?" I ask, taking the wooden wolf and turning it in my hand. The carving is remarkable—I can see individual strands of fur and the fierce intelligence in the wolf's eyes.

"Aye," Kieran admits, suddenly looking almost shy. "I worked on it during the nights while Rachel was waiting for the wee one to show himself. Needed something to do with my hands besides wearing a hole in the floor pacing."

It's amazing how much things have changed. When I first met Kieran MacTaggart, he was ready to run me through with his claymore for daring to look at his daughter. Now he's carving toys for our son. Life has a funny way of working out.

"It's the symbol of our clan," Rachel explains, touching the wolf's head with her fingertip. "For protection and cunning."

"He'll need both," Kieran says. "And he has a father who will do anything for him as well as a strong mother who will do the same."

The great-aunts walk into the room, and they have two visitors with them—Dale and Norma, Rachel's grandparents on her mother's side. They still enjoy living in the village of Loch Fairbairn. But I'd bet they'll come back to Dùndubhan a lot more often now. Plus, I'll make sure Rachel and I take the wee tyke to the village occasionally too, once he's old enough to travel.

Kieran ducks out of the solar again. I don't notice how long he's gone since we're all having too much fun baby-talking to the kid who's asleep in

Rachel's arms. The aunts brought him baby clothes and plush toys. Dale and Norma fuss over their grandson just as much as Alyssa does.

A few days later, a contingent from Clan MacLeod shows up at the gates, which we had left open in case chieftains from other clans want to pay homage to the sweet little boy who recently came into the world. But we never expected the MacLeods—and especially not Alisdair. But there he is, politely standing beside his father.

Kieran and I approach the two men, but Rachel comes running up beside us.

"Where's the baby?" I hiss.

"In the solar with his grandmother. Alisdair is here because of me, so I should be at your side."

"Okay, fair point. But stick beside me."

She nods her agreement.

Eanraig MacLeod bows his head deferentially to Kieran, though only for a moment. "Madainn mhath, MacTaggart. We hope your kin are doing well, especially the new bairn." He turns his attention to my wife. "I'm glad to see you here, Rachel. What Alisdair needs to tell you is important and should have been said long before now."

Rachel eyes Alisdair with a hint of suspicion. "I reckon I'll hear it, then. But mayhap he should have made his apology months ago. I assume that's the reason for this meeting, aye?"

"That's right," Eanraig confirms. "Will you hear my son's apology? I would understand if ye dinnae what to."

Rachel lifts her chin and rolls her shoulders back, looking every bit the braw, strong lass she is. "Alisdair, you may tell me what you wish to say."

Alisdair MacLeod shifts uncomfortably as if he has fire ants in his trews, his gaze shifting from Rachel to me, then back again. The arrogance I remember from our first meeting is gone, replaced by something that looks suspiciously like genuine remorse.

"Rachel, I…" he begins, then stops, clearing his throat. "I've rehearsed this speech for months, but now that I'm standing here, the words feel inadequate."

"Give it a try anyway," I suggest, not unkindly, but firmly. Nobody hurts my wife and gets away with a half-assed apology.

Alisdair winces, then squares his shoulders. "I behaved dishonorably. When you rejected my advances, I should have accepted your decision with grace. Instead, I let my wounded pride turn to anger, and I spread falsehoods about you throughout the clans."

He hesitates, but his daddy gives him a reproving look.

Alisdair swallows hard. "There is no excuse for my actions. I dishonored not only you but myself and my clan too." His voice wavers a touch, but he meets Rachel's gaze directly. "The things I said were untrue and spoken out of spite. You were right to reject me, and I was wrong in every way that followed."

Rachel's posture remains rigid, but I can feel the subtle shift in her mood. My wife has a generous heart, sometimes too generous for her own good. I slide my hand into hers, squeezing gently.

"Why now?" she asks. "After all this time?"

Eanraig steps forward. "The birth of your son has reminded all of us of what truly matters. Clan feuds can poison generations if not addressed."

"And I could not bear the thought of your child growing up hearing lies about his mother," Alisdair adds, his voice softening. "I have spent these past months reflecting on the man I wish to be, and that man is not one who lets pride destroy the reputation of an honorable woman."

Rachel's fingers tighten around mine, and I can feel the subtle tremor running through her. This apology means more to her than she'd ever admit. The whispers and sidelong glances from other clans had hurt her deeply, though she'd faced them with her chin high.

"It took courage to come here," Rachel finally says. "I cannot say all is forgiven, Alisdair, but I acknowledge your apology and appreciate that you made it publicly."

He smiles tightly. "Thank you, Rachel."

My amazing wife holds out her hand to Alisdair, waiting until he cautiously accepts—with a genuine smile. "We look forward to seeing you at the *faidhir* our family plans to hold soon, here at Dùndubhan."

Alisdair grins. "Aye, we will attend the fair and purchase the wares being offered."

"The MacLeods are welcome to bring their own wares to sell."

With that, we say goodbye to Eanraig and Alisdair.

The future holds incredible promise these days, and I can hardly believe our good fortune.

As Kieran strides back into the house, Rachel slides her arms around my waist. "Care to visit the *abhainn na daoine maithe*? My mother is taking care of the bairn. And something about motherhood has begun to make me extremely aroused."

"Hmm, what should we do about that?"

"Is iomadh rud a nì dithis dheònach, Joey." She winks. "That means two willing people can do many things."

"Damn, you know how to get me hard fast." I cup her ass with both hands. "Let's get naughty on the banks of the Ashray river, baby."

We race through the courtyard hand in hand, laughing as race to the waterfall. And we do exactly what I suggested.

The Ashrays must be blushing.

The Hot Scots will return!

Anna Durand is a bestselling, multi-award-winning author of contemporary and paranormal romance. Her books have earned bestseller status on every major retailer and wonderful reviews from readers around the world. But that's the boring spiel. Here are the really cool things you want to know about Anna!

Born on Lackland Air Force Base in Texas, Anna grew up moving here, there, and everywhere thanks to her dad's job as an instructor pilot. She's lived in Texas (twice), Mississippi, California (twice), Michigan (twice), and Alaska—and now Ohio.

As for her writing, Anna has always invented stories in her head, but she didn't write them down until her teen years. Those first awful books went into the trash can a few years later, though she learned a lot from those stories. Eventually, she would pen her first romance novel, the paranormal romance *Willpower*, and she's never looked back since.

To get exclusive content, join Anna's Facebook group, Anna's Romance Addicts, or sign up for her newsletter.

VISIT ANNADURAND.COM TO SIGN UP.